# BLOOD PROPHECY

*Three: Queen's Ascension*

# BARB JONES

This is a work of fiction. Names, characters, places, and incidents are products of the author's imagination or are used fictitiously and are not to be construed as real. Any resemblance to actual events, locations, organizations, or persons, living or dead, is entirely coincidental.

## World Castle Publishing, LLC
Pensacola, Florida
Copyright © Barb Jones 2020
Paperback ISBN: 9781953271013
eBook ISBN: 9781953271020
First Edition World Castle Publishing, LLC, August 17, 2020.
http://www.worldcastlepublishing.com

### Licensing Notes
Cover: Steven J. Catizone
Editor: Maxine Bringenberg

# Dedication

This book is dedicated to Arianna and Kaiden, "Thing 1 and Thing 2."

And to Steven J. Catizone, one of my favorite artists. Thank you so much for my covers and everything. You are a big part of this world!

It is also dedicated to my fans - to each and every one of you for making Blood Prophecy a part of your world.

*"In the hour of the wolf will come the queen of reconciliation. In the birth of her death, the joining will commence, and great will be the hatred of her words…"*

# Prologue

*Elizabeth Hexham, England, 1564*

Elizabeth Hexham was a woman of piety. Since the days of her girlhood, she had known she was destined to live her life for a higher purpose. She devoted herself to Him.

With the pages of the Bible etched into her mind, she would recite verses to whoever would listen — inside the church, outside the church, during her walks, in the drawing room — anywhere sound carried her voice.

Elizabeth Hexham was an outstanding example of what a faithful follower was believed to be. This sentiment was true until the day she came across a young boy named Sammael. Not one soul was in sight, save for the boy. She found him sitting at the edge of the dirt road, alone and scared. A sad sack of skin and bones, it seemed as if he folded into himself, a painful feat indeed.

Hoisting up her skirts, she knelt by the boy. "What is thy name, child?"

Void of any expression, he looked up at her with his pools of dark brown and eyed her satchel, which was firmly placed in her hands. She reached inside, pulled out a piece of day-old bread, and offered it to him. Without hesitation, he grabbed the bread from her fingers and tore into it hungrily. Crumbs fell from his mouth, only to follow the long path from his shirt down to the ground.

"Sammael," he said with his mouth full. "But ye will know me as many names, thy mother."

Repulsed by his audacity, Elizabeth's eyes widened, her mouth slightly agape. "I know not what you sayeth. I am a God fearing woman. I do *not* speak such filth."

Elizabeth was ready to move on, but she found that her feet would not walk away. She was rendered immobile, and the boy rose, standing in front of her. Terrified, she held her hands together, looked up to the heavens, and prayed for salvation. Deep inside within the pit of her stomach, however, she felt this was the devil's work at hand, rather than that of He who she worshipped so profoundly.

Sammael looked up at her, his eyes double in size, too big for his face. Dear Elizabeth opened her mouth to scream, yet she was unable to. It was as if her voice was stolen from her. Clutching her throat, she attempted to speak, to scream, but her efforts were fruitless. Sammael fell to the ground, not in pain but rather with a purpose, his stare never wavering as he moved to all fours.

Right before her eyes, Elizabeth witnessed how Sammael's body gradually transformed into that of a black goat. What was once his skin was now fur, his brown eyes now black, his hands and feet now hooves. The goat stood before her and remained transfixed as he stared into her soul.

Suddenly, Elizabeth heard a voice — Sammael's voice — in her mind. He commanded her to undress. Despite pleading eyes, she failed to resist, and removed her skirts and shift, letting them fall and pool around her feet. Ashamed as she was, she used her hands to cover herself.

"Thy mother will not cover herself," the voice demanded. She opened her mouth to speak, yet couldn't once more. Traveling through her ears and invading all her senses, the voice grew stronger, more persistent. "Thy mother will head the family of witches. From thy line, a dark path will be born. Ye will practice and will grow more constant with each of my visits. As the years pass and ye age, similar visits will be made to thy children, relatives, and neighbors. To conjure the destruction of light, it is ye that will lead the dark. I will guide thee till thou art dead."

Just as quickly as the goat had appeared, it disappeared, the body morphing into a human figure once again—not a boy, not Sammael, but a tall, dark man—a man with the same deep brown eyes. His tall frame towered over her, his shoulders broad and wide, his sinewy body rippling with muscles that he didn't dare hide, especially in his nude state.

Elizabeth stood there, silent, not for the fact that she couldn't talk, but because she chose not to. For the very first time in her life, she was near a man, who was not even her betrothed, and naked before her. She couldn't collect her bearings. Her mind raced with the most impure thoughts, and at this, a warm blush heated her entire being. He stepped closer, inches away, a sinister smile on his lips as if he could hear her thoughts. Elizabeth continued to stand in a frozen state, but her fears, dreams, fantasies would not rest. *Does he want me? I have never been with a man.*

He stood there, naked and ready. She gasped at the contact, skin against skin.

"Ye shall not sign thy name to my book, but instead will take my seed and give birth to the next, and will continue to do so on my visits to you. No other man will have you. You are mine, as will be your offspring."

Before she could resist or even worry about being discovered by prying eyes, the man did what he had been set to do the moment he saw Elizabeth. She closed her eyes and willingly took what he was giving her. His body covered hers. With his lips against hers and tangled limbs and sighs of pleasure, the deed was done, and he was gone.

His body no longer providing the heat she never knew she needed, she opened her eyes to see that she was naked and alone in the middle of the dirt road.

Her virtuous behavior was no more.

*Many Years Later....*

Elizabeth found her home occupied with her children and grandchildren, each one different but strong in the practice. Oftentimes her thoughts wandered to that very day she'd found him. *Or did he find me?* She remembered each word that fell from his lips and every thrust from his hips to hers. She remembered what he said and how he'd felt, and she wondered when he would return in the flesh to see her. But deep down, she knew he always visited her while she slept based on the numerous pregnancies she'd had. He was true to his word.

Her question was answered when her youngest daughter, Alison, returned home talking excitedly about meeting a boy who could magically shift into a dog.

He was back, and she, his ever-loyal servant, would be ready and waiting to help him.

The line of Hexham witches would grow stronger, and Elizabeth knew the devil's work was at hand. She had been his servant since that day she met him and turned away from the Almighty Creator. It was she who was the mother of his many offspring. She had fulfilled his request and loved her strong line through him.

~*~

Forty years passed, and Elizabeth was a woman whose mind

was still quick, as was her tongue, yet her body didn't fare well. Her hands shook as she held the heavy pot of broth. So weak were her bones that she lost her balance, the pot slipping from her grasp, until....

The face of the man who invaded her dreams was there, tangible and in person.

She gasped, "Sammael."

With his presence, time froze—the birds were caught mid-flight and the pot mid-fall—everything and everyone except Elizabeth and him. He looked the same as the first and last day they had met. Her eyes shone, overwhelmed with emotion. He walked to her and pulled her close as he once had long ago, and he whispered in her ear.

"Listen closely, Elizabeth dear."

His hot breath made her entire body shiver with anticipation as she slowly nodded.

"The Hexham line of witches are and will be critical to my plan."

"Plan?"

"From your womb and my seed will arise the world's most ruthless witches of all time and space. Boundless will their power be: three women—one of the past and two of the future. The Alchemy of Three will lead to the opening of a new world—*my* world. Is that not divine, Elizabeth?"

She nodded once more, her head against his chest, taking in his scent as he played with her hair.

"In my world, all desires will be fulfilled, with no room for guilt or sin—love and lust, chaos and conceit, all for the taking. This world would cease to exist, but I need *your* help. Can you do that?"

"Anything—I'll do anything."

# Chapter 1

*Amber, Seattle, Present Day*

It had been hours since Thana appeared. Michael lay in the bed, fighting his own personal demons. In the library, surrounded by all the magic books and grimoires she could find, she took copious notes, hoping to find a way to save Michael. With Chloe's help, she had made quite a dent in the research, but as Chloe tried the spells, they didn't seem to work to wake Michael from his slumber.

Thanks to Malakai's job as a museum curator, he had his own personal collection that involved the supernatural—he didn't want the humans to stumble upon something that was completely unexplained. He, like the Order of Taliesin, took it upon himself to protect all magical artifacts, and therefore, knowledge.

Amber riffled through the pages once more as Chloe looked at her with tired eyes. Knowing that look, the one on the brink of giving up, Amber knew she had to push through. In her bones, she knew she was strong enough to overcome this hurdle. She'd seen her past lives and knew what she was capable of.

"Any luck, hon?"

Amber shook her head, her body weak from not feeding.

"C'mon, let's go get Marcus. You two need your strength if

you wanna help Michael."

"But—"

Chloe grabbed Amber's arm and pulled her up. "No buts. You're going because I said so." Amber smirked in response, and Chloe asked, "What?"

"You totally sound like a mom right now."

"Whoa, you're right. I'm still not used to it. I say things like that, and I feel like I'm turning into my mother. But then when I see Zaraquel, there's an infinite amount of love, and there's nothing like it in the world. I don't know how to explain it. She was my destiny."

"So, let's recap—you're a mom, and you write cards for Hallmark?"

Chloe bumped shoulders with Amber as they walked toward the door. "Shut up. You're just snarky 'cause you're hungry."

Amber stopped in her tracks and looked dejectedly at the ground. "And lonely."

Chloe wrapped her arms around her friend. "I know, sweetie. But remember you're not alone, okay?"

They hugged, and Amber thought to herself, *How did I get so lucky for you to find me when you did?*

~*~

*The Order, England, Present Day*

Deep within the labyrinth-like hallways of the old castle and the stone staircase, hidden behind one of the bookcases, was a room concealed to all but Sebastian Rowe. In this room, the deadliest of artifacts were kept, its existence known only to a select few.

Sebastian waved his hands with a wordless plea to open the door. The entrance sprang open, the cold air attacking with a harsh welcome. Adjusting his glasses on the bridge of his nose, he looked far into the massive gateway and began to take notes as he always did on his daily trip down to "The Pit."

There was a shift in color, a slight variation from that of yesterday — a dark plum before, and now, a scanty reddish tint, as if burnt from being so deep within the depths of the unknown.

Enchanted with the strongest and most powerful of barrier spells was the portal. The portal leading to Hell? Heaven? Another dimension? No one knew really, but to risk finding out was a fool's errand. For there was one individual, one who possessed great potential to do the unthinkable, who had tried, but he was eradicated from existence.

Nonetheless, the one thing this star pupil had managed to do was to successfully carry out the first part of his plan: to open the door.

~*~

Within the superb and wonderfully preserved corridors of the ancient castle, Sebastian sat hunched over his desk in his personal office. The books — too dangerous for use, too troublesome for the inquisitive minds of the young scholars — along with the most tempestuous of artifacts, were kept inside his office under lock and key.

Despite the room being dimly lit, Sebastian, with his glasses sitting on the tip of his nose, rifled through the books upon books that were stacked beside him. He flipped furiously, as if looking for something specific. He stopped.

"Ah, there it is."

The book splayed open to the page with the symbol from the vial that had caused an incurable coma in several of his students. It was the symbol of the unicursal hexagram — a six-pointed hexagram. Never would Sebastian have imagined that he would see people in that kind of helpless peril, their eyes silver, their bodies motionless, and their minds trapped.

His cautious hands trembled as he read through his tiny manuscript from so long ago.

*Those marked with the unicursal hexagram will await a fate worse than death. First, their physical bodies will wither, then it is their souls that will remain. Alas, not under their own free will, but under his, the ruler of demons. His army will rise.*

His finger followed the words as he read them, but abruptly stopped when he found that the following pages were ripped from the seams, nowhere to be found. Sebastian sat back in his seat in silent defeat, cradling his heavy head in the palms of his hands. Taking a breath, he grabbed the rotary telephone on the corner of his desk and dialed a number.

"McPherson, keep looking. The pages aren't here."

~*~

*Bradley McPherson, Seattle, Present Day*

With the phone nestled in his ear, McPherson listened intently to Rowe as he supervised Rae and Zaraquel with their potion making in the kitchen. The two girls were inseparable despite the impending battle with the dark forces. Meanwhile, Miss Arianna cleaned the kitchen, keeping a close eye on the girls.

"It is absolute!" declared Rowe. "You *must* find them, for they hold the truth to defeating the wicked him."

McPherson raked a hand through his hair in frustration. He turned away from the girls to hide his antsy disposition, not wanting to alert them of any misgivings. They were still children, despite their roles in the prophecy.

"Look, Rowe, I know. I am fully aware of the gravity of the situation." His voice lowered to a whisper, cautious of his company. "They are more powerful than we could've imagined. With each passing day, they continue to amaze me," McPherson whispered into the phone the best he could."

~\*~

Rae's ears perked up at the sound of McPherson's urgency to the person on the other end of the line. Rae was so invested in hearing the other part of the conversation that she dangled an incorrect ingredient above the pot, but Zaraquel managed to stop her just in time. She grabbed ahold of Rae's wrist, and in response, Rae whipped her head at Zaraquel.

"What the heck, Z?"

Miss Arianna interrupted. "Now girls, you know we don't use violence against each other."

Zaraquel pleaded with Miss Arianna. "It's not like that, Ari." She focused once again on Rae. "Notice anything that's *not* in the recipe?"

Rae looked around the room, her stare lingering a bit longer than it should on McPherson. She shook her head.

"Your hand, Rae. That sage? It's not part of the spell."

Rae's gaze wandered to the fistful of sage in her hand. "Shoot!"

"Whatever Uncle Mac is talking about, it's not any of our business."

Rae rolled her eyes and stirred the pot. "Yeah right, Z. You're just saying that because you probably already know what it's about—y'know, because you're the almighty avenging angel. Am I right, or am I right?"

Zaraquel nonchalantly shrugged and threw a smug smile in her friend's direction.

"I like how that sounds, 'almighty.' It has a nice ring to it."

The girls, along with Miss Arianna, shared a laugh but were soon interrupted by Rae as she suddenly fell off her stool and onto the floor. Her body seized, her mouth foaming, her muscles stiff as her limbs contorted to positions that weren't humanly possible.

Zaraquel and Miss Arianna screamed in panic, while McPherson dropped the phone and ran over to see the commotion.

Sebastian's concerned voice could be heard. "Hello, hello…. Is everything all right? Bradley? Bradley, what's wrong…?"

McPherson crouched down to check on Rae's vitals. She was hot to the touch, her heart beating rapidly. As she was squeezing her eyes shut, he pried them open, and he and Zaraquel shared a look of solicitude — Rae's eyes were anything but hers. They were a rich black.

"Oh, dear God," exclaimed Miss Arianna, her voice wavering.

Clutching her head in discomfort, Rae's vision blurred as Miss Arianna, McPherson, and Zaraquel towered over her, worried. Rae gave in and blacked out.

Zaraquel held on to her precious friend's hand as McPherson leaped to his feet to immediately concoct an awakening spell. So concerned with Rae's wellbeing, Zaraquel had a peculiar feeling that something was not right. She closed her eyes and silently prayed as she so often did with Jerome.

A shadow-like entity escaped from Rae's limp body like smoke, slinking away on the floor before it could be seen by anyone in the room as if summoned by an unseen force.

~*~

*Pandora Tudor, Los Angeles, 1993*

A young woman, so lovely she could have been a Botticelli painting come to life, was chasing after her friends through the bustling streets of Hollywood. Her black, pixie, face-framing cut and glittering slip dress shined brightly as the fast cars drove past her. Inebriated and high on the chosen delight of that particular evening, she tripped. The heel of her shoe stuck in a divet of the rocky surface. With her sight dulled by the drugs in her system, she was as helpless as a human.

"Shit," she muttered as the contents of her purse spilled onto the concrete. She kneeled to pick them up, and in reaching for the tube of her lipstick, she saw it move.

"What the —?"

It moved all on its own — there was no wind, and no people passed. She reached for it again, and again it moved on its own volition. Like a child in chase of a toy, the young woman followed it into a dark, narrow alleyway.

The click-clack sound of her heels bounced off the brick walls of the narrow passage. The hair on the back of her neck stood as she felt a cold chill run up her spine. She turned, and in her periphery saw someone — something — move among the shadows with incredible speed.

Her heart raced in her chest, and her palms became sweaty as she began to chant a spell. But before she could finish it, a tiny hand jumped from out of the darkness and clutched the young woman's throat. Dimly lit by the streetlights above was a child — a girl who'd caught a witch.

This little child, lanky and frail in appearance, held the young witch with a great force that wasn't normal for a human child. The grip on the witch's throat tightened, restricting her airflow, her weight causing her to crash to the ground.

"Bow before me, *witch*."

The girl's eyes morphed into a deep bottomless pit of black. The witch's eyes widened in fear, the scream lodged in her trachea.

A silky baritone voice spoke out from the obscurity. He spoke with a slight English lilt as if he were attempting to mask his accent. "Enough, little demon."

The acheri demon squinted her eyes in a silent rebuttal, not wishing to let go. The man stepped out from behind the demon. He was tall, with a head of dark hair and an air of mystery around him that simultaneously frightened and intrigued the young witch.

"I said, *enough.*"

With a snap of his fingers, the acheri disappeared, but not before kicking the witch. Her head smacked down, hard, against the rocky asphalt. She was positive a nasty gash formed at her hairline. The man squatted down, gently took her hand, and helped her up. Although she didn't wish to admit it, she liked the feel of his rough, calloused hand against her soft skin.

He smiled a small smile as she drank him in despite herself. Dressed in a simple white tee and leather jacket, with jeans and steel-toed boots, he looked like he belonged in the city where the stars were made. He was beautiful, almost strikingly so—but then again, so was she. They'd look good together, she knew this.

The slight curl of his hair that fell onto his face; the scar across his eyebrow and the piercing on the other; his deep-set hazel eyes—a perfect mix of light brown and green with a hint of yellow. She was sure she saw the color in his eyes shift the moment she looked at him, but she brushed it off. He was a foot taller than her, but she didn't mind.

She didn't feel the blood till it trickled down her forehead. With his hand, he caressed the injury, healing her instantly.

"H…how'd you do that? I mean, you didn't even say a spell."

"It's all about the intention. No words are needed for that."

"How'd you know that?"

"I'm a professor of sorts."

She looked at him with awe and blushed as her body felt keenly aware of how close they were. He smirked knowingly and softly massaged the base of her neck.

"The name's Briar." A chuckle easily escaped his mouth, which instantly put her drug addled mind at peace. Such a harmonious sound could only result in one thing: he captured her heart and soul.

"What's your name, little witch?"

Enchanted by his power, his words, and his essence, she responded with the only two words she knew by heart.

"Pandora Tudor."

~*~

*Rae, Seattle, Present Day*

Rae felt as light as a feather. With her body like air and her problems gone, it made her feel weightless. She looked down at her hands and realized they were transparent, her whole being floating in the atmosphere. And like a ghost, she took in the scene below — Zaraquel on her knees praying beside a distraught Miss Arianna, while McPherson frantically cooked up a potion.

He quickly mixed it and poured the brew into a vial. He knelt beside Rae's lifeless body and placed the vial underneath her nose for her to smell it. And she did — her spirit self could smell the incense, but her body never reacted. They pulled her eyelids open, and she saw what they saw — her eyes: black, empty.

Rae witnessed a smokey sort of essence worming its way out of her body and disappearing as if it were never there to begin with.

"What the — ?"

Her attention was caught by that weird entity that once resided in her body. She then saw the panic in their eyes as Bradley immediately lifted her body into his arms and took her out of the kitchen.

Feeling the need to run after them, she floated down, still unseen, and followed them through the estate. Passing by the guards and the waitstaff, the wolves and Jerome, they reached the tower with incredible speed. However, from the corner of her eye, she noticed a pair of angel wings that looked nothing like

Zaraquel's. And that's when she saw him—Loquiel.

Loquiel looked ethereal, his wings so large and wide he could cocoon both himself and Zaraquel and still have room to hide someone else. He possessed this glow, but a glow that was set on dimmer. His light was fading—it was faint, but still present.

She ran and reached to grab ahold of one of his wings. He jerked in response and was surprised to have physical contact with anyone besides Zaraquel. He looked back at Zaraquel and noticed that she was preoccupied with Rae, whose body was being carried up the steps.

He stopped in his tracks. "How's this possible?"

Rae quirked her brow, her hand shaking. "How the hell am I supposed to know? I'm literally in two places at once right now." She began to pace back and forth. "I...I don't even know what's happening. How is this happening?" She stopped and took a couple of steps closer to him. "What did you do to me?"

"Me? What did I do to you? Nothing! I'm just here to...."

"To what?"

Rae saw he was distracted as he looked up the stairs to where Zaraquel entered the tower room. She squinted her eyes, instantly suspicious of his motives. But before she could question him, he disappeared before her eyes. Gone.

~*~

*Loquiel, Seattle, Present Day*

*Loquiel, where are you? I need you.* He heard Zaraquel call for him via mindspeak and found her in her room, waiting for him unbeknownst to everyone in the manor. *Loquiel, I'm worried about Rae. What if she doesn't wake up?*

*If you believe she'll wake up, she will. Besides, I'm sure she's fine.*

*How do you know?*

He hated seeing her in distress, only wanting to make her

feel better. He inched closer to give her a hug. She sighed in relief as she leaned in.

*Because you're there to help her, Zaraquel.*

*I can't be of much help without fulfilling my destiny. I must have a kill. My wings are hurting just thinking about it. I still don't understand why you took me away when you did, but you are my best friend, and I forgave you.*

Loquiel was a fallen angel who had fallen deeply in love with her. But more importantly, he had a purpose from the Tall Dark Man. He was to watch and report, and as always, the command was obeyed.

But it came at a cost. Loquiel couldn't let her serve the prophecy for the wrong side. He was invisible to everyone but his beloved Zaraquel. Sometimes the thought crossed his mind to tell her the truth, but fear kept him from doing so. When he became visible, and otherwise "human" to others, he was rather handsome, with dark hair, blue eyes, and a strong muscular build—nothing out of the ordinary.

*Zaraquel, you are about what age now? I lose track because you grow so fast.*

*I think I look about fifteen or so. Amber says my body is that of a teenager. Will you help me?*

He nodded, yearning to fulfill yet another small plea for her. He'd do just about anything for her.

*Your wings are not red yet. What kind of kill do you need to do?*

*I think it needs to be justified, so I must find someone. I'm gonna ask Auntie Amber to help me find someone to save. If you steal me away again before I complete it, I will never forgive you, and we won't be friends anymore.*

Loquiel gulped upon hearing those words. His job of watching and reporting was getting tougher by the minute.

*I promise. You will have your first kill.*

Even though he promised, he knew the Tall Dark Man would be angry with him. The master strongly forbade him to let her follow the path of his enemy.

~*~

*Zaraquel, Seattle, Present Day*

Zaraquel watched him closely, but couldn't quite put her feelings together. She was young despite her physical appearance. But she'd promised Uncle Mac and Auntie Amber that she would always keep her guard up. She knew she had to, even with her best friend. Rae, however, was starting to fill the gap in the friendship she was missing with Loquiel. Close in physical age, she felt connected to her.

Since they met, she'd felt that Rae was a special gift sent to help her and Auntie Amber. She learned potions, spells, incantations, and more, all the gifts from the light. The light gave Zaraquel such power and purpose that she was anxious for her first kill. Feeling a little better, she let her wings emerge, and her hair began to shine as it fell against her wings.

She noticed that Loquiel watched her closely but didn't say a word. She really cared for him, but she questioned whether she should tell him or remain silent. After all, he did take her away from her first kill. The kill was essential to begin her journey to the light. She needed to help Amber in the battle—that was her destiny, nothing else.

From the time Zaraquel was born, her life had been impeccable. She remembered the moment of her birth and the love her parents had for her. The fact that Chloe drank from the wolf Malakai was essential to her path.

She even kept secret the fact that she snuck out of the manor each night, walking the streets of downtown Seattle, searching and waiting. Occasionally she would catch a walking corpse and send it back to hell, but it wasn't a justified kill, as it was already dead.

Zaraquel recalled meeting a man who was more of a mist than a physical form. She sensed his great importance but was a bit shy towards him. She remembered that meeting very well, however brief it was. Perhaps this was the time to tell Loquiel about the new friend she had made, and despite her hesitance, she plowed on with her confession.

*Loquiel, I have something to tell you. I…I, uh, I met another friend. He isn't like me or you. I mean, I can see right through him, and he says he knows all about the prophecy, my destiny. I think he's like a ghost or something. He has a funny name – Kabos, or something like that. I want to meet him again. So, do you want to come with me?*

Loquiel was noticeably quiet, and she waited for him to respond, but as he remained silent, she decided to tell him more.

*He's Michael's father, so he's kinda ancient, like Rae calls old people. And he knows more about what I am and all about Michael and Amber. He said the prophecy is really a battle that has to be fought between two forces – light and dark. But only Amber holds the key to fulfilling the prophecy, though nobody really knows how it will end. Pretty cool, right?*

She looked at him, at his blank expression, and continued.

*Then, he says that the dark force has all these creepy people watching and trying to stop certain events from happening. Maybe you and I could help him find these creepy people. Whaddya say? He told me he could use my help in saving the world.*

~*~

Loquiel sat still for a moment as he tried to process everything she had just told him. If he didn't assist her, she might become suspicious of his true motives. So, he decided to accomplish what his master asked of him: to observe and report, like the good soldier he was.

He nodded in agreement and knew he would've made the same choice just to see the smile that appeared on Zaraquel's face.

# Chapter 2

Amber sat alone in the room she shared with Michael and glanced out the window overlooking the vast, empty grounds. She looked up at the dark abyss, overflowing with stars that night. Yet, despite this seemingly peaceful respite, Zaraquel's words were forever cemented in her memory. They played in a constant loop in her head.

*There's a battle. Everyone will be watching. But no one will see the knife that is thrown. It lands in your heart. Your blood will fall into a cup. A pretty cup. But then Michael rips open your chest. He pulls out your heart. You die.*

*Die.*

*Die.*

*Die.*

Fearing her death would be imminent, Amber squeezed the amulet in her hand so tightly that when she opened it to admire the stone once more, she found that her hand was bleeding. She wasn't in agony—rather, she was amazed by the sheer amount of blood that came out of such a tiny, insignificant part of the human body. She willed her body to heal itself, and it did.

She saw Michael lying on the bed, comatose. Closing her

eyes, she was instantly hit with the image of Michael hovering above, smiling and stealing kisses. But his face soon transformed into that of his current visage, one of anguish and hopelessness. Longing to be by his side again, she wished for his pain to cease, her heart aching.

She dropped the amulet, and as her eyes sprung open, "Oh, Michael," slipped from her lips.

The quiet plea quickly escalated into an unrelenting sob that shook her core. She could no longer hold back the tears she so bravely attempted to hide. She felt like *Alice in Wonderland*, drowning in her own tears. If one were to look at the sad picture that was Amber at this moment, one would only feel a never ending sense of melancholy. She felt like her whole world was ending, so much so that she was physically shaken, violently.

"Amber."

A voice, first a whisper, called out to her. She stifled her cries in hopes of better hearing the voice which called her back. Then she noticed a blurry figure in the distance walking towards her. The man was gaining traction, drawing closer.

"Amber."

Straightening herself, she stood on her feet, attempting to gain some semblance of balance.

"Michael?"

She rubbed her eyes to focus her sights and was awakened by a concerned Malakai, protectively crouching over her. His thick hair, tousled into a ponytail, was the first thing that caught Amber's attention. The second was the look on his face—he looked as horrible as she felt. *But why?* She thought.

Malakai, reading her thoughts as he always could, heard her confusion as he placed a loose strand of hair behind her ear. She leaned into his caress, and a few rebel tears escaped from her eyes, down to her cheeks. He wiped those away.

"Don't fret, my queen. Please don't lose hope, we'll find a way to save him. You are strong. I *know* this to be true."

Malakai held onto her as she wept in his arms.

~*~

*Michael, Seattle, Present Day*

Dripping of sweat and shoulders sagging from the weight of the battle he was enduring, Michael stood in front of both Alaric and Valentine. He knew his body was safe, as his love and trust in Amber reminded him of this. It was his mind that was on the brink of breaking. He knew it; he could feel it. He didn't know how much more he could endure.

As if sensing Michael's despondency, Valentine smiled. "Michael, give it up and join us. Forsake your beloved. The prophecy has already been determined. And this torture? Well, this is just for fun at this point."

He and Alaric laughed at this sentiment.

Alaric picked up the conversation. "It's been days without blood for you, and still you cling to that nasty idea that she is coming for you. Pathetic, weak fool."

"Shut up. Let my mind go. Amber is strong, and with Zaraquel at her side, nothing will stop her."

As Michael was too weak, he failed to notice that as Alaric circled him — like a vulture before mounting on its prey — his hands shook. Tremor after tremor, Valentine regarded this and paid attention to his allegiance's truly fragile state.

"Michael, fool. Choose us or die, it's that simple. We have the power to kill your body as well as your mind. Face it, you lost; you're broken. You. Are. Nothing. The queen bitch and that little child cannot save you now."

Michael covered his ears and screamed as he fell to his knees. Tears flowed down his cheeks, and screams of pain continued.

"Michael, all you need to do is kill her and bring us her blood in the chalice. That is all we require of you, and then you will be free of our imprisonment." Alaric stood in front of Michael. "Besides, if your love is as strong as you believe it is, why is it that *your* Amber is in the arms of another?"

Michael blinked away his tears and found his voice once more. "You're lying. Amber would never betray me like that."

Alaric simply clapped his hands, and a vision of Amber currently seeking solace in Malakai's arms immediately appeared before them. Valentine and Alaric shared a look of joy, as the potential for their victory was so close they could taste it. Michael's eyes were glued to that image of Malakai and Amber as his face fell, finally broken.

~*~

*Chloe, Seattle, Present Day*

Chloe sat cross-legged on the wooden floor of the tower, surrounded by candles. Meanwhile, Rae lies unconscious in front of her. Her chants become louder, and objects rose into the air, participating in a chaotic dance as they floated about. The candles' fire grew brighter and more intense while Marcus stood back, utterly amazed and proud of his wife.

With the book Bradley had given her propped open, she tried spell after to spell to awake her cousin, to no avail. Bradley lent his assistance, yet he too was unable to wake up the young witch.

Chloe placed the tips of her fingers on either side of Rae's temples, hoping to get a vision. She often didn't have to try hard, as they would hit her like a bolt of lightning—instantly, since Zaraquel's birth. Chloe felt her powers grow day by day, and she wasn't sure if she felt dread or excitement at that prospect.

She applied pressure and....nothing. *How odd*, she thought to herself.

Taking a few calming breaths, she recentered her focus and tried again. Her mind was flooded with blurred and out of focus images proceeding in fast, successive flashes. She saw her aunt, Rae's mother, holding hands with an unknown man. And then in the clearing of a forest, an inhumanely large goat stood on its hind legs, holding a baby in each hand — twin girls.

As the vision filled her mind, the room around her was frantic — the shutters flapped, the drawers opened and closed, the lights switched on and off. It was like a poltergeist. Chloe's eyes sprung open, and all ceased. It was quiet, eerily so, for everyone was stunned to silence. She looked at her daughter's worried expression and mindspoke with her.

*I'm okay, honey. Don't worry.*

*You're a horrible liar. I saw what you saw, Mom.*

*Don't say anything until we can get a better understanding, okay? We have enough going on right now.*

*You're right. Consider me a vault.*

Chloe silently chuckled at her daughter's unique sense of humor. As if it were an ordinary occurrence, she hopped to her feet and let out a sigh of frustration. All the candles blew out. Zaraquel found her mother in low spirits, given Rae's state.

"I don't know what I'm doing wrong. This is the tenth spell I've tried."

Bradley flipped on the light switch and illuminated the room once more. He stood next to Zaraquel as she nervously played with the tips of her long hair. Miss Arianna sat beside her, solemnly looking down at Rae. Marcus walked toward Zaraquel and held Chloe in a reassuring embrace. He nuzzled her neck and gave her a kiss.

"Hey, Chloe?"

She looked up at him expectantly, waiting.

"You're doing all you can. I'm sure you, McPherson, and little

Z here can figure something out. Right?" He directed his look at his daughter and her mentor, and they nodded in response.

"See, you just have to believe in yourself as much as I believe in you."

He gave her a peck on the cheek, and a giggle escaped from Chloe's mouth like a schoolgirl. At that moment, Zaraquel realized what she wanted. Yes, she wanted to be the avenging angel she was meant to be, but she also wanted someone to share the pains and joys of life with. She smiled happily as she made her way to her parents. She gave them each a hug.

"Dad's right, Mom—we'll figure something out."

Amber walked in and witnessed the loving familial scene. She had always known she wanted a family, but now that she was a vampire, along with the fact that she held the fate of the entire supernatural community in her hands, she had a feeling that wasn't in her future.

Malakai placed his hand on her shoulder, rubbing small circles with his thumb, and for some strange reason, this action seemed to comfort her.

~*~

*Illyris, Ancient Greece, 324 AD*

Illyris stood on a cliff overlooking her land and the busy townspeople working hard down below. Her long red hair shone brilliantly in the sun as it blew in the wind. Her stance was one of power, and she held an authoritative aura around her. No one dared question her at any moment in her reign as queen.

In the near distance, she heard footfalls. With speed and agility that were no match for anyone of her kind, she attacked the man, and they both tumbled to the ground. All her weight was on him, and she was certain she'd crush him, but all she heard was a hearty chuckle.

"It would be wise to look at the face of your attacker before pummeling him," Giorgos smirked. "My queen."

She looked at his face, always so kind and genuine that she melted above him. "You must forgive me, Giorgos."

The queen, about to become trapped in a loveless marriage, shared all the love she possessed with the wolf, the man beneath her, and knew he was hers and she was his. He caressed her face with one hand, and with the other rubbed gentle circles on her shoulder.

"There's no need, *i zoí mou,* for we are one, and that will forever be true."

She became overwhelmed with a passion that knew no bounds and kissed him as if it were the only thing she knew how to do.

~*~

"Amber?"

Amber stood there in a dreamy stupor, grinning as she was caught in the wonderful vision that Illyris—well, she—had once lived. It always felt so incredibly real, she never got over the fact that it had occurred in her past and *not* in her present life. At times she was envious of Illyris's intense passion. But she *was* Illyris, so that same passion burned inside her, somewhere.

Malakai cleared his throat, attempting to hide the smirk that lingered on his lips as he, too, remembered that particular memory. Their souls and lives were permanently linked. He missed how their bodies fit perfectly, intertwined, one with the other. How he wished he could see her eyes light up when she saw *him*, and not her consort. He knew it, felt it in his bones that he was fated to her, but who was he to break her heart? Certainly not Malakai Ridgewater.

He leaned in to whisper in her ear and could feel the warmth radiating off her cheeks. "Amber, are you all right?"

She heard a faint "*I zoí mou….,*" as if the memory itself carried life, and looked over her shoulder only to come face to face with Malakai, their noses almost touching. They could feel the air crackle with electricity, their breath in sync with the other, and with the fire that was growing inside them.

~*~

A rush of cold wind entered the room, and Amber and Malakai quickly separated. No one noticed their intimate exchange aside from themselves. With Rae's body still on the floor and the family of three huddled in each other's arms, they were astounded at the sudden change in temperature, while Bradley stood near the window with his arms at his sides, unfazed. He sighed, resting his forehead on the palm of his hand.

Via the current, a filmy effervescent being was seen floating in the air, as if he, himself, was riding along with the flux of incoming zephyr and magnetism. Sebastian Rowe appeared before their eyes.

Bradley slowly clapped at his friend's theatrics, as the rest look on, puzzled. "You always were one for a dramatic entrance, weren't you?"

Rowe chuckled as he brushed off some lint from his coat and adjusted his spectacles. He threw a mischievous wink in Zaraquel's direction, and she smiled in return. She walked up to him, and as her parents tried to stop her, she reassured them.

"He's a friend."

All eyes were on Sebastian, and consequently on Bradley, as Zaraquel shook Rowe's hand with a firm shake.

"Hello, Mr. Rowe. My name's Zaraquel Tudor. I believe you are here to help us."

Telepathically she sent him images of what had transpired with Rae and Michael, hoping that would give him a better understanding of their current predicament. He nodded knowingly, a slightly proud glint in his eye as he witnessed the amazing power of the child born from the prophecy. He knew of the legend, but he'd never expected to live long enough to see it.

Rowe addressed the room with a calm and kind manner, knowing that was what they needed to feel in that moment. He emanated that through a transference spell — a spell that would do no damage but would settle their frazzled nerves for a bit.

"Yes, as the child said, I am nothing but an ally."

~*~

Rae walked around the room, no one knowing she was there. She saw their panic and worry, felt it even; she, however, felt as if all her problems were nonexistent. Not once did she blackout or feel the acheri's urges. She didn't feel the darkness simmering on the surface, waiting to be unleashed.

For the first time in her life, she felt free. She was happy to be liberated from the darkness that drew her in. The thoughts that flooded her mind, the unhappy ones that she knew weren't hers, were gone. They'd left with the acheri.

*How could this be?* Rae thought, completely perplexed by her situation.

~*~

Ever since he was a boy, Sebastian Rowe could see what others couldn't, or what they simply didn't want to. He saw far beyond his mind's eye and into the realm of the fantastical, and this, aside from his other extraordinary gifts, made him a great friend, but an even greater adversary.

Sebastian could see the little girl that deemed herself a ghost. He saw her confusion, her need for answers. He wanted to guide her to find the answers she sought, so he knelt and gently grabbed her body's hand. He looked at the spirit of Rae and urged her to do the same.

"Y...you can see me?" He nodded as she quickly came over

and sat beside him. "Who are you?"

Sebastian communicated with her via mindspeak. *Dear child, you were conceived from both light and dark, and now you are tethered to this realm and to one of the spirits. But fair warning, child – the path you seek may not always be the one you yearn to deal with. Proceed with caution.*

He took her spirit hand and placed it on her flesh.

~*~

The instant her selves made contact, a bright light filled the room, brought on with such great power that everyone, except for Sebastian, was pushed back against the walls by a strong magical force. Her body convulsed on the floor. She became one, her spirit and her body now combined. The room was filled with gasps, the tension palpable in the air.

Marcus looked on with fear, never having seen anything like that in his lifetime. "What's happening to her?"

Bradley came to Sebastian's aide and knelt on the other side of Rae's body. She continued to violently shake; slowly, but gradually her body began to levitate. Amber's eyes widened, and her pulse raced. Without a second thought, she found Malakai's hand and held it. He felt her fingers intertwine with his, and all he wanted was to protect her.

Zaraquel clutched onto her parents, her eyes watering. "Is Rae gonna be okay?"

Chloe hugged her daughter tightly. "Of course. Mr. Rowe and Bradley are going to help her, right gentleman?"

Sebastian, fascinated by the phenomenon, rolled up his sleeves and inspected the parameter. "I assure you, Mrs. Tudor, that I will do everything in my power to help this child. For a fate such as hers is of paramount importance to the prophecy. Please take my hand, and I will instruct you on how to help save her."

She stepped forward and took his hand, and memories from

Sebastian's past life crashed into her like a wave. She saw who he truly was, and he gave it to her freely, knowing he could trust her with his secret.

"You've experienced the transfiguration into a wolf, yes?"

Still in awe of what she had just experienced, she tentatively nodded her head in agreement.

"Perfect. You are a vessel of magnificent power, which is extremely rare, but useful in this case. You will use it to anchor your cousin, who is fragile. Then McPherson and I will be able to determine what it is that has her in such a cursed state. Understand?"

"Yes."

"Now take a hold of her hand and don't let go, no matter what. If you were to sever the link, the side effects would be catastrophic."

Amber, not accustomed to feeling useless in any situation, offered her assistance. "Is there anything I could do, Mr. Rowe?"

He smiled warmly at her evident love and care of this family of witches. "It would be my honor if you would simply observe, for now."

She frowned, somewhat deflated. He shook her hand and whispered in her ear, "The time for you to help is near, but is it neither here nor now."

~*~

Puzzled, Amber walked back to Malakai's side. She closed her eyes, attempting to focus and read Sebastian's mind, but she couldn't.

"Amber, what's wrong?"

"Sebastian Rowe. Have you met him before?"

Malakai took a closer look at the gentile elderly man. "No, but he's well-known, if not an enigma, within the magical community. Why?"

"I don't know. It's just I have a weird feeling he's not telling us something, something important."

"Read his mind, then you'll know with certainty."

"That's the thing—I can't."

# Chapter 3

*King Alaric, Seattle Underground, Present Day*

The exorcism from the demon Ysric had taken a toll on Alaric's body. Since his return, the flesh he called his own was failing him. Having his current body and his past life in the same plane of existence had its drawbacks, none of which Lilith had mentioned to him.

Having control of Michael's mind was the only thing that made him feel as powerful as he once was. Alaric enjoyed knowing he could still inflict pain on those he deemed worthy. It gave him such an adrenaline rush, almost better than conquering his victims and sucking them dry — almost. That and knowing he was close to the demise of that bitch of a queen. He loathed her with every fiber of his being. The gall of such a wench to choose a mangy dog over him, a king!

~*~

*King Alaric, Babylonia, 1032 BC*

It was the night before their wedding. He knew it had been arranged to merge the families of great power, and wealth was the goal, but the young king still believed he could make his new bride and soon to be wife love him.

Alaric was a man of pride, but he was also one of domineering control. What he sought, he always managed to succeed in getting, whether it was a pool full of blood or an endless number of servants waiting at his feet. He was king, of course — it was his prerogative. For who would lead the race of the bloodthirsty and rid the world of every other filthy creature if not him? Lilith gave him purpose, gave him life, and he lived that life in a way that only he knew how: with an unbridled passion.

That's when he saw her standing underneath the gazebo, her brilliant red hair long and flowing against her white sheath dress. She crouched down, and Alaric decided to hide, obscuring himself from being seen. He could smell it before seeing it, the pest of a beast and his nostrils flared while his blood boiled. Yet he waited to see what Illyris would do next. She patted the wolf on the head, and the gigantic creature growled in delight as if he were enjoying the touch of her skin on his fur.

"That bitch traitor," Alaric said as he ground his teeth, his fangs protruding.

Steadily she took a few steps back, and Alaric saw the transformation from wolf to man firsthand. Repulsed by the nature of this monstrosity, he felt dirty, wrong, as he witnessed the unnatural metamorphosis. A man shouldn't be anything less than what he was: a man. If anything, he should be superior, greater than his predecessor. And an animal, especially a wolf, belonged to the lowest of castes, lower than the dirt beneath their feet.

Despite seething with anger and hate, Alaric waited and watched as Illyris was embraced by that *thing*, known as Giorgos. Their hands roamed each other's bodies as if they simply couldn't wait to be together. He lifted her up, and she wrapped her legs around his waist, and they kissed intensely, without abandon, as if they were starving for the other's touch. Despite the distance between them, Alaric could hear their gasps and moans of pleasure as they became one. His hands became fists at his sides, and his legs began to thrust him forward, toward the amorous couple.

Giorgos said something to Illyris and playfully bit her, to which she leaned back and laughed.

Alaric froze.

That sound, her laugh. She never, in his presence, had laughed so freely. He became mesmerized by the song-like quality of her hilarity. Now, more than anger, more than disgust, he felt wicked envy invading every inch of his body, his eyes redder than the fire he'd once felt for her.

He retreated as he meticulously came up with a plan to kill Giorgos, thus killing Illyris in the process. If he couldn't be happy, no one could.

And so he thought, *I'm going to tear that abominable being limb from limb, its flesh from its bones, till its blood washes every crevice of my kingdom. And she'll be there. She'll see every horrible thing done to her dog, waiting for me to move on to her. But no, I won't kill her — not in that way. She'll live with the memory of knowing she couldn't do anything to save him.*

~\*~

*King Alaric, Seattle Underground, Present Day*

When in extreme distress, Alaric's hands would tremor and jerk uncontrollably. The only one that seemed to notice this was his majordomo, whom he heard was planning a coup against him. He spotted him in the kitchen, preparing the hors d'oeuvres for tomorrow's Avalani gathering: jugs of blood sorted by the preference of blood type — O, A, B, and all the other in between.

With his arms crossed across his chest, he stood behind the majordomo and let him finish placing the cups into the refrigerator. Startled, he turned and faced Alaric with sudden fear in his eyes.

"Ah, Your Majesty, forgive me. I didn't see you there."

Alaric walked up to him, slowly, each step deliberate. "For the exact reason that I didn't wish to be seen."

The majordomo cleared his throat and walked over to the sink to wash his hands. Undeterred by the faucet running on high, Alaric heard his once loyal servant gulp deeply. He smelled the scent that emanated from his tired, aged body. Drawing closer to him, he saw the veins on his neck pulse violently. Loud and clear, he could hear the majordomo's heart racing — *thump, thump, thump.*

Alaric lunged onto him, clutched his nails into the majordomo's shoulders, and sank his teeth into his neck. Frantic screams filled the room, the majordomo's body twitching as he fought for his life. The delicious, rich blood coated Alaric's tongue. It tasted like a fine wine with hints of bitter and sweet notes. Alaric grew deliriously happy and found that he couldn't contain himself. The bloodlust was too overwhelmingly strong. With his last remaining gasps, the man's body went limp, but Alaric continued until he sucked him completely dry. What was once a body that flowed with sustenance was now a skin sack, heavy with bones that weighed it down.

Alaric dropped his recent kill and sloppily wiped off his lips with his forearm. Moments later, his leg jerked. He was losing control of his body.

~*~

*Michael, Seattle, Present Day*

The image of Amber with Malakai haunted him. He'd seen it, her nestled in Malakai's arms, over and over and over again. That's what filled his vision, and that's what killed his hope of finding his love once more.

Michael couldn't help but wonder if the sentiments between him and Amber were real. Or did he just happen to feel them because he'd been told of them countless times due to the prophecy? Because he was her consort? He didn't know, and the uncertainty caused him severe anxiety.

He felt emotions that were foreign to him, a deep pit in his stomach that never seemed to fully disappear while trapped in his mind. Michael kept spiraling down a deep, dark hole he was afraid he'd never get out of. He'd ruminate, his thoughts consuming him.

*Does she love me?*

*Do I love her?*

*Why do I thirst for her like no other?*

*Will I ever be free?*

~*~

*Zaraquel, Seattle, Present Day*

"Now, let's get started, shall we?"

Sebastian spoke with unrelenting confidence that filled the room. Zaraquel listened to the adults conversing about Rae's condition. She tried to access her thoughts to make sure she was okay, but there was something, someone that kept her from doing so. She didn't know what or who it was, but she knew it was evil — so much so, she felt chills all over her body.

She couldn't help but think that if she'd had her first justified kill, she wouldn't have to deal with all these unnecessary roadblocks. As the Avenging Angel, it was her duty, her destiny, and she needed to protect and save the innocents. Rae was her friend, and she was the definition of innocence. She hadn't chosen for the acheri to possess her — she didn't even have control of it.

*It isn't fair!* She admired Rae's tenacity, her fight to be good and seize the light magic within her, rather than be overcome with the darkness that came with the circumstances of her birth. She nervously rubbed on the friendship bracelet Rae had made for her — she'd made Rae one as well — and her gift of sight allowed a vision to pass through her.

She saw Rae's spirit self float about the room, and then with one touch to her body she was transported back into it. Zaraquel could sense the darkness no longer possessed her friend's body as if the demon child no longer inhabited Rae. In her mind's eye, she saw Rae wake up, alert and breathing, only to see her body convulse and fail seconds latter. She gasped so loud her father heard her.

~*~

Marcus, hearing the intake of his daughter's breath, gave her shoulder a comforting squeeze — he didn't realize she was in the middle of experiencing a vision.

"It's gonna be all right, sweetie."

As the words came out of his mouth, he wasn't sure if he'd said that to reassure her or to convince himself that everything was actually going to be okay. Nonetheless, the moment he felt Zaraquel hold on to his hand, he felt somewhat relieved. He was amazed that he not only had Chloe in his life, who was resilient and powerful, but Zaraquel, who had acquired those same qualities from her mother.

~*~

Still deeply into her vision, Zaraquel saw herself place her fingers on Rae's wrist to measure her pulse — nothing.

Rae was dead.

Zaraquel's eyes sprung open at the sight of the horrifying image.

"Something's wrong with Rae. What is it?"

Zaraquel's mind wandered in thoughts of despair until

she heard Amber's voice bringing her back to the moment. The moment of Rae's death.

"Zaraquel, what do you mean? What's wrong with Rae? Zaraquel, answer me!"

Looking at Amber, Zaraquel began to cry. Then she noticed the look of concern on Amber's face. One look said it all. Amber looked as if she couldn't believe what was happening, but she knew she had to say something. After all, her best friend was now dead. She didn't know what to tell Amber.

"Amber, Mom – I can't feel her pulse. I think Rae's dead. I...I... just can't do this."

~*~

Sebastian, however, was right beside her, performing a discovery spell, and confirmed Zaraquel's suspicions.

"The child is right." He arched his brow in confusion and looked at Bradley. "You said this child, too, was special—half witch and half acheri, correct?"

"Yes, why? What is the problem?"

"This." He closed his eyes and softly chanted an ancient spell. His hands gestured as if he were clearing a table, and what had been visible to only him was now visible to everyone in the room as they gathered around Rae's floating body.

A glowing light filled their vision, bright and white like the sun. They felt warm, exhilarated, the sort of excitement that was felt when they knew this was a once in a lifetime experience. This sort of magic was palpable, so much so, the hair on everybody's arms stood to attention. A sudden buzzing rang in their ears from the intense energy in the room.

But when their eyes adjusted, they saw it—Rae at the center, her face almost peaceful, placid; her hair flowing around her; her body aglow, phosphorescent. Each with their respective look of shock and awe took in her image, almost divine in its likeness—

the guardian to the Avenging Angel and her queen.

Chloe gasped, "She's all white light."

Sebastian nodded. "Yes, it seems that the acheri demon is no longer in the girl's body."

"That's good, isn't it? I mean, that's why she came to me for help."

Zaraquel chimed in, "She wanted to control it. She was so scared."

Sebastian took in all this information in hopes of compiling his thoughts. Once he came to a conclusion, a worried expression crossed his face. "That's what I'm afraid of. If she couldn't control it, how is it that the acheri is now out of her system, as it is presently? She had to have assistance from someone with great power."

They all turned to Chloe in hopes of gaining some kind of explanation. She responded with a shake of her head. "It wasn't me. With Michael in the state he's in," she gave Amber a look of commiseration and continued, "I've been so busy helping Amber and Zaraquel—we've been trying to find her first justified kill—that we haven't had much time for Rae." Her hands began to shake, and she almost let go of Rae but remembered she couldn't sever the link, so she held on. "Oh my God, is this all my fault? Did she seek help from someone else, someone with dark magic?"

Marcus stopped her spiraling. "It's not your fault, Chloe."

"Your husband is right, Mrs. Tudor. Gather around, everyone. Closer, she won't burn you." They did as he suggested and collectively inched in closer. "Now, do you see that, behind her earlobe?"

It was a black mark as if etched in—a symbol. They all nodded in understanding. If they squinted, they could see it. It was so small—if Sebastian hadn't pointed it out, they wouldn't have noticed it.

Malakai inspected it. "It looks like a B. I don't know, it's fading."

"So it is," Sebastian said matter-of-factly. "Every witch, whether they know it or not, has a signature. Each spell they cast and potion they make is engraved with their signature. A witch's signature is their own, literally one of a kind. It's like a brand, a mark, which I can see you are all familiar with." He gestured to the marks on everyone's respective bodies.

"And have you seen this one signature in particular?" Malakai gestured to Rae's fading mark.

Sebastian scratched his head as he collected his thoughts, but continued. "I'm afraid it is beyond my reach, and I have to look into it." He quickly glanced at Bradley, and they shared a knowing look.

Amber pensively rubbed her chin, curious. "So, a witch—we don't know who exactly—cast a spell to rid Rae of the acheri. Why? I mean, can't we break the spell? As a group, I really think we could do it."

Bradley sighed in response, obviously frustrated by the gravity of this situation. "Unfortunately, it's not that easy. An enchantment of this magnitude is difficult to break. Magic is a science—every spoken word, ingredient, and hand movement must be meticulously done. If it isn't—well, we don't want to know the repercussions, do we?"

~*~

*Kabos, Seattle, Present Day*

During his time with Mozart, Kabos grew increasingly worried as to what his son's role was in the Tall Dark Man's scheme. They spent long nights walking the cemetery grounds, attempting to figure out a way to rid Mozart of such a horrid gift.

*Why on Earth would he give him the ability to raise the dead?*

He desperately wanted to save him for, despite some of the choices he was forced to make, Mozart was one of the good ones.

"Kabos, all I ever wanted to do was create music — write it, play it — and not this," he said despondently as he raised a couple of corpses from the dead with a swing of his violin bow.

The zombie's hands crushed through the fresh earth and slowly began their ascent. Like in a Romero film, their bodies moved in slow robotic motion, their movements deliberate. The men watched in stupefaction as these zombies began to roam the city, ready to ensue chaos at every turn.

"There must be something you can do. What if you choose *not* to play? Is that not an option?"

Mozart kicked a loose stone on the ground as they continued their walk. "I ask you this: can a vampire not consume blood merely because they do not wish to?"

"I see."

"It is not as simple as it appears, Jacob. You think I like this, being a slave to such great evil?"

"No, I never as —"

But Mozart prattled on vehemently before Kabos could complete his share. He so wanted to share his thoughts, his sentiments over his ill-fated fortune. He placed down his violin and leaned against a tombstone as if his own thoughts weighed him down.

"I must do this. Not for him or because I feel like I'm compelled to, but for the prophecy."

Kabos stood in front of him. "I don't understand. The prophecy? In all of Michael's search, he never once mentioned the possibility of raising the dead."

Mozart laughed bitterly. "Oh, Jacob. You really think *Michael* would know the prophecy in its entirety?"

Kabos heard the jealousy evident in Mozart's voice. "Look...."

"No, not a soul, save for the cosmos, knows the complete prophecy. That's its design, I believe. Why risk having the possibility to stop the prognostication by one individual? Power is not the ability to raise the dead or live forever, for that matter — it's knowledge."

At that moment, Kabos realized his sad friend was right. He had to do something, he just didn't know what or how.

"Or at least that is what the man told me, something to that effect."

"What man? The Tall Dark Man?

"No, the old one with a long majestic white beard who freed me."

Not only did Kabos have to protect the prophecy as well as Michael, but he now had to discover who this old man was.

~*~

*The Avalani, Underground Seattle, Present Day*

Krieg, the stone demon, Valentine, and Thana convened at Alaric's castle, but he was nowhere to be found. They stalked the grounds, somewhat frustrated, as it was he who had summoned them to his abode. The grounds were eerily quiet and dimly lit. They roamed the halls, looking for Alaric and the majordomo, who was typically always there to help them.

Impatiently looking at her freshly painted red nails, Thana said, "And we're still here because…?"

Krieg, loyal to Alaric, sneered at Thana's crassness towards the king of the vampires. He began to stalk towards her, picturing how it would feel to choke her. "Listen here, you little bitch."

She raised a mocking brow and smiled at him, her eyes sparkling mischievously as she dodged his failed attempt at attacking her. He fell to his knees, but quickly stood, much angrier than before. He ran, quickly transforming into solid stone before ramming Thana into the wall.

Blood dripping from her lip, she wiped it off with her finger and licked it. With a violent shake of her hands, her nails grew to the size of talons and were sharp like knives. She lunged forward but was stopped by Valentine, who twisted her wrist behind her back.

"Enough. Stop acting like petulant children, and let's get this over with."

She yelped in pain but managed to scratch him when she escaped from his grasp. She stopped, suddenly alert. She stood, her nose high, and while sniffing the air around them, she picked up a scent. "Do you smell that?"

"What? Your defeat?" Krieg snickered, while Valentine rolled his eyes.

Thana ignored him as she walked down the hall, following her senses. She'd know that scent anywhere — the metallic, almost sweet smell of blood travelling up her nostrils. Thana grew intoxicated by it. The hunger turned her eyes a brilliant red, and she licked her lips in anticipation.

"It's blood, tons of it."

Valentine and Krieg followed her as she made her way through the hallways, and in every room, they found mountains of bodies, drained of blood, just lying there on the floor. It was a grotesque and ghastly sight, the faces of the bodies turned down, limbs upon naked limbs on top of each other.

Thana saw one of the humans gasping for breath, and with the heel of her shoe, crushed his larynx. She bent down and finished him off, sucking the life out of him.

Blood spatter covered almost every inch of the walls — it had been a truly vicious massacre. If one were to walk in, they would assume the blood was red paint. The walls appeared as if they were sweating blood from their pores. It slid down the walls and onto the floor until there was a thick pool. Their feet sloshed around as if they were walking on water.

~*~

All the years of his life, Krieg had never seen so much blood spilled in one place. He'd succeeded in getting the chalice for Alaric, as well as completing various other tasks for him over the years, but nothing compared to seeing the massacre he now saw within the walls of the king's castle. Given their years, a sort of unlikely kinship had formed, and at the sight of this onslaught, Krieg became somewhat concerned for the king's wellbeing. He spotted a trail of blood leading to Alaric's bedroom. Not one of his comrades would ever have committed such a gruesome and vile act. Krieg arrived at the king's bedroom, lit by only a few candles, and the stench of blood filled the room. Dead and mutilated bodies were strewn across the room—tangled in the sheets, on the floorboards, on the couch—everywhere. He found Alaric at the foot of the bed, his body covered by a silk sheet and drenched in blood.

Krieg could feel Valentine and Thana behind him, taking in the scene of Alaric's disposition just like he was. Even though he'd consumed tremendous amounts of blood, Alaric still looked as pale as a sheet. And it wasn't just his hands that shook—his entire body began to jerk as he, for the first time since they'd stepped into the room, made a sound. His screams echoed in their ears as his eyes rolled back in their sockets. Never in what seemed like an eternity in Krieg's life had he heard a more horrifying sound than these screams. Then he noticed Valentine hunching over and vomiting all over the floor.

"Valentine, you foul hunter. Get a grip on your insides. We have work to do."

# Chapter 4

*Amber, Seattle, Present Day*

With the windows propped open, the curtains billowed through the room. It was a cold night, the stars nowhere to be seen. Despite the ruckus that had occurred earlier, all that was left was silence.

Amber sat on the edge of the bed at Michael's side. He was sweating profusely, so she had a towel and continually wiped his forehead. She told him about the occurrences in regard to Rae, and then her thoughts drifted to their own current situation.

"Sometimes I wake up in the morning thinking you're going to be there looking down at me, smiling. And then when I open my eyes — well, you're not. It's really hard having you right next to me, even though you're not really here. And I know — I know it's only been days, but it feels like months, Michael — months. I really don't know what I would do if I lost you."

She bit back the cries that threatened to come out of her mouth, and quietly sobbed into her hands. Without her knowing, her amulet began to glow a low, soft light.

~*~

*Michael, Seattle, Present Day*

Michael heard her cries and wanted to jump out of his skin, yearning to wake up. He had to get out of his head somehow, but he just didn't know what to do. He heard his voice again, Alaric's, even though he wasn't present and hadn't been for a while. But Michael still heard him, haunting him, taunting his sanity. He heard it so much he began to hear it morph into his own voice. It was a kind of desperate pleading, not to escape from this hell, but to kill Amber. That's what scared him the most, to succumb and listen to the voice.

His bloodlust was unquenchable. He pictured room upon room filled with human bodies just for his taking. All he saw was red — red walls, red floors, red hands. Red filled his vision. Suddenly all he felt was a wave of uncontrollable anger as he saw that standing above him were Valentine and Krieg, the demon who'd stabbed him, as well as a female vampire he failed to recognize. All three looked at him with a mixture of disgust and pity. And — anger? He looked around the room and realized it wasn't his room they were in. Michael looked down at his hands, only to find that those were not his own either.

The demon spoke, a deep and gravelly voice. "Wake up, Alaric. Alaric?"

*Alaric?* Michael thought. *What the hell?*

Michael closed his eyes and shook his head. He opened them to find himself once again in the torture chamber. His voice quivered in fear as he cradled his head in his hands. "What is happening to me?"

~*~

*Amber, Seattle, Present Day*

When her time wasn't spent in the library or in the field practicing her magic and combat skills, Amber found herself in the kitchen. She couldn't very well taste the goods she was baking, but it kept her hands and mind busy.

That morning she made a feast for her newfound family. Jerome served as her sous chef from time to time; however, she found herself telling him to sit down and enjoy the company for once. She didn't like seeing him so hard at work. The part of his life wherein he worked to live should have been over.

"I'm not sure I'm fond of this arrangement, Ms. Stone." He stood behind her, overlooking her shoulder as she quickly whisked some whipped cream.

"Whatever do you mean, Jerome?"

"Now, don't be coy. It's simply unbecoming."

Amber chuckled in response to his obvious discomfort. "Enough of this Ms. Stone nonsense. That's my mom, J."

"Ms. Stone—I...I mean, Amber—I cannot be idle. I must do something. Anything to assist?"

Amber sighed dramatically. "If you insist, you can help with the table settings, God knows how many people live in the house. I mean with the staff, Chloe, Marcus and the girls, Malakai and the wolves."

"Don't forget the witches, Bradley and Mr. Rowe."

"Right, *them*."

There was still something about Mr. Rowe that didn't instill the most trust in her. She was wary of him and surprised that nobody else questioned his presence in the estate at this very tumultuous point in their lives.

Jerome looked at the spread before them in the kitchen as she placed the whipped cream into a decorative dish—a vast array of savory dishes: frittata, bacon, hashbrowns, sausage, ham, scrambled eggs; along with sweet treats such as pancakes, waffles, French toast, muffins, with a side of fresh berries.

"My, that's enough to feed an army."

Amber laughed at the irony. "Well, technically I am, J."

He looked at all the food and then smiled proudly up at Amber. "I must say I am genuinely impressed, and that doesn't happen often."

Now it was Amber's turn to be uncomfortable. She still wasn't accustomed to receiving compliments and blushed so hard it almost matched the color of her hair. "Well, J, you sure know how to sweet talk a girl, don't you?"

"All I am guilty of is speaking the truth." He smiled, nodded, and walked off into the dining room.

~*~

Everyone gathered around the table was a happy sight, even if it was just temporary given the stressful circumstances concerning Michael, Rae, and the upcoming battle. Zaraquel went straight for the sweets, her plate overflowing with pancakes, French toast, and whipped cream.

Chloe's eyes nearly bugged out at the sight of her daughter's plate. "Whoa, slow down. That's literally diabetes on a plate!"

Zaraquel shrugged. "I'm just copying Uncle Mac." The Tudor girls looked at him shoveling a muffin into his mouth, his plate mirroring Zaraquel's.

He spoke through a mouthful. "I have low blood sugar."

Chloe replaced some sweets on Zaraquel's plate with eggs and potatoes. "Right."

Sebastian sipped on a cup of tea while enjoying some fruit. Seated next to him was Jerome, who had a plate of pancakes. The men were enjoying pleasant conversation when the dire wolves came bustling through the doors, all dressed in appropriate workout gear. They howled excitedly as the smell of the food wafted up their noses.

Sabre entered last, more composed than the rest of the pack, and spotted Amber taking in the scene of everyone reunited. She saw the sweat on his forehead and handed him a napkin.

"How was the run?"

"Perfect, thank you. This meal, Amber, it is much appreciated, albeit unnecessary on your part. A queen cooking? I've never heard of such an idea!"

She playfully smacked him on the arm. "Oh hush, Sabre. It's the 21st century. Women are capable of *anything* they set their minds to."

"I meant no offense, my queen." She brushed it off with a wave of her hand. "You did forget one thing, however."

She raised a brow in contest. "And what's that?"

"Women can do anything they've set their minds *and* hearts to."

She shook her head and smiled. Amber skimmed the room, looking for Malakai, but he was nowhere to be found.

"Um, Sabre, Malakai came in with you guys, right?"

"Yes, he was right behind us."

"I'm just, uh, gonna look for him. Make sure he knows the food's ready."

She took off in a brisk jog towards the door.

~*~

She spotted him in the foyer, the sunlight casting a sort of halo around his head. He was on the phone having a heated discussion, so she hid behind a wall to give him some privacy. Amber cocked her head, for she had never seen anything but a smile or concerned look on Malakai's face.

"Look, I know you want to see me, but I just can't right now," he said in anguish as he spoke into the phone.

She didn't like to hear him in any kind of distress. Since Michael's condition and even before then, she'd felt a peculiar closeness towards Malakai, a bond like she'd known him her whole life. But she stood there with her apron and flour probably everywhere, realizing she didn't really know him at all, and her thoughts began to spiral. A thousand questions per minute ran inside her head.

*Who wants to see him? A girlfriend? I mean, why should I care that he has a girlfriend, 'cause I don't. God, no one can hear me. The only one I'm trying to convince is myself, and — well, I don't think I need convincing. Do I?*

A loud pounding from the other side shook her from her thoughts. She stuck her neck out and peeked through to see Malakai with the phone still near his ear while his other hand ran through his hair in frustration.

"M, I'm sorry, dear."

Amber's eyes widened. *Dear?*

"It's just not the right time. There's a lot going on, and I…I have people here that need me."

*I really shouldn't be listening to this,* she thought. But as she turned to walk back to the dining room, she bumped into the side table, and the vase fell. She closed her eyes, cringing at the thought of being caught.

Malakai cleared his throat, his phone now in his pocket. She looked up, ashamed, and knelt down to pick up the shattered pieces of the vase. He walked over to her and proceeded to help her.

"So…."

"So."

"Amber?"

With her hair in her face, she blew a puff of air to set it back in place. "Yeah, well. Uh, I was just here, y' know, to tell you breakfast was ready. There's a bit of everything, sweet and savory—I kinda got carried away, I think. And—"

Malakai carefully gathered the pieces and chuckled. "You're rambling."

She stood up straight, defensive. She noticed the flour on her jeans and wiped it off. "I am not! I'm merely talking in a jumbled and rapid fashion."

"So, rambling." A smirk slipped onto his face.

She sighed in defeat. "Yep."

As they walked side by side, she avoided looking him in the eyes.

"Is everything okay?"

"Yeah, why would you say that?"

"Because, believe it or not, Amber, I know you. And I know something's up. So, what's up?"

They stopped walking and reached the door of the dining room. Amber looked down at her shoes and then nervously played with her amulet. She looked through and across the room, her stare lingering on Chloe and Zaraquel laughing as Marcus tried to juggle some oranges. Malakai followed her gaze and saw the yearning in her eyes.

*That's beautiful, isn't it?* she said through mindspeak, knowing he could hear her.

*It is. And you'll have a chance to have that too.*

*Will I? I don't even have a good track record with my own family — my birth family, I mean.*

*Amber I —*

*Don't get me wrong. This prophecy thing is great and everything, with the unification of species. And everyone is all for it and happy. But....*

*But, you're not?*

*God, now I sound selfish, don't I?*

*No, Amber, you sound human, and that's completely normal.*

She looked out at the dining room again, the dire wolves in their human forms, fighting over the last piece of bacon. At that instant, with a snap of his fingers, Sebastian muted their voices. It was quiet, and the wolves were panicking. Another snap and the pieces of bacon multiplied, and suddenly the table had plenty.

*Nothing about this is normal, Malakai.* She gave him a pat on his shoulder. *You should get something to eat before there isn't any left. I'm gonna make a plate and take it up to Arianna.*

She left him, a sad smile on her face.

~*~

*Valentine, Underground Seattle, Present Day*

He left Thana and Krieg back at the castle to clean up Alaric's mess. He didn't want to deal with all the bloody filth and needed the time to decompress. Valentine leaned against the brick wall outside, his fedora hanging low. He took a cigarette from his pocket, lit it, and inhaled a long drag. He released the puff of smoke, and through the filmy screen of the grey, he saw the Tall Dark Man standing before him.

"Valentine, the vampire hunter."

The Tall Dark Man himself was an obscure figure as if he were a shadow come to life. Valentine felt a strange combination of hot flashes and cold chills attack his body. He threw down his cigarette and proceeded to step on it, smudging it into the ground.

"The one and only," Valentine replied nonchalantly.

"So, you're the one that hates my dear Lilith's creation of her little bloodsucking pets that roam the earth?"

"What do you want?"

"I want what you want, of course. To get revenge on Michael."

Valentine narrowed his eyes in suspicion. "Why is that?"

"Were you to succeed in stopping him from returning to the queen…well, let's just say things will then go on according to my plan."

"And if I were to decline your offer?"

Suddenly a rush of cold air hit him. He came face to face with the darkness before him, his life being physically sucked out. As the Tall Dark Man held him in a tight chokehold, Valentine could barely breathe and felt his life fading away. His bones protruded in a disturbing manner; his skin was seconds away from flaking off; his eyes sockets were nearly hollow.

With a blow of hot breath from the Tall Dark Man onto Valentine's face, all was as before. Valentine gasped for inhalation, alive and panting.

"I believe you still owe me your answer, Valentine."

"I...I accept."

A tiny spark appeared in the air. It moved and composed a lazy scrawl as if Valentine were signing his name in light. A dark hand reached out and caught it.

"Perfect. You must follow my instructions to a 'T,' understood?"

Frightened to refuse, Valentine nodded and listened carefully as the wicked man gave him step by step instructions for the ritual.

~*~

*Briar Hexham, Los Angeles, 1994*

With the release of their album, *Smash*, The Offspring held a private show for Hollywood's elite. "Self Esteem" blared through the speakers of the jam-packed bar. Alcohol and cocaine were abundant, as were the bumbling bodies that danced around the room. The music was loud, and the partygoers were even louder as if they were involved in an unspoken competition.

With his perfectly coiffed jet-black hair and piercing hazel eyes, Briar looked as if he hadn't aged a day since he met Pandora that night one year ago. He had a timeless air about him, an authoritative aura emanated from his being. He was eternally youthful in appearance, but mentally he was most likely the smartest person in the room, perhaps every room he'd enter.

He sat at the end of the bar, alone, just the man and his whiskey. Nearing the end of the song, the two girls that had been eying him the whole night finally had the courage to come up and talk to him. They were both Xerox copies of the Kate Moss wannabees — thin and tall, with long hair. Fluttering their eyelashes and smacking their lips together in what they assumed to be an attractive manner, they stood before Briar. He gave him a quick once-over and proceeded to investigate the dancing crowd. Either high or drunk beyond their minds, the girls didn't take a hint.

"So, what's a total babe like you doing here all alone?" The redhead said, her speech incredibly slurred.

He rolled his eyes as the blonde saddled up on his side and began to grind herself on him, to the beat of the music, no less. He abruptly stood and peeled her off him. When she persisted, Briar flicked his finger in the air, and the blonde was pulled back by some force.

She looked at him, clearly freaked out. "What the fuck?"

"Who said I was alone?"

Briar ignored them and continued to look out into the crowd, where he saw — as he parted the sea of people with a movement of his hand, just like he had before — Pandora dancing the night away, her hips seductively swaying to the rhythm. Her miniskirt and handkerchief top fit her body like a glove, her curves on full display. When he looked at her, he saw only her, like tunnel vision. He had never felt like that towards any of his lovers, male or female. Pandora was the only one — *his* only one. She was the only one that quenched his thirst for power. He knew he had to return to his reality to fulfill his duty. But she was there with him, and he wanted to make that last.

~*~

Pandora met Briar's eyes from across the room and smiled. She stuck out her hand and wiggled her finger in his direction. He slowly walked up to her and wrapped his arms around her tightly. The band began to play a cover of "Crimson and Clover."

She nestled herself into the crook of his neck, and he gripped her waist with his hands. She whispered into his ear, "I love this song."

He smiled, "I know," and closed his eyes. The room went dark and suddenly filled with smoke; in a blink of an eye, everyone disappeared save for the band, who remained oblivious to the magic around them. They softly played in the background, leaving only Briar and Pandora on the dance floor.

With roaming hands, their passion ignited. They made their way out the door and continued their make-out session against the walls in the alleyway. It was reminiscent of when they first met. Even though they were out in the cold night, the air began to feel hot and dense, their bodies slick with sweat. He leaned into her and bit her ear as she growled with intense pleasure. She wrapped her legs around his waist, her hands scratching at his shirt, persistent.

"Off. Now."

She bit his lip and helped him lift up his shirt; seconds later, it was on the ground. Her hands splayed across his chest, and she smiled, elated. Her rapid hands went for his pants, but with a flick of his hand, she was stuck to the wall, arms clasped above her head and legs spread apart.

He looked at her, ravishing every bit of her willing body. "Now, you know, babe, I don't like you telling me what to do."

She hung there as if held to the wall with magnets, as he covered her body with his. His lips kissed her neck and down to her chest; meanwhile, his hands worked their way underneath her skirt. The instant she felt him, she groaned loudly. Briar smirked as he peppered Pandora with kisses all over her body.

"Don't stop," she breathed in soft pants, her body hazy from the fervent attack.

As he thrust his fingers harder into her, he said, "Never."

~*~

*Marcus, Seattle, Present Day*

Marcus and Amber sat in the very back of *Mordere*, a restaurant owned by his friend and fellow vampire, Sofia. Sofia Bonetti was an Italian chef and restaurateur who, with her thick brown hair and even thicker curves, commanded attention the moment she entered the room.

The restaurant was classic and elegant, with white linens and impeccably dressed waitstaff. It was dimly lit, mainly since their clientele consisted of the glitterati vampires, such as Michael and Marcus. It was filled to the brim with starving vampires.

Sofia instructed her waitstaff to set down dozens of plates of gourmet food composed of blood—either liquified, fermented, poached, baked, the works—all meticulously prepared. Driven by hunger, their fangs slithered out, which Sofia saw as the utmost compliment.

"Now, as you Americans say—uh, 'Dig in.'" She clapped her hands enthusiastically. And that they did; Marcus and Amber enjoyed every bite as they ate with gusto.

"Where's Michael? Another trip around the globe, is it?" Sofia chuckled, aware of her friend's luxurious spending habits.

Amber froze and met Marcus's tentative gaze. He nodded, and she stood, trying to keep the tears at bay. "Excuse me, I have to go to the ladies' room." She walked off, leaving Sofia concerned.

"*Mi dispiace*, did I say something wrong?"

"*No per niente*, Sofia. Amber has a hard time speaking about

Michael since...."

"What's wrong with Michael?"

Marcus sighed, not quite sure how to explain their predicament. "Well, he's in a magically induced coma."

"What? For how long?"

"It's been a couple of days now."

She suddenly smacked him on the arm, offended. He leaned back, not from the pain, but from the surprise. "Why did you not tell me sooner, Marcus?"

"To be honest, we're all still trying to process what happened, let alone trying to figure out how to wake him up without damaging him."

"Are you any closer to a solution for our dear friend?"

"Yes. No. I don't know!"

Sofia gently patted him on his forearm as Amber arrived to hear the last bit of the conversation, her expression mirroring Marcus's hopeless outburst. Sofia ordered more food for them.

"Sofia, that's really sweet, but—" Amber started to say.

"No buts. You need your strength for what's to come, bella— both of you. I'll pack it up for you to go, eh? How's that sound?"

Amber felt extreme gratitude towards her new friend. "That sounds perfect, thank you."

~*~

*Bradley McPherson, Seattle, Present Day*

Bradley stood beside Sebastian as they observed Rae, with Miss Arianna dutifully waiting in the background. He began to pace the room rather impatiently, back and forth across the room.

"I just don't understand how the acheri is out of her body. And if that is the case, how is she still alive? How could she survive a spell that powerful? She's eleven, for God's sake!"

"It seems the imbalance tipped to the side of light for this child," Sebastian thought aloud. "And that is, perhaps, what saved her."

She floated a few inches from the floor, much lower than before. Her hair drooped down, as did her hands and feet. It appeared as if she were being held by a thin string tied around her waist, like a sad ornamental doll, forgotten as it hung.

"But for how long? You see it, don't you? Her skin is losing its color—she's almost as white as a sheet."

"It's almost as if her body is rejecting all the light. It isn't enough to...."

"To what, keep her alive?"

Sebastian solemnly nodded, not bothering to correct McPherson. Miss Arianna quietly sobbed in the corner at the sound of such miserable news.

"What are you saying?"

"To keep her body from failing, she needs to be reunited with the dark force that has been giving her life—the acheri."

~*~

*Michael, Seattle, Present Day*

Down on his knees, Michael's head hung low as Valentine brusquely lifted him up by the hair on his head. Michael yelped in pain.

"What the hell, Valentine?!" Michael's fangs and nails whipped out at the sudden burst of pain in his system.

"Up on your feet." He held the chalice out as Michael begrudgingly stood.

Furious that he wouldn't give up a fool's errand, Michael gritted his teeth as he spoke. "I will NEVER spill Amber's blood! Do you hear me?"

He strangled against the shackles as Valentine smacked his lips together disapprovingly. "You won't, but the king will."

"What?"

Before Michael could say another word, Valentine knew it was time for the Tall Dark Man's ritual to commence. He smiled wickedly, and his hands glowed a bright ember. Michael eyed him, more terrified than anything.

"Wh—?"

Michael's sentence was cut short when Valentine plunged his glowing hand into his chest. Michael's eyes grew wide, and he screamed in pain. The veins on his neck and forehead became visible. His body convulsed violently. Valentine held Michael's beating heart in his left hand and in his right the chalice.

He squeezed the heart, pulverizing it as the blood poured and filled the chalice.

~*~

His tragic state mirrored his waking life as Michael's body began to sweat and shake vigorously. Amber leaped onto the bed in an attempt to keep him still, or at least wake him up. She climbed on top of him, placing all her weight on him.

Nothing worked.

"Michael, love, you gotta wake up! Michael!"

She tried to communicate with him telepathically, but she was ambushed with his loud and heartbreaking screams.

~*~

*Chloe, Seattle, Present Day*

"No. No, absolutely not."

Chloe was adamant when she heard Rowe and McPherson's plan to summon the acheri demon and place it back into Rae's body. She stood by the window and watched as Marcus played tag with Zaraquel. It was impossible, really. Despite Marcus's speed, he was no match for Zaraquel, because she could fly. But Marcus didn't stop trying.

Sebastian Rowe interrupted her thoughts. "It's the only way I could think of, at least for now, to prolong the child's life."

She strutted towards him and could feel the magic of the wolf tingling in her blood. Her facial features began to shift, her eyes a piercing yellow, her teeth now fangs. Bradley gently held her by the shoulder, holding her back as she growled in Sebastian's direction.

"How is that possible? You're one of the most powerful wizards of all time! You're freaking *Merlin*! You should know what to do," she hissed.

Bradley looked between them, shocked that she was aware of one the Order's most treasured secrets. "You told her?"

Rowe nodded, trying to rectify the situation. He took off his glasses and cleaned them, only to place them back on the bridge of his nose. "If you want to keep the child alive, we must take the necessary precautions before we can find a permanent solution. This is very old and very powerful magic — we must tread carefully."

She began to physically appear as herself, via calming breaths.

"Do you trust me, Chloe?"

She looked into his eyes and saw genuine honesty, and she did trust him.

"Good. Assume your position as you did before, take her hand, and I'll take yours. For this to work, you have to want this to succeed, to have faith. Do you?"

She nodded.

"Close your eyes and open your heart. Listen."

~*~

*King Alaric, Underground, Seattle*

Valentine entered Alaric's room and found him alone, still on the floor passed out, Thana and Krieg nowhere in sight. As if sensing the aroma of blood, Alaric slowly lifted his head and found Valentine with the chalice full of Michael's blood.

Like a dog with a bone, Valentine teased him, waving the cup around. Alaric's eyes greedily followed it.

"That's it, just like the animal you are. Want it?" He raised the cup higher, and Alaric raised his neck accordingly. Valentine laughed, enjoying mocking him.

Alaric's nostrils flared, and he found the strength to pounced onto his feet. In one swift movement, Valentine slit his throat, catching the spilled blood in the chalice.

The Tall Dark Man appeared, and before the cut on Alaric's throat could heal, he took one step and crushed Alaric's head. It burst like a watermelon, blood splattering onto Valentine's face. He handed the dark one the chalice.

"Perfect, Valentine, job well done."

The tall, dark man dipped his index finger into the blood, giving it a good stir. The blood of Alaric and Michael became one. Michael's blood, once red, intertwined with that of Alaric, whose blood was black.

With a snap of his fingers, the Tall Dark Man and Valentine arrived in Michael's mind dungeon. His body was laid out on an alter encrusted with the unicursal hexagram. A deep gouge colored his chest.

~*~

*Sebastian Rowe, Seattle, Present Day*

As a young man, long ago, he'd promised himself he would never meddle in the dark arts — that was then. Now, a young girl's fate rested in his hands, and he felt that to ensure the realization of the prophecy, he had to act. He held onto Chloe's hand as she held on to Rae's, a human chain, and they were linked.

*"Darkness once buried, never gone*
*Return now and fortify the bond.*
*From demon to child*
*From dark to light ever wild."*

He chanted this until it became nothing but a soft murmur leaving his lips. Chloe opened her eyes to see various objects flying across the room. She focused in on Rae's body, which vibrated intensely, and only then did she see the acheri crouched down in the corner.

The acheri demon crawled on her knees, her neck twitching as she looked up at Chloe and the body she used to inhabit. The objects in the air froze, and a second later, they crashed to the ground. Chloe shook in her skin, while Bradley and Sebastian remained calm and collected. The demon child neared Rae, mere inches away, then pulled her down and climbed on top of her. The demon dissipated into her skin.

Rae's body crashed to the ground, a resounding thud vibrated through the room, and her eyes opened, an obsidian black.

~*~

Amber tried with all her might to keep Michael still as Marcus arrived with a water bottle.

"Here, Am—" The bottle floated out of his hand; the cap snapped off and poured itself onto Michael's face. They waited a moment for him to react.

Nothing.

Amber looked at Marcus helplessly as tears brimmed in her eyes. She fell onto Michael's chest, right above his heart, and froze.

"His heart. I...I can't hear it."

~*~

Michael felt Amber's body on top of his, and for the first time in days, he was able to breathe again.

He spoke her name with a faint whisper. "Amber."

# Chapter 5

*Amber, Seattle, Present Day*

Amber lay on Michael's chest. She first felt the intake of his breath, and then, she finally heard the words she'd been dreaming about: her name from his lips. She rose to see his eyes flutter open, and a watery smile painted her face.

"Michael," she said, her voice small as she quietly sobbed into her hands. She was so happy and relieved she didn't know what to do except make sure this wasn't a dream, and it was, in fact, very real. She reached out to caress his cheek, but he beat her to it, and with a shaky hand, he wiped the tears from her face, as he'd seen Malakai do days before.

"Amber? The queen…," he softly whispered.

"Yes, yes, it's me. Are you okay?"

"W…where am I? Who am I?"

She took his hands in hers and held them tight as if she never wanted to let him go. "I don't understand. You know me, but you don't know who *you* are?"

He nodded and looked at her a little longer than she was comfortable with. There was something about the way he held her stare, like he was analyzing her, that didn't sit right with Amber.

Rattled by the shock that he didn't recognize his own bedroom, let alone who he was, Amber looked back at Marcus, who leaned against the doorframe, his expression mirroring hers.

~*~

*Marcus, Seattle, Present Day*

Marcus had a difficult time processing what he was witnessing. He saw Michael sit up and take in his surroundings—he seemed lost, disoriented. When his gaze shifted to Amber, it was cold, calculating—different than the Michael that had created him.

*How peculiar*, he thought, not sure how to voice his opinions aloud. Marcus leaned back, slid down the wall, and sat down with his head resting on his palms. He sat back to collect his thoughts. *If he doesn't remember himself, what are the chances he will remember me? Will he fulfill his role in the prophecy?*

He was so consumed by his thoughts that he failed to hear Amber as she called out to him. Marcus felt a slight nudge on his shoulder and turned to face her.

"Yeah?"

She was knelt down beside Marcus, concern etched on her face. In his peripheral vision, Marcus saw Michael stand and face his mirror. Marcus saw him touch his face, pulling his skin as if that would spark a memory. He could see the hunger in his eyes, which was natural given his comatose state. Nevertheless, a darkness lurked that wasn't there before.

~*~

*Michael, Seattle, Present Day*

As he stood before the mirror, he raked a hand through his thick blond hair and was pleased that it was soft to the touch. As if wanting to commit his face to memory, Michael examined his visage—his lips, his nose, his cheeks. Everything seemed the same, but it felt different to him now.

His gaze wandered to Amber and Marcus on the floor. He could see Amber's figure in the background reflected in the mirror. Her body seemed soft—no sharp edges, just curves; her skin smooth, not a blemish in sight; her neck, his favorite, slender and a perfect fit for his hands. Michael saw her and only felt one thing, primal and animalistic—an unrelenting bloodlust. He licked his lips, entranced by the pulsing veins in her neck.

He caught Marcus looking at him, a multitude of warring emotions evident on his face, ones he couldn't quite place. Fear? Revulsion?

*What gave* him *the right to judge?*

~*~

*Marcus, Seattle, Present Day*

Struck by the way Michael stared at them, specifically Amber, Marcus was alarmed at the sudden shift from the Michael before the coma and this version currently in the room with him. Something didn't feel right—it was like they were two different people.

Marcus saw Amber wave her hand in front of his face. "Hello, Marcus?"

He shook his head. "Yeah, sorry. You were saying…?"

"Aren't you the least bit worried that he doesn't know who he is?"

He tried to diminish her worries. "I'm sure it'll come back to him. He just needs time." He said those words, even though he didn't honestly believe them. But he gave the best imitation of a warm smile that he could muster.

He saw the hope in her eyes and didn't want to be the one to take that away from her. Both she and Chloe, and Michael, for that matter, had been through more than enough to ensure the prophecy was fulfilled.

When it came to Michael, Marcus had to be completely sure and sought to confirm his suspicions. But how to do so without Amber or Chloe finding out? The last thing he wanted to do was place them in more danger than they already were.

~*~

*Rae, Seattle, Present Day*

The air was so incredibly thick, Rae coughed up a storm as she struggled to sit up. She saw Zaraquel and Chloe at her side, waiting tentatively as if through a filmy silkscreen, their appearance grainy in her eyes. She rubbed her eyes and opened them to see much more clearly. That one simple act made everything significantly better, like a windshield wiper on a dirty car.

Everything was brighter, more vibrant as if she had somehow been reborn. She slowly turned to survey the room—Zaraquel and Chloe beside her, as Miss Arianna was happily sobbing into a handkerchief. McPherson stood looking at her from overhead and smiling, and beside him was an old man she knew she didn't know but recognized anyway.

*Who is he?* The thought crossed her mind, and he flashed a knowing grin her way.

It hit her suddenly, and out of nowhere, she saw the memories of her spirit hovering above her body in the kitchen, and then subsequently in the tower. Rae recalled meeting the old man and feeling safe with him.

The safety she felt with him didn't amount to the happiness she'd felt when the acheri left her body. Rae had felt what she assumed everyone else felt—normal. She remembered feeling light and without burden, but she knew now that was not the case. In the pit of her stomach, Rae was positive the acheri had made its way back into her body, like some sort of bad poison she just couldn't get rid of. She just didn't know why — why did the acheri leave? Why did it return? She didn't know.

Because her confusion met no bounds, Rae turned to her cousin for guidance. She was aware that Chloe and Zaraquel were speaking to her, as their mouths would open and close, but she couldn't hear a sound. Rae attempted to stand, but her body had another idea: she shook, her limbs weak from immobility. Zaraquel and Chloe caught her just in time before her face met the floor. After a few moments, her hearing returned, but she still felt weak and somewhat unbalanced.

"Chloe? Z? W…what happened?" Her confidence was gone, her voice small, as they held her up, their arms around their shoulders.

McPherson brought a chair over and helped her sit, and she nodded in appreciation. Chloe crouched down to Rae's level, meeting her eye to eye as she held tightly onto her hand.

"Rae, sweetie." She looked down briefly and then back to Rae's watery eyes. "Somehow, someone cast a spell to remove the acheri from your body, and when they did that…well, you didn't react well."

"I don't understand."

Despite the difficulty, Chloe continued. "In order to keep you alive, we had to put the acheri back."

Reeling from the disappointment, Rae slumped forward. "Wasn't there any other way? I mean, couldn't I live without her inside me?"

She looked at Chloe, and Chloe looked up at McPherson and Rowe as they motioned for her to continue with the truth. "Well, that's the thing, Rae. You were born with the acheri already inside you; thus, the imbalance, the dark versus light battle within you. You need the acheri to survive — you can't live without it. We've already seen what happens when you do."

Rae felt the tears threatening to fall. Zaraquel pulled her into her arms as she sat on the arm of the chair.

"I don't get it. Did someone want me to die? Is that why they took her out in the first place?" She sobbed. Instinctively she leaned into Zaraquel's embrace as Zaraquel ran a hand through her hair, trying to soothe her.

"Don't talk like that, Rae," Zaraquel admonished her.

"Then, why?" The volume of her voice began to rise. "I need someone to tell me why!"

Rowe approached her. "Now, don't fret, child. We will find the culprit who did this to you. As we will help you find the balance you need. Remember your path."

She nodded, remembering what he had told her when he helped her return to her body — that her path wasn't an easy one, and she must remain strong no matter the outcome.

~*~

*Kabos, Seattle, Present Day*

As a spirit, Kabos was free to do as he wished. He floated about and wandered through the world, looking for a solution for Mozart's predicament of creating corpses. He knew his son was unhappy, but he also knew he had yet another son that was alive, more or less. With a cautious mind, he entered the estate and felt a strange pull to one bedroom in particular.

With a blink of his eyes, he automatically appeared where he was meant to be. He was drawn to the presence of his son, Michael. But as he looked at him, still unseen in the middle of the room, he saw Amber asleep on the bed beside him and felt a sense of unease. Michael peered at her as if he were a lion, and she was a lamb, defenseless in her most vulnerable state. This man was not his son, he was something else. He was the selfish and lustful man that he had been before he became a vampire.

How was it possible that he reverted to his prior self? He sat down in the lounge chair across from them. His gaze wandered down to his ankle, where he saw the mark he was born with — the mark of the gypsies.

~*~

*Kabos and the Romani, Venice, Italy, 1600*

Nineteen-year-old Kabos sat near a canal, shaded underneath the bridge, where he gathered a small pile of stones. The gravel felt cold beneath the thin cloth of his pants. Carefully and methodically, he tossed one stone into the water, causing it to skip. It made two complete jumps before plummeting into the water. He grabbed one more stone and was about to throw when he heard the laughter of a group of girls behind him.

Kabos turned at the sound and smiled in their direction. One of the girls, Flora, a voluptuous girl on the edge of seventeen, with a head of thick brown curls cascading down her back, blushed furiously as she motioned for the girls to keep walking along. They left, leaving Flora and Kabos alone. She looked at him, her light brown eyes sparkling, a sort of mischief evident as she walked towards him.

Her voice was soft, like a song. "Tossing stones again, Kabos?"

He chuckled. "It clears the mind and keeps the hands busy."

She sat down beside him, her feet dangling almost close enough to touch the water with the tips of her toes.

"So young, Kabos, yet it seems as if you have an old soul."

"And you, Flora, so soft-hearted and coy, but your eyes tell a different story."

He looked out into the water, a sort of unease washing over him, his lips turned down. He threw a stone, not even trying to skip. It fell in with a *plop.* Flora tentatively touched his shoulder, and he met her concerned scrutiny with a sigh that escaped his lips.

"It is me you can trust, dear Kabos. What troubles you?"

"Oh, precious Flora. It is the sad, bitter truth, but it seems that nothing weighs more than the destiny one is bestowed."

"And the burden is great?"

"Very much so."

As a young man, he always knew the gift his mother possessed was one of great sight. Birna's accuracy was impeccable. He remembered, when he was a child, that he could never hide anything from her, nor she from him. Their blood was their bond, as was their native tongue.

Since the day of the vision that fated Kabos to his destiny, he felt as if fate followed him wherever he went. It was at times like these he wondered, had he not known about his future, would he still be following that path? Thoughts like these consumed him, ruined him to no end.

~*~

*Malakai, Seattle, Present Day*

With the betterment of both Michael and Rae, Malakai was glad that they were well and fine; nevertheless, he needed some time to decompress. All the magical commotions that had occurred were too overwhelming for him. He needed some sort of release.

He enjoyed the brisk jog in the park, as he cut through the sharp wind of the cold night. But this did nothing to lift his spirits. He was happy that Amber's smile finally met her eyes. That was all he'd ever wanted for her: happiness, that's it. There was nothing more he could ask for—she was his priority. Yet, in the back of his mind, as in his heart, he couldn't help but believe the ancient legend that he'd heard so long ago was the certifiable truth, as it was written in Eschmun's scroll.

*...her fate is tied to the true alpha of the wolves. A blood drinker will stand formidable, but it is the nature of the child to call upon the true alpha and bring him to the queen's inner heart.*

*Could this be the truth?* he often wondered as he traveled the world collecting artifacts and evidence supporting this notion. Yes, he'd crafted a reliquary, quite accidentally, and people assumed it was to keep the magic insulated, away from the humans. But that wasn't the case, at least not for him. He so wanted to believe, just from the sheer fact that it was said in the scroll. But Malakai was a man of logic, driven by cold hard data. Although wanting to romanticize that his destiny was tied with Amber's, he needed confirmation. He wanted validation for the strong emotions he was feeling.

~*~

*Zaraquel, Seattle, Present Day*

Walking the cemetery grounds as she so often did without the knowledge of her parents, Zaraquel wandered at a leisurely pace. She whipped out her phone and checked the time which read midnight. Her brow quirked in confusion, as she had expected Loquiel some time ago. With her long hair styled in two braids and her bright red coat to keep her warm, she sat down on a bench.

She was elated that her best friend, other than the one that was currently running late, was alive and breathing. Rae had given Zaraquel a terrible fright, for she had never known the death of someone close to her heart. She shook, not from the cold, but from remembering the tragic vision she had of Rae's demise.

A throaty growl awoke her from her thoughts. She heard the fast footfalls of someone, something, running toward her, and she put her fight training to use. Zaraquel spun around, so much so that her wings unfurled. But that did not deter the undead man from attacking her. His decaying flesh was a sight she instantly wished she could unsee, but she had to fulfill her duty and protect the people, which meant ridding the world of this monster.

She punched him in the stomach as her father had taught her, but that did nothing to stop him from throwing his fists at her. She dodged his poor attempts at aiming for her and grabbed his arm, twisting him around, so he fell to his knees. Her weight on his back caused the corpse to fall to the ground. It growled in anger, shaking its head savagely as if it couldn't wait to get back to its feet. Zaraquel, however, had plans of her own. She stood briefly to step on his neck to keep him from moving and whispered a spell she'd learned from a book.

*"Capite obtruncato intestinisque extractis."*

She heard the cracking of his bones, the stretching of his skin; with a *pop!* his head flew off, gore spattering in every direction. His body went limp, as it was before he had risen from the ground.

Zaraquel sighed in frustration as she walked off, disappointed from another unnecessary and unjustified kill. She continued to walk the grounds and felt a rush of warm wind, the kind she felt every time Loquiel was near. She turned, and there he was, right behind her.

~*~

*Loquiel, Seattle, Present Day*

Before he landed on the ground and because he spent so much time with his beloved, he felt something was awry. He didn't know why or how, but he was completely sure something was wrong, as certain as he was of his love for her. He passionately believed they were linked — a special bond between angels that the two seemed to share. He landed softly but knew she felt him, so he stood behind her and waited, oblivious to the bloody beheaded corpse on the soil.

Loquiel felt the earth stand still for a moment when she turned around to look at him, blood spatter on the delicate features of her face. His eyes widened at the horror he was witnessing. He knew what the Tall Dark Man had in store for Zaraquel, but the sight of something unwholesome, such as blood, just seemed wrong and out of place. She looked too pure and innocent for the darkness that came with the act of killing.

"Sweet Zaraquel, what happened to you?"

He palmed her cheeks to clean her face, but she shrugged off his touch and took a step back. Loquiel flinched, unaccustomed to such rejection, especially from her.

"You were late, so I had to take care of things myself," she said flippantly as she eyed the body on the ground.

He followed her gaze and saw the pool of blood at the site of the decapitation. It was truly a gruesome sight — the spinal cord detached from the cranium was something he'd never seen before. How could such an ingenue commit such a gruesome act? He looked at her again. Despite the red that colored her face and the anger that clouded her eyes, she still maintained an essence of beauty he couldn't quite put into words. He was amazed by her. Unfortunately, he could never act on his feelings — they were forbidden. His master would never permit such a union.

"It was not my intention to be late. I…I was held up."

She pouted indignantly and crossed her arms over her chest. "Doing what? Huh, Loquiel? What were you doing?"

He avoided meeting her eyes. If he did, he wouldn't be responsible for the words that fell from his lips. Loquiel turned away, his thoughts wandering to moments before their meeting.

~*~

Loquiel stood, not quite cowering but not quite firm either, in front of his master. The Tall Dark Man, still in his shadow form, as chimerical as ever, sat on what appeared to be his throne. Perfectly crafted from the lingering skulls of lost souls that inhabited his dwelling, their faces were molded in screams of anguish—their jaws wide open, their orbitals, black holes.

Meanwhile, Loquiel stood there, nervously awaiting his master's reply. The Tall Dark Man tapped his fingers on the arm of the throne. *Tap. Tap. Tap.*

Deep and guttural, like a beast barely waking from hibernation, the master spoke. It was harsh, like gravel. "So, this child, *not* the scepter, saw you in your natural state?"

Loquiel nodded meekly.

His master gave him a once over, his eyes squinting. "Help me understand this. How is it that you can pay your respects to me if you are not kneeling?"

Immediately Loquiel dropped to his knees, ashamed of his foolishness. He bowed his head down and pleaded for forgiveness.

The master waved his hand in the air dismissively. "Go on."

"It was not Zaraquel, but a relative of hers. Rae. Rae Tudor."

"Ah, one of the Tudor witches."

"Yes, that is correct, Master. But she isn't just a witch. Half of her is home to a demon, acheri."

The master leaned forward, perked up and interested. "Is that so? She may prove of some use to me."

Pleased that he finally had done something the master approved of, Loquiel continued with his report of his latest findings of the estate filled with the magical beings of the prophecy.

"And the scepter? Have you kept her from the prophecy?"

At the mention Zaraquel, Loquiel's nerves got to him, and his wings began to twitch uncontrollably. He did not meet his master's eyes.

"Uh, n…no, sir. She hasn't had her first justified kill."

"Keep it that way. Now, return to your post, Loquiel. You are to report back the moment you acquire new information, understood?"

Loquiel had no other choice but to obey his demands.

~*~

Since he still faced away from her, she walked over and stood in front of him, tapping her foot as she impatiently waited for an answer. "Well?"

He lifted his hand to her face to wipe off the blood, and her expression softened. "Forgive me, Zaraquel. I had some business to tend to."

"What kind of business?"

"The kind that could save the world."

"Sounds important. How can I help?"

He wrapped his arm around her as they continued to walk around the grounds. He looked down, and a smile slipped onto his face as he was amazed by her. "Just by staying here with me, you're already helping me."

A blush crept onto her cheeks, and her giggles filled the space around them. "Oh, Loquiel, you say the weirdest things."

# Chapter 6

*The Avalani, Underground Seattle, Present Day*

The stench of blood still lived in the air, wafting around their noses and staying there; it smelled dry and putrid. The vampire king's castle now served as the Avalani's headquarters. And there they sat, the Avalani — Krieg, Valentine, and Thana — waiting for further instructions.

Valentine sat at the end of the table, which Alaric had occupied days before his demise. He looked around the room. To his right stood Krieg, somewhat forlorn since the death of his master, and to his left sat Thana, unamused by the pomp and circumstance of the meeting, since she'd much rather be out sucking the blood out of humans.

They all sat around the table, waiting for the guest — their new head of operations — to arrive, the tension palpable. Thana impatiently tapped her manicured nails on the table, the sound echoing across the empty hallways.

She rolled her eyes at the men beside her. "Must we really wait this long?"

"We must do what is necessary," Valentine said sternly, frustrated by her nonchalant attitude.

Krieg angrily slammed his rocky fist into the wall. "I can't sit here with you chickenshits and chitchat. I have an army to run!"

Thana scoffed. "What? Your group of rogue amateur vampires?"

"Yeah? And what are you doing? Besides sitting on your ass."

She stood abruptly, planting her hands on the table. "You know very well what I am doing. It's just taking some time," Thana said through clenched teeth.

Krieg slammed his hands on the table across from her. "What? Having troubles with your brother?" He snickered as a slow smile appeared on his lips.

Finally, Valentine stood, significantly taller than both of them. "Enough! Enough, both of you. You're insufferable." He paused and took a step back and spoke in a calm, soft tone. "We all know *who* called this meeting and what *he* can do. You will sit the *fuck* down and wait."

~*~

*Amber, Seattle, Present Day*

Sprawled amidst the sheets, Amber lay on her side. She reached her arm to try and touch Michael in his sleep, but she couldn't. She turned and found the left side empty — Michael was nowhere in the room. She tried to call for him telepathically, but once more, she found that she couldn't. He wasn't on the estate, and the moment she realized that she sat up and sprung to her feet. She quickly changed and charged out of her bedroom. In doing so, she ran straight into Chloe.

"Whoa, whoa, slow down. What's wrong, Amber?"

Amber frantically looked around Chloe, but not at her. "I don't know where Michael is. He's not in the room, and I tried calling him — y'know, with my powers — but he's nowhere. And I don't know what I'll do, Chloe, if I lose him again. I...I just don't know."

As she powered through her ramble, tears filled her eyes and fell down her cheeks. Chloe rubbed her arms, comforting her.

"Hey, he couldn't have gone far. We're gonna find him. You hear me, Amber? You're not going to lose him."

"I just got him back, Chloe."

"I know, sweetie, I know. Let's go and see if Marcus knows where he is."

Amber nodded as she and Chloe frantically walked down the hallway.

~*~

*Bradley McPherson, Seattle, Present Day*

Bradley looked down at the scrap of paper that Malakai had written on to depict the witch's signature from the curse placed on Rae. He held it and crumpled it in his fist. He threw it across the room, thwarted that he couldn't figure out the symbol. It looked so familiar to him, but he couldn't place it.

"Damn it! Where the hell have I seen this?"

The paper ball rolled across the floor, stopping at Sebastian's feet as he entered the room. He bent down to pick it up and unfurled it. He saw the mark, and with a wave of his hand, it disappeared from the paper.

Rowe approached McPherson as he sat crouched down on a chair. "What seems to be the problem, Bradley?"

McPherson rose and began to pace the room. "I've seen that signature. I know I have."

Rowe patted his shoulder, gesturing for him to take a place on the couch next to him as he sat down.

Bradley continued as he raked a hand through his hair, a habit when he became nervous or stressed out. "I feel like I'm going crazy because I swear to God, I've seen that sigil somewhere."

"The mind is a complex organism. Perhaps it is something that cannot be remedied," Rowe said dismissively.

McPherson looked up to his mentor, desperate for an answer. "Surely that's not what you believe. There must be something that *you* can do."

"Now Bradley, you're not proposing that I dig around your mind, are you? Because that is not something someone can just dabble in, even me. It's a delicate bion, and it can have damaging effects."

"I don't see what else we can do to find who did this to Rae. You saw what the spell did to her. Whoever cast the enchantment knew what he or she was doing, and they were good at it."

"Yes, that's a frightening thought, isn't it?"

Bradley looked at Rowe's demeanor. "Unbelievable. You know something, don't you?"

"What I know is that mark is extremely powerful, and we must be cautious. We have the symbol to be vigilant for, but we also need to find the missing pages."

"Right, right. We've been so caught up in this mess that I completely forgot. I'll look around the estate."

"Don't fret, Bradley. I'm positive we will find the pages, as well as that mark, and track it down to the individual."

"And Rae?" Bradley asked, clearly concerned for the girl's safety.

"Why yes, Miss Tudor. We must bring her along and keep her under observation."

"Bring her along where?"

"To the Order — we're going back at once."

"You really think the answer is hidden in that old castle?"

Rowe chuckled. "That's where the best things are hidden, amidst the old that are thought to be forgotten."

~*~

*Alexander the Great, Macedonia, 343 BC*

At thirteen years of age, Alexander sat leaning across his stone desk. He admired the display of the vast land in front of him. The hills were green and luscious, surrounded by the sparkling blue water that Macedonia offered.

His thoughts of running through the fields with Bucephalus, his trusty steed, were interrupted by the slamming of a wooden stick on his desk. He looked up and saw a bearded old man with an aura of intelligence standing in front of him, his brows furrowed.

Alexander sat up straighter and pushed the stick away from his desk, in clear defiance of his teacher. He quirked a brow and snickered. "I have one question: is that treatment deserving to the next in line to the throne? Is it, Aristotle?"

"Were the future king to pay attention and comport himself in a polite manner, then the treatment would be reciprocal."

Alexander glared at him as he turned his back and continued to look through his material for today's class.

"Now, today's lesson regards syllogism."

Alexander raised a brow as if to say, "Meaning?"

Aristotle took a seat in front of him and continued. "All men are mortal. All Greeks are men. Therefore, all Greeks are mortal."

This notion got Alexander thinking. He sat back in his seat, somewhat perplexed and somewhat in awe as if he were on the cusp of discovering something new.

He thought to himself, *What if all men weren't mortal?*

~*~

*Chloe, Seattle, Present Day*

With Amber beside her, Chloe spotted Marcus training outside. He moved with agility and dexterity as he practiced his combat skills with Sabre and the other dire wolves. She watched, somewhat amazed, as it appeared everyone was a part of some dangerous dance, all in motion, all anticipating the other's moves.

The girls approached them, and the fighting ceased. Wiping the sweat off his forehead, Marcus saw the concern etched on their faces. "What's wrong? Is it Zaraquel?"

Chloe shook her head. "No, no, Zaraquel is fine. She's helping Rae recuperate with Miss Arianna."

"What is it?" Marcus asked once more.

Amber fought through the tears, her voice trembling. "It's Michael — he's gone."

The dire wolves, along with Marcus, grew attentive at the news. Marcus attempted to gather his thoughts. Meanwhile, Sabre was the first to speak. "And you have no idea where he's gone? He didn't say anything to you?"

Amber angrily looked at him as if he were crazy. "If he had, do you think we'd be here?" She felt the magic tingle at her fingertips, her blood boiling with frustration.

Chloe held her by the shoulder, trying to hold her back. "Amber, he's just trying to help. You know that."

Gaining her composure, Amber closed her eyes and took a deep breath. She opened them to face an empathetic Sabre. "Sabre, I'm sorry. I didn't mean to snap at you."

He patted her shoulder and nodded. Chloe looked at Marcus for a possible answer, and the rest followed suit. Marcus ran his hands over his face and looked up to the sky, in hopes of finding a miraculous answer from the heavens above.

"I don't know where he could've gone."

"You have no clue?" Chloe prodded.

"Look, he's probably out feeding right now. Maybe he needed space." Chloe looked at him, not convinced, but he continued. "With everything that's going on, I can't believe it's easy on him.

Who knows what was done to him while he was trapped in his mind?"

"I never thought of that," Amber said quietly, barely above a whisper, but Chloe heard her.

She looked at her best friend and could see how this situation was affecting her. Even though Michael was awake and alive, Chloe sensed that not everything was as perfect as it seemed. This disconnect between their dreams and their reality only brought Chloe to think about her little cousin Rae.

She could still not grasp what on earth would possess someone to harm a young girl, an imbalanced girl at that. What concerned her, even more, was the fact that she—who had held an incredible amount of power since her daughter's birth, who had transformed into a wolf—hadn't detected that something was wrong with Rae.

After all, it was Rae that had come to her for protection in the first place, and she couldn't even do that. Chloe was going to make it up to her. She had to protect Rae, for she and her family had been through enough tragedy already.

~*~

*Mona, Yakima, 2014*

Mona was the image of Rae; however, they were exact opposites. Where Rae had long dark hair, Mona had long blonde hair. Rae had light skin, and Mona had a sort of cinnamon mixed in, as the darker tone favored her father. Other than that, the girls were identical.

She was sitting across from her sister at the table when she noticed something was wrong. She saw Rae grip the table tightly, and a voice spoke, though not hers.

*"This witch will ban me to silence, but I am both the light and dark. No one will harm the instrument of peace and unification."*

Mona looked at her sister, terrified. She looked into the acheri's eyes and knew she was not her sister. And just as soon it started, the vacant look in her eyes disappeared, and Rae became cognizant.

The coven's overlapping voices invaded Mona's ears, and she couldn't stand all the hate directed at her sister. Rae's acheri side was unpredictable and unstable, but it wasn't her fault she couldn't control it. Mona knew deep in her soul that Rae was a good person, an innocent bystander who was dealt the wrong cards.

When they were younger, it was Rae who had brought in the stray cats. She fed them and took care of them when it seemed no one else would. She was always there for the coven. Whatever they needed — help with a potion, a reading using the sight, or a simple hug — it was Rae. Despite her sassy and sarcastic exterior, her sister was the most loving and honorable person she knew.

Mona was taken away from her thoughts when suddenly she was on her feet, led by Rae. She saw her sister shaking in her boots, their expressions mirroring each other's. They were both frightened of the possibility that they may not see each other again. They ran up the stairs and into their room amidst the chaotic yelling around the dining table.

Mona watched as her sister hurriedly packed some clothes in a duffle bag. She zipped it up and opened the latch to the window, but Mona grabbed her hand to keep her from leaving.

"Rae, what are you doing?"

Rae looked out the window and then back at her sister. "I have to, Mona. You heard what the coven wants to do with me. They're summoning the leader as we speak."

"But—" Mona's eyes filled with tears.

"I don't want to go, but the acheri is getting stronger, and... and...."

"I know, Rae."

Mona pulled her sister into a tight and warm embrace. They held each other, afraid to let go, for they had never been separated before. They weren't just sisters, they were twins, magically bonded for life.

Rae was the first one to let go and looked into Mona's eyes. "I'll be back for you, Desdemona. I promise."

They linked their pinkies together and kissed their respective hands, something they'd always done to seal their promises. Rae turned and walked to the window, gave one last look to Mona, and jumped out. That was the last time the Tudor sisters were in the same room.

~*~

*Michael, Underground Seattle, Present Day*

Michael confidently walked down the narrow alleyway into the underground castle as if he had been there a million times before. The floor was wet with sewer water, the gravel thick with trash, yet he didn't mind the smell. He opened the door and strolled in without a second thought.

It hit him hard, like a punch to the gut—the scent of dried blood. He stopped and inhaled it deeply as if he were taking his very first breath. Walking to a door and slowly twisting the knob to pull the door open, he came face to face with Valentine, Thana, and Krieg. He was the new face of the Avalani.

They looked at him, perturbed that he was the one the Tall Dark Man had sent. Michael took his seat at the head of the table and surveyed the room, seeing each member wearing a look of hatred as well as intrigue.

Krieg was the first to speak. "What? Come back for more torture?"

Michael narrowed his eyes at Krieg and growled, his fangs

on full display. "Silence, Stone Demon. Now, tell me if the army of rogue vampires is ready."

He looked at Michael, confused. "What? How the hell did you know about the army? Only Alaric knew—"

Michael tsked, waving his finger in a "No" gesture. "Knows. Alaric knows." He tapped his temple on the side of his forehead. "He's in here, as he always has been. I know everything."

Thana and Krieg looked in Valentine's direction as if to verify this new wave of information. In response, Valentine nodded and gestured for Michael to continue.

"Krieg, you will continue to follow through with the army; keep it growing, for the queen, and her people are strong. They have incredible magic on their side. Thana, look for Kabos and keep him busy, whatever it takes."

"I know how to do my job," she sneered in his direction.

He stood and leaned over the table, his eyes aglow. "Then do it. Keep Kabos away." Michael shifted his attention to Valentine. "And you, I have a special assignment for you, Valentine."

"Which is…?" Valentine began to lose his patience as he gripped the sides of his chair.

Michael sat back down in his chair, calm and collected as if nothing had occurred. He scanned the room, weighing their every move, every facial expression—analyzing them.

A slow smile appeared on his lips as he noticed his guests were uncomfortable, growing angrier by the second. He milked every second of their unease. It wasn't his role to make their lives easier. If anything, he was up for the challenge.

"Valentine, you have the special opportunity to kill Marcus."

At the sound of Marcus's name, Valentine grew suspicious. "Why?"

"Unfortunately, to my dismay, he has the uncanny ability to know whether Michael is behaving like himself or not. I need

Marcus out of the way."

Puzzled, Thana couldn't quite place the pieces together. "But isn't Marcus your son, Michael?"

Michael whipped his head around to face her, and with great speed, raced to meet her. The blood rushed to his face, boiling hot and tempestuous. He gripped her tightly by the neck, and with magnificent strength, lifted her from the ground, her feet dangling.

"Did I ask you?" he hissed, furious with her idiotic question. Gasping for breath, Thana could not speak or form a complete thought, the oxygen depleting from her brain.

He let go, and she dropped to the floor. He slowly walked to the head of the table and stood there in silence, the anticipation building.

Valentine was the brave one and dared to speak. "And Amber?"

He looked up at them, his eyes blood red. "Leave the queen to me."

They turned to retreat, but he growled to command their attention, and they stopped in their tracks.

"It's Machiel."

~*~

*Merlin, Camelot, 1276*

Deep within the woods surrounding Camelot, Merlin, a strapping young man with sharp blue eyes and dark black hair, and knowledge that surpassed his years, ran through the trees, darting past the shrubbery in hopes of reaching his destination.

Out of breath, he stopped in front of a wall of foliage and flowers. With a wave of his hand, he whispered, *"Eowan,"* and revealed a hidden door within the cobblestone wall. A charge of wind pushed his hair back as he entered the passageway, and behind him, the wall was sealed once more.

With every step he took, fire illuminated his path, until finally, he reached the opening, a large room filled with herbs and ancient ingredients. The rickety shelves on the walls were lined with books and scrolls.

He eyed the cauldron within the hearth and said, *"Ignis flamma,"* and a fire lit underneath the kettle and quickly started to bubble. Merlin racked the shelves looking for a specific book he had in mind.

"Aha." He found the volume and reached for it. In his hands, he had a delicately crafted book, made from worn soft leather with embossed writing which read, *Balocræftum*. He blew on the cover to rid it from the dust and cracked it open. While perusing the pages, he flipped through eagerly. Merlin found what he was in search of.

In the middle was a hole gouged out from the pages. He reached inside and pulled out an amulet, magnificently encrusted with all sorts of gems and diamonds. It radiated light and glowed. He pulled it up to his face and inspected it, the jewel aglow in his visage. His eyes sparkled in admiration.

# Chapter 7

With the power to control objects with her mind, Amber distracted herself by practicing and preparing for the ultimate battle, as was predicted in the prophecy. She stood outside, surrounded by different obstacles displayed on the grounds. There were bows and arrows set at varying distances in front of their respective targets, scraps of metal from a junkyard, as well as a vast array of weapons to measure her adroitness.

As she lifted a car door from the ground, she could feel her blood pumping, her heart racing. Amber pushed her body and her mind to the limit. She moved her hands as if she were stretching some invisible fabric. Right before her eyes, the car was pulled apart slowly — she heard the crunch and crackle of the metal. The anger of the past day and the overall frustration of her situation culminated into a heart-searing scream as she shattered the car door. The pieces were vaporized into tiny fragments that floated across the air. She placed her hands at her sides, and the steel fragments fell like hail.

Her surge in power emulated how she felt. How could Michael abandon her when she had fought incredibly hard to get him back? She felt just like the bits of ore that fell upon her, shattered. Amber couldn't wrap her brain around why he was acting the way he was. Her mind was riddled with unsettling thoughts.

*I love him. Why'd he disappear? Did I do something wrong? I mean, how could I have done something? He literally just woke up. I don't understand what's going on. The situation with Rae and Zaraquel fulfilling her part of the prophecy – it's just too much. I don't know how to handle it.*

Her hands trembled as the anxiety inched down her throat and into her stomach. With her stress at an all-time high, the objects around her — the weapons and equipment, the fallen leaves, her hair — all levitated.

She heard him before she saw him. "Am I interrupting something?"

Amber turned to see Michael with a smirk on his face.

~*~

*Michael, Seattle, Present Day*

He snickered as he saw her ears turn red to match her hair. Amber's nostrils flared, the hail pounding harder onto the ground. He walked towards her, unfazed, and she marched up to him, clearly offended. A tennis ball flew in his direction, but he stealthily caught it with one hand.

"Is something bothering you, dear?" He eyed her mischievously.

She walked up to him, their noses almost touching. He could feel her hot breath against his skin, inhaled it even.

"*Really*, Michael? That's the first thing you have to say?"

A piece of metal fell on his shoulder, and he flicked it off nonchalantly. "Relax, Amber. I just went for a walk." He took a few steps and walked around her.

She took off to follow him. "Hey, I'm not done talking to you,

Michael!"

He gritted his teeth at the sound of the word that was once his name. He clenched his fists, feeling his nails transform into his claws and embed in his skin. He had to control his anger or the plan would end before it began.

Michael took a few calming breaths and turned around. "*Mi amor.*"

He cringed as he said those words, but continued, nonetheless. She raised a brow, waiting for a response. He took her by the shoulders and imagined squeezing her so hard, her skin would crush beneath his force. Michael shook those thoughts away.

"Amber. I needed to clear my head. I—"

"You were gone for more than half the day! I went crazy, looking everywhere for you. Day and night, Michael, I was by your side, worried sick about you. And you just walk off? Nowhere to be seen. I mean, I know you're older, but have you heard of this invention called the cellphone?"

He resisted the urge to roll his eyes at her melodrama. "I know, I know, and I apologize. But I had to collect my thoughts."

He sighed dramatically, wanting to sell his part. He took the chance to sit on the bench behind him and pulled on Amber's hand so she would do the same. He needed her to feel like he wanted her. This had to work. His plan to make her stay in love with him was crucial, so he could crush her heart—just as she had done to him once before, when she was Illyris and was in love with Giorgos.

Grabbing her hands, he placed them on his lap and felt her soften with his touch. Perfect. "With everything that occurred with my memory, I needed to figure out who I was, even if it was for a couple of hours." He looked down as if he were terribly sad.

Amber lifted up his chin with the tip of her finger till he looked up at her. "It's not your fault." She looked at him with sad eyes. "I guess I overreacted. But Michael, I was worried."

She placed her hands around his neck and played with his hair. It took everything he had not to push her away. Being close to her, all he could see was red. He hated her. So much.

"I don't want to lose you. I just got you back." He inhaled her scent as she scooted in closer to him, practically sitting on his lap. Their lips touched as she whispered, "I love you."

He closed his eyes, anguished as if he were being burned with the contact of her lips against his.

~*~

*Pandora Tudor, Yakima, 1995*

Pandora's hair was cut into a chic shag framing her face. Dressed in a tank top, baggy overalls, and Dr. Martens, she was the epitome of grunge. Her expression matched her mood — brows furrowed, stiff lips. She was pissed.

Weeks before she'd reached out to her coven — her family, specifically her mother — for some financial support. Their answer was a definite no. She walked in the woods leading to the backyard of her family house. The wind rustled the fall leaves as they fell, and specks of orange, yellow, and red filled her vision. Her hands jittered from the withdrawal of the drugs in her system.

The sunlight hit her silver bracelet and shone in her eyes. It caught her attention, as it remained a permanent fixture on her wrist since Briar had given it to her. It was an intricately crafted silver cuff embossed with florals and ancient writing, one that she couldn't quite piece together.

She felt a stronger connection, as she was magnetically drawn to him, not willing to part from him longer than a couple of days. Pandora had tried it once, one day longer than she usually did, and remembered feeling ill, sick to her stomach — her body weak, her hands shaking. That was the only time she'd risked being away from her beloved.

She felt as if this was a sign from the gods, from the stars, from the fates, that she was meant to be with Briar. After all, this was what she had always wanted, always wished for when she blew out the candles — to be loved, greatly and passionately. And that he did — he loved her. Pandora felt his love with every fiber of her being.

Waving her hands above the tall, unkempt grass, she let the wind hit her body as she neared her destination: her childhood home. Before she touched the doorknob, the memories ambushed her in waves. Running through the hallways with her sister, Marlene, as a young girl; giggling under the covers of their adjoining beds as they played with an ouija board; their mother teaching them incantations. That's what she had missed most during her time away, her family.

Noticing the track marks on her arm, like bruises on her pasty white skin, Pandora placed a cloaking spell on them. "*A facie abscondam.*" The marks disappeared before her eyes. She twisted the knob and found it to be locked, and whispered, "*Patentibus,*" hoping the door would open with a simple spell — but it didn't.

"What the hell?" Pandora opened her mouth to speak once more but saw that the knob was turning from the inside.

A young girl, about ten years of age, with black hair cut her to her shoulders and big round eyes, opened the door. "Can I help you?" Pandora saw the young girl tapping her foot, waiting impatiently.

"Who's at the door?"

Pandora remained still, as she would recognize that voice anywhere — her sister. As if she had conjured her with the mere thought of her, she appeared behind the young girl. Her eyes widened in surprise at first, quickly followed with disappointment.

Her eyes never leaving Pandora's, she talked to the girl, her tone harsh. "Go to your room, Chloe."

Pandora eyed the girl. "Chloe?" Then she looked at her sister. "That's Chloe?"

Marlene gently urged Chloe to go on upstairs, but not before Pandora met Chloe's confused stare before she disappeared into the hallway.

Pandora stood before her sister, taking her in. She looked the same — long hair, bohemian style of dress, boots. But her eyes were different. They were no longer kind or understanding — they were cold, distant.

"What do you want, Pandora?"

"Wow. I mean, Chloe's really big — like, whoa." She chuckled as she anxiously scratched her arm.

Marlene glared at her, not buying the act. "Yeah, well, a lot can happen in five years. What do you want?"

"C'mon, Marlene. Don't be like that. You know things are complicated."

"What I know is that the person I'm looking at is *not* my sister. I mean, have you looked at yourself lately? Really, Dor. It looks like you've barely eaten, and you're shaking."

Pandora felt like her insides wanted to come out and make an appearance at her sister's words.

M sighed, heartbroken by what she'd told her sister. "Look, I've given you money over the years, and I've tried more times than I can count to get you into rehab. But if money is what you want now, that stops today. I can't anymore."

"I know you and Mom —"

"Mom's gone."

Pandora looked up at her sister, mouth open in shock. "What do you mean, gone?"

Marlene looked down at her scuffed boots, and then, with watery eyes, back up at her sister. "I called you, Dor. I called you so many times, and the one time you did pick up, it was clear you were high out of your mind."

Taking a couple of steps back, Pandora shook her head in denial. "No, no. I would have remembered."

"Would you, though?"

The truth sank in, and she realized she really wouldn't have, and she felt the tears fall down her face, her whole body shaking as she fell to the floor. Her sister knelt down in front of her as they cried together for the first time in years.

She choked back the tears but spoke anyway. "I'm sorry."

Her sister took her hand in hers and held it tight. "I know, sweetie. I know." They sat on the floor embracing for a while. It could've been hours or more, they didn't know.

Marlene was the first to break the silence. "Come home. It's time."

Pandora took a moment to respond. "I...I can't."

She felt the cold air ambush her as her sister stood up, gave her one last look, and closed the door.

~*~

*Bradley and Rowe, Seattle, Present Day*

Bradley and Rowe walked in tandem as they spotted Chloe in the garden, cleaning up the mess that Amber had made during her practice session. They saw her lift her hands and chant, "*Resurgemus et pœnitentiam age*," and the material rose and began to return to its original form.

Rowe clapped, clearly amused by her growing powers. She looked back, startled, and the objects fell to the ground once more, shattered.

"Darling child, continue," Rowe assured her in a kind

manner. Chloe raised her hands and completed the incantation. She rubbed her hands on her billowing skirt as if there were some invisible residue that she wanted to get rid of.

They saw the concern on her face as she turned to face them. "Is something wrong?"

Bradley shook his head. "Quite the opposite, actually." Rowe and Bradley shared a look of quiet confidence, hoping their plan would come to fruition.

Chloe raised a brow, not one for pleasantries at that moment. "Well?"

Bradley cleared his throat and stood a bit taller as if he were ready to present something. In fact, he was.

"Chloe, I have been at the estate for only a short while, and I have—well, we, really—have witnessed incredible feats of power not only from Amber and yourself, but from the rest of the women in your family."

"You mean Zaraquel and Rae?" she asked for confirmation.

He nodded, then proceeded. "Yes, them indeed. And it's our…," he gestured to Rowe, whose eyes glittered with anticipation, "sincere hope that you will accept this as an invitation to the Order of Taliesin."

Chloe sputtered in response. "Uh, as in *the* Order? It's real?"

Rowe let out a good, heartfelt chuckle, the kind that originated from deep within the pit of his stomach. His smile was so incredibly genuine that his eyes crinkled at the edges.

"The Order is more or less essentially a person," Bradley said, glancing in Rowe's direction.

Chloe followed his gaze, and her eyes widened. "No way. Whoa. I heard stories about it as a girl."

Rowe followed up with a smile. "You and the girls will join us, develop your powers—grow them, nurture them—and in turn, figure out who it was that cursed Rae."

"Well, that sounds wonderf—"

"Great, so we'll make arrangements to leave tonight." Bradley cut her off before she could finish her sentence.

The sound of that particular bit of information seemed to sober Chloe up from her excitement. "Wait, wait. Tonight?"

"Yes, we need to leave as soon as possible before things take a turn for the worse."

"Bradley, you don't get it, do you? I can't just up and leave. I have a family. Amber. I have responsibilities."

"You're right. It is your responsibility to protect your family, and that is what we are trying to do. The Order is the safest place you three could be right now."

"That…. I don't know. I mean, Marcus is my husband, and Zaraquel still needs to find her first justified kill for the prophecy. I still don't know how to control my transformations, and… and…."

"Chloe—"

Rowe placed his hand in the air, interrupting Bradley. He calmly grabbed Chloe by the shoulders and looked her in the eyes, calming the raging storm she felt within her. He eased the tension out of her body, out of her mind, and she stood there waiting to listen.

"The Order—*we*—would like nothing more than to help you, but we cannot if you are not physically there."

"Why does it matter if I'm there or not?"

"The castle of the Order is special. It was built on the remains of the enchanted forest, Broceliande. It is protected by the purest of magic, and therefore the oldest and most sacred. If one is physically there, their power, their magic, will be more powerful, truly capable of reaching its full potential. Do you wish to protect your loved ones?"

Chloe nodded her head, and without hesitation, responded,

"Yes."

"Then please, come with us."

Her uncertainty escaped via a heavy sigh, as the decision weighed on her shoulders.

"Can I bring Marcus along?"

Rowe and McPherson shared a look that didn't fair well for Chloe.

"What? Can I?"

The great witch looked at her sympathetically and approached her softly. "I'm afraid, my dear, that your husband is still a creature of the night, and as such, is prohibited from entering the castle."

"I don't understand," she said, barely above a whisper.

"Long ago, before your time, before Bradley's even, precautions were established to keep vampires and werewolves alike out of the premises. If they happened to stumble upon the grounds, an indestructible blaze would set them on fire. No one can tame it, not even I."

"Oh." Her eyes filled with tears that threatened to fall.

And with that, the men left her to make an impossibly difficult decision.

~*~

*Malakai, Seattle, Present Day*

Wandering through the aisles of the supermarket, Malakai had a cart full of provisions, from sweet and savory to necessities like bread and different cuts of meat. This was his weekly run, as he oversaw gathering the groceries. He didn't have to, but he liked to keep himself busy. He'd volunteer for anything to keep his thoughts from wandering to Amber.

He didn't like putting up a wall that separated them, especially since they had gotten so close, but he felt it was essential. She had

Michael back, and Malakai needed to realize that she didn't need him like that — they were merely friends. He could deal with that, but he just needed time to adjust. Or at least, that's what he kept telling himself.

As he was perusing the cereal, a scent caught his attention. It wasn't the typical smell one would find in a supermarket. Not that anyone would notice it, but given that he was a wolf, that made Malakai the exception.

He dropped the cereal box in the cart, not really minding what kind he picked out; rather, he let his nose lead him. The scent was different as if it was aged and matured somehow, yet the more he focused in on the fragrance, the more familiar it felt, like he'd smelled it somewhere before and just couldn't place it.

*Like campfire and wood,* he thought.

Pushing the cart around, mindlessly it seemed, he bumped into customers who stuck up their noses and glared in his direction, but he didn't mind. He had to find where that odor was coming from. He knew he wasn't crazy. He had smelled that scent before — the wolf in him *knew* it.

The adrenaline kicked in as he got closer and closer to the scent in question. He spotted a man — tall, with a muscular build. The man turned, and Malakai caught sight of his profile.

"It couldn't be," he whispered, completely in shock — so much so that he stopped dead in his tracks. He felt his heart in his throat, the handle of the cart bending beneath his tight grip. "Nikoli?"

He saw him across the room, as clear as day. As if sensing that someone was watching him, Nikoli turned and looked at Malakai. A blank expression crossed his countenance, seeing right through him, past him. Just as quickly as he'd turned in the first place, he turned away and began to walk once again.

Malakai discarded the cart and sent it flying, causing horrified screams of the customers in the store. A crowd emerged, blocking him from reaching Nikoli, if that really was him. He pushed them away with one goal in mind: to catch Nikoli.

Nikoli got lost in the sea of people, and Malakai lost sight of him. He ran outside the store to see if he could find him once more. All that was left was the faint scent of campfire and wood. He scratched his head, utterly confused. He began to think what he'd seen was a figment of his imagination. But to him, it seemed so real. Utterly puzzled, he returned to the store to collect his cart.

~*~

*Briar Hexham, England, 1986*

Settled in his childhood home, Briar was alone, as he had been since the death of his parents three years ago. An orphan at the age of thirteen, he was left to raise himself with books as his only teachers and companions. The folks in town were cautious when it came to Briar Hexham. They didn't know what to think of him — the tall, lanky loner who listened to punk music loud enough to wake up the entire neighborhood. The Clash and The Sex Pistols played in a constant loop, alienating him from the adolescents, who failed to understand him.

Mystery and rumors surrounded him — that he sacrificed animals and ate them for breakfast; that he was a shaman with spirit friends; that he walked the night in women's clothing; that he murdered his parents.

His parents' death was a sudden and inexplicable one. One day they were happily in love and dancing around the house, and then the next, they were nowhere to be seen. Never one that was terribly close to his parents, Briar didn't think much of their disappearance. To him, it seemed as if they had finally decided to leave, for they hadn't asked for a son who had dark predilections and could create things out of thin air. It was not like people asked those questions on the adoption form.

He'd never really felt like he belonged, even with the people who chose to love him. When he realized this, he became detached and calculated. By sixteen, he wore his emotions like a mask that he could take off and put back on when convenient. The girls loved him, and some boys too, but most despised him.

It was all an act. He wanted to perfect the performance of being normal, and when he did so, when he smiled and laughed and hung out at the chip shop, those around him seemed to be more open to the idea of accepting him, forgetting his questionable past.

Despite the fact that he pretended, the dreams that kept him up at night reminded him that he was not "normal." They seemed so real but as fantastical as they were, he knew they weren't. The dreams consisted of the supernatural, magic, and an unexplainable urge to collect things—everything: rarities, knowledge, power. He felt he was meant for something bigger in the world than merely fixing clocks and televisions that the locals brought him. Briar wasn't just a fixer, but a creator.

One dream, or rather a nightmare, haunted him almost every night. He stood in the clearing of a forest—was it the one behind his house? He never could tell, but there he was on his knees, waiting, for what felt like hours—days even. His eyes were open, but he couldn't see or hear anything, as if stuck in a bottomless void. Then he heard the hooves walk around him, then in front of him.

*Click. Clack.* Twice, then three times.

Then suddenly, his vision worked as it had before he fell asleep, and he could see. But what terrified him—which spoke volumes, for he was rarely scared—was what he saw each time he closed his eyes.

He saw a giant goat standing on his hind legs, eyes red and

glowing, holding a baby in each hand. Their cries were more like torturous screams that seemed better suited to the underworld than the clearing of a forest.

Each night the outcries woke him up, his skin slick with sweat.

~*~

One night when he was making his rounds in the forest to see if he could find any scraps tourists left behind when camping, he heard a soft whisper.

"Briar...."

He stilled at the sound of his name and turned around to see no one or nothing in sight.

He was alone.

In the dark.

So, he crouched down and continued to shine the flashlight.

"...Hexham."

He stopped once more and looked over his shoulder. His forehead crinkled with lines of confusion. "Hexham? Who the hell is Hexham?" His voice was thick with an English accent.

The bodiless voice laughed, and the closer he listened, the more definite the voice became. A woman's voice spoke to him loud and clear as if she were standing right in front, having a conversation with him.

Briar's voice quivered, partly from fear and partly from fascination. "Who are you? *Where* are you?" He shined the flashlight but saw nothing. Complete darkness and trees, that was it.

The woman's voice laughed mockingly in return. *"Who I am is not important — for now. But I am everywhere and nowhere, all the same."*

As the voice spoke, Briar felt a sense of ease overwhelm his body. The fear and anxiety dissipated. For the first time in his life, he felt like he belonged, truly and deeply, just by the sound of her voice.

*"You do belong. We are family, a family of witches. The most powerful to have walked the earth. We lost you, but now you are found."*

He looked out to no one in particular, but his shock was evident. "Witches? That's ludicrous."

*"If that were true, how are you speaking to me and vice versa? I see you; I hear you and respond. But you can only hear me, as that is my intention. I can control things at will. I am standing right before your eyes, yet you show no indication of seeing me."*

And he couldn't. He waved his hands in front of him to where she supposedly stood, and there was a great temperature change—it was colder, significantly so.

"This can't be happening," he muttered to himself, still in disbelief.

*"The dreams, the girls—they are very much real."*

His breath caught in his throat. *How could she know?*

*"You, Briar Hexham, are important to his plan,"* the voice said, all too knowingly.

"Plan? What plan? *Whose* plan?"

"All in good time. The master will reveal himself."

# Chapter 8

Tapping her fingers on the tabletop, Chloe took another hefty bite of a leftover muffin she'd managed to save from Amber's breakfast fest. She sat there, consumed by her thoughts of the conversation she shared with McPherson and Rowe. She still couldn't believe the Order was real. That was literally the stuff of legends, a bedtime story her mother had told her to quiet her always racing mind.

And here she was, years later as an adult, seriously considering the prospect of joining—along with her daughter and cousin, of course—but the invitation was lingering in the air, nonetheless. Her skin crawled with anticipation at the thought of controlling her powers and possibly growing them as well. Her life as a full-fledged witch was a fact she thought was fascinating. Chloe didn't recognize herself—she was far from the girl who'd loved to party and loved to love. She was a completely different person.

Never in her wildest dreams had she believed she was going to marry, period. And a vampire, no less. That, and she was a mother, something she would never change in the whole world. She'd do anything to protect both Zaraquel and Marcus, even if that meant leaving one of them behind.

Her heart had broken the instant they told her that he was forbidden from joining them in the Order. At one moment, she would've smirked at the idea of a forbidden rendezvous between her and her husband, but not if it guaranteed his death. She would not risk it. Despite herself, she'd fallen for him — and hard.

As if her thoughts summoned him, he came strolling into the kitchen with a wide smile on his face. However, the second he saw her forlorn expression, it faltered.

"What's wrong, Chloe?" he asked as he sat across from her, so close their knees kissed.

"We have to talk." The words came out like gravel, slow and grueling. She ran her hands through his hair, lingering as she touched his face, committing it to memory.

He took a hold of her hands and held them tight in his. "Hey, whatever is going on, you can tell me. Forever, remember?"

She nodded at the certainty of his voice, of his words, which gave her the courage to continue. "Rowe and McPherson invited Zaraquel, Rae, and I to go to the Order's castle."

"Sounds important. Is that good?"

She chuckled, the excitement getting to her. "It's great, actually — surreal. You don't understand, Marcus, Rowe and Bradley are extremely well regarded within the witch community. They're immensely powerful — I mean, you saw what they did with Rae."

His face lit up at her apparent enthusiasm. "That's great, babe. What's the problem?"

"We leave tonight."

His brows furrowed in confusion. "That's a little short notice, but I'm pretty sure we can pack up fairly quickly."

She squeezed his hand, clutching it as if for dear life. He looked down at their clutched hands and then back up at her.

"There's something you're not telling me. What is it?"

Her voice broke. "You…you can't go."

His hands fell and curled into fists as they parted ways. He stood, slowly creating distance between them. Marcus spoke in a low, eerily cool tone. "What do you mean, I can't go?"

She stood, following him around the kitchen. "It's not that I don't want you to, Marcus. You cannot be there—it's physically impossible."

He tried to control his anger. She could see him taking calming breaths—up and down his shoulders went. She walked around to cup her hands over his face. She didn't like to see him sad, that was the last thing she wanted to do. But she had to tell him the truth, he deserved it.

"Listen, the Order's castle is protected by a spell that keeps the witches safe inside, and…well, the werewolves and vampires out. If you even tried to get in, you'd burn alive."

"What about Rowe and McPherson? They can't—I don't know, break it?"

She heard the hope as well as frustration in his voice, and she hated that she was the cause of his misery. "No, I'm afraid they can't."

"And you're still planning on going? Tonight?"

Her emotions were fraught, she couldn't speak. She didn't.

"I see. So, your mind's made up, isn't it? We're *partners* in this marriage, Chloe. *Bonded*, don't you get that? I can barely be away from you for two hours without feeling an ache in my chest."

The tears flowed freely now. "I know. I know. I feel it too. But I can't pass this up. I have to go."

"For *your* powers."

That remark lit a fire. She was angry that he thought she could be so selfish. She felt her magic sizzle at her fingertips and saw him become slightly alarmed.

"No. For Zaraquel and for you. The fact that even crossed your mind shows how little you know me. And that? That *hurts*." He opened his mouth to reply, but she shut his mouth with a snap of her fingers. "I am not done," she growled.

He glared at her, and she knew he was angry that she'd used her powers on him, but she didn't care.

"I'm not going to lie and say that going there is not going to make me more powerful, because it is. And I need to be. Zaraquel and Rae, for that matter, need to learn how to protect themselves, and even more, how to defend themselves. I don't know everything, and God, at times, I wish I did, but I don't. I need help, and I can only get it there, at the Order. And I'm sorry, Marcus, but we're going even if you can't. I must. I have to protect you, Zaraquel, Amber—everyone—and I need to be ready."

She snapped her fingers to restore his ability to talk once more and gave him a soft kiss on the lips. She walked out, leaving him behind.

~*~

*Krieg, Seattle, Present Day*

He had heard stories, horrified accounts surrounding the life of Machiel. To Krieg, the illusive Machiel was known as the ripper, for he ripped up the bodies of his prey, leaving them unrecognizable. He was the epitome of a monster. Krieg smiled at the thought of the Michael he'd stabbed, the self-righteous white knight persona that he carried himself with.

"And now look at him. He reverted back to his bloodthirsty ways," he chuckled to himself as he took a sip of his whiskey from his cup. "We're so fucked." His eyes glittered with mischief, picturing the destruction he was placed in charge of. He was prepared—he had the people, the weapons, the motivation. He just needed to know the day, and he was ready to bring the fight on.

He was lost in his thoughts, plotting and calculating, when Fydor, Ivanna, Nataliya, and Demetri entered, gaggling like a bunch of schoolgirls. Krieg rolled his eyes, tired of their recklessness. They drank and indulged in drugs and sex way too much for Krieg's liking. They had a mission, and it was his prerogative to bring that to completion.

"Listen and listen good, you little shits."

The group stopped in their tracks.

Krieg continued. "The time has come to stop all your pussyfooting and get to work. I don't give a damn how you get it done, all that matters is that you do. It's time to raise the army."

Demetri scoffed. "What army? Alaric's dead—there's no reason for us to listen to his *bitch*."

The group behind him laughed amongst themselves but soon grew silent when Krieg charged in Demetri's direction, crushing his throat in his stone fist. Ivanna moved to approach them, but Krieg whipped his face in her direction and snarled, "Don't even think about it."

She stopped, her eyes wide with fear as she glanced over to Demetri. She quickly retreated.

"Alaric is not dead. He has just been…reborn. This work still needs to be done. It has to be. I don't particularly need you." Krieg applied pressure to Demetri's neck, which made him gasp for dear life. Krieg didn't stop and squeezed harder, a glint in his eye. He was enjoying this.

Nataliya screeched, "You're killing him!"

He let Demetri go, and he plopped to the floor, unconscious. Meanwhile, Krieg surveyed the room, meeting each one in the eyes. "Do not question me. Do as you are told and follow orders. Is that understood."

All three nodded, terrified to upset the tyrannical Krieg.

~*~

*Amber, Seattle, Present Day*

Anxiously pulling the hem of her dress down, Amber sat across from Michael at *Mordere*. Taking his time looking over the menu, Michael hadn't paid any attention to her since the moment she returned from the restroom seconds ago. She stared at him and tried to get his attention by clearing her throat — to no avail, it seemed. For some reason, unbeknownst to her, he was ignoring her.

*He's so different. Why? I just can't put my finger on it,* she thought as she took a sip of her wine. Amber looked up at him once more and saw that he was looking at her, glaring just for a second, and then just as quickly as it appeared, it was gone. It was replaced by a small smile that didn't really sync up with the rest of his face. He was staring off at the other end of the room, smoldering. Amber knew that look all too well — his bedroom eyes on full display. Turning to follow his gaze, she saw a beautiful blonde, a Gigi Hadid look alike.

*Well, he can look all he wants. He's not getting anything from me tonight.*

She scoffed and chugged down her wine till there was nothing left. She decided it was time for her to enjoy herself, despite Michael having a stick up his ass and looking at other women, *in front of her*. She'd give him his time, but was going to stop feeling sorry for herself, which she found she was doing more often.

She wasn't a fan of this version of Amber, sulking and demure. That was not her. No one, not even Michael, would succeed in changing her into someone she wasn't. Like Illyris and Bircenna before her, Amber was fiercely strong and independent.

Spotting Sofia through a window leading to the kitchen, Amber got up from her seat. Michael craned his neck to look up at her, displeased by her abrupt departure. He grabbed her forearm to keep her from leaving. "Where do you think you are going?"

Looking down at the tight hold he had on her, she glared at him and roughly shook off his arm.

"Unhand me, Michael. *Now*."

He met her glare with equal intensity until finally, he let go. "*You* invited me, Amber. And you are *leaving*? That's ridiculous."

She scoffed, practically fighting back the laughter that was bubbling within. "We've been here twenty minutes, Michael, and you've barely said a word to me, let alone looked at me." She glanced in the direction of the beautiful woman, who waved at Michael, to prove her point.

He stood, straightening his jacket. "Is it really my fault? I mean, she has eyes — I can't blame her."

Her eyes felt like they wanted to bug out of her skull as the anger radiated off her. Suddenly the lights in the restaurant began to flicker uncontrollably. Everyone inside the restaurant, including Sofia, looked around to see what was causing the disturbance; murmurs and questions filled the room. Amber's eyes were set aglow, her hair floating as if underwater. She felt a hand touch her shoulder gently. She turned her head violently, only to face a frightened Sofia.

"What's wrong, *dolcezza*? Is everything all right?" She looked back and forth from her to Michael, who, with a clenched jaw, couldn't look more upset.

"Amber, calm the fuck down," he whispered, low enough that only she and Sofia heard. He was seething.

"Calm down. Calm down? *Me*?" She unclenched her fists and threw her hands up in the air, tired and frustrated with his cavalier attitude, causing all the bulbs to burst. Some of the guests gasped while others groaned, upset that they couldn't finish their respective meals.

Sophia took Amber's hand in hers. "Hey, *bella*? Why don't we take this outside, huh?"

Michael led the way out the back entrance, the girls following him, a substantial space between them.

Amber shook her head and sighed, slightly embarrassed by the scene she had caused. "I'm so sorry, Sofia."

"Don't worry. All couples are prone to a lover's quarrel occasionally. It's the makeup sex that will make all this worthwhile."

Sofia chuckled, but Amber couldn't find the humor in this situation. She could see Michael ahead of them as he got into the driver's seat, and worry painted her features.

"It'll be fine, Amber. You love him, no?"

She nodded in response, not able to trust herself to speak.

"Love, that's all it takes, bella," Sofia said with confidence.

She waved goodbye to Sofia and made her way to the car. *I sure hope so,* she thought to herself. She hopped into the vehicle, and Michael sped off into the street.

She nervously rubbed her amulet, hoping the worries would disappear.

~*~

*Briar, England, 1989*

*You forgot the arrowroot.* Briar heard the woman's voice in his mind, as he had heard her for the past three years since they "met." He didn't know her name. He never asked, nor did he want to. She, if she even was a she, was an enchanting eidolon that was there for the sole purpose of helping him, or so it seemed.

For once, he felt special, and not like a freak. She made him feel special as a mother would have — or so he thought since he'd never experienced the love of a maternal figure.

It was she who convinced him to apply to join the illustrious and arcane Circle. The Circle was a school for the magically gifted, particularly witches, hidden in the depths of England. Only those with a special alchemic forte were accepted, and for Briar, this was where he excelled. Since he'd been young, he'd always dabbled in creating things that appeared as if out of thin air. He practiced in the silence and comfort of his home, for he didn't want to be a novice. He didn't need another reason for people to judge him. And so, under the guidance of his protector, he succeeded in gaining a spot within the deeply coveted Circle.

It was a boarding school packed with rigorous study, not for the faint of heart. The only things that flooded the school more than magic were the drugs and alcohol that made their way into the rooms of almost every student. Who could blame them? They were expected to be the best of the best, and if they faltered, they were kicked out, never to return. Not only that, but any memory of their time spent at the Circle would be erased. It was Briar's main mission, according to his advisor, to stay in the school and excel. He could not fail her, for she had given him a purpose, a life, and he would not let her down.

Therefore, through long days and even longer nights, he voraciously studied and gained the knowledge he needed to be the top student, as he had been for the two years he'd been in attendance. He had one more year, and he aimed to maintain the spot. If there was one thing Briar didn't like, it was losing.

Most of the time he was burrowed in the library, and subsequently gained the reputation as the misunderstood recluse. Nevertheless, given his charisma and the perfection of his "act," he was popular with the female population. They fell for his rare smiles and glittering eyes, which was his intention; however, when it came to his studies, he preferred to be alone.

The one exception was his roommate Mick. He understood that Briar needed his space to think, to create, and he respected that. He didn't push or prod him, just merely accepted him for who he was. They both admired the power that books held, and spent most of their weekends at the library analyzing and learning spells and then putting them to the test in the forest outside the school's grounds.

One afternoon, while the rest of the students were out celebrating the annual Winter Solstice Festival, the boys were hanging out at their usual spot near two trees that were twisted into each other in the forest. Mick was struggling to correctly annunciate a spell to change the gloomy weather into sunshine. Briar sat on the ground, furiously taking notes in his notebook. He scribbled in his broken scrawl a spell to enchant a bracelet or a cuff that held the ability to block a witch's power. A rough sketch of said item was detailed at the bottom of the page. He scratched his head, stuck on the quandary of how to prevent the witch who wore it from figuring out it was enchanted. It didn't help that Mick's incessant rambling was all he heard.

"*Huc veni…. M-mane-bo…,*" Mick sputtered, lifting his hands in the air.

Briar rolled his eyes. "Really, Mick? It's a spell, they're not that hard. It's *huc venit soli nunc manebo.*" As soon as he said the words, a burst of light parted the clouds.

Mick looked up, mouth agape. Peeved that he couldn't achieve it on his own, Mick picked up a tiny pebble and launched it in Briar's direction, hitting him on his head. "Perhaps not hard for you. You're every professor's wet dream."

He brushed the pebble off his shoulder and quirked his brow, smirking at Mick. "Even Professor Hambeldon?"

"God, yes. Especially Hambeldon. Did you see that shirt she

was wearing? So low-cut, every time she leaned over her desk...." Mick playfully bit his fist and groaned. "She probably did that on purpose. Evil temptress."

Briar laughed at Mick's antics. "Before you start plotting ways to seduce our dear prof, don't you think you should at least — I don't know — gain some experience? I mean, have you had someone give your todger a proper tug? Besides your own hand, of course."

"Fuck off, mate."

"You've been doing plenty of that on your own for the both of us."

"You're a serious wazzock, you know, that right?"

"All I'm saying is that you wouldn't be so stressed if you got out of your head. Or, in your case, get some head." He laughed at his own pun.

Nervously Mick ran a hand through his hair, not meeting Briar's gaze. "Is it really so bad to wait?"

Briar took a moment, considering his response, but relied on his snark instead. "Ever the romantic, Mick. Didn't know you had it in you." Briar snickered as Mick's face began to flush. But that quickly changed when he met Briar head on, seriousness painting his features.

"You've got a balls-up view on relationships, mate. It takes more than the physical shit to make a legitimate connection with someone. But what would you know, right?"

Briar stood there, slightly taken aback by his words. Who would've thought Mick would grow a set and confront him? *Him?* But then again.... *He was right,* Briar thought to himself. *What would I know?*

He didn't know how to love, how to be loved. He wasn't wired that way. The only sort of affection he felt was for the woman he'd never met. She wanted to protect him, like a mother, and he didn't know what to make of it.

"You're right."

Mick looked at him, shocked by the admission. Briar shook his head and began to walk off in the direction of the school. When he saw that he wasn't being followed by his friend, he waved him over.

"C'mon, Mick, pick up your jaw from the ground. That's the only time you're gonna hear it."

"Right, right then." Mick followed Briar, not wanting to be left behind.

~*~

*Marcus, Seattle, Present Day*

His body was drenched in sweat as he jumped back and forth on the balls of his feet. Marcus stood in Michael's home gym, cautiously approaching the punching bag. Despite its rapid palpitations with every hit to the punching bag, Marcus's heart broke even more. It had been hours since his conversation with Chloe. He loved her with every fiber of his being—she was the mother of his child, the love of his life. But right now?

Right now, he was angry.

He could not believe she would leave him—leave with Zaraquel and *not* him. He punched the bag repeatedly as memories sped in his mind. They hit him in quick, successive flashes.

The night they first met, her long black hair cascading down her back, her hiding her smile from him.

*Punch.*

Zaraquel's birth. He'd felt the tears well up in his eyes as he looked down at his girls.

*Another swing and a punch.*

Chloe freaking out as Zaraquel took her first steps, as he

sat behind them, recording her with his phone. He laughed at Chloe's childlike expression as she clapped her hands.

*Punch. Punch. Punch.*

And now when Chloe approached, hands shaking, tears in her eyes. He'd known something was wrong the moment he walked in. He saw her, head down and feeling blue. The words she was speaking were foreign to him. As he went over every sentence, she'd said, the anger bubbled inside of him.

*"I need help, and I can only get it there, at the Order."* Her voice rattled in his head.

Did she not think he was good enough for her? To protect her? He unfurled his fists, letting his claws out, his eyes red with fury, and went for it with the punching bag. Feeling the material rip before him, he saw the sand pour out and hit the mat.

~*~

*Malakai, Seattle, Present Day*

Still out of sorts from his outing to the supermarket. Malakai wasn't sure what or who he'd seen. He couldn't wrap his head around the mystical occurrence. Was the undead real? He'd heard rumors within the supernatural community, but he hadn't believed the whispers—until he saw Nikoli. Well, at least he thought that was Nikoli.

He whipped out his phone to call Miriam, but he heard something hit the floor, hard.

Malakai stopped in the hallway and peeked through the door into the home gym. What he saw was Marcus pounding the floor like a lunatic. He ran in to keep Marcus from hurting himself.

~*~

*Marcus, Seattle, Present Day*

Clawing at the mound of sand on the floor, Marcus simply

couldn't contain his anger. He felt a strong force push him back and arched his neck to look up at him. It was Malakai. He did not have time for his platitudes of being the good guy — he wanted to stew in his anger. He pushed him back as he rose to his feet; meanwhile, Malakai extended his hands in defense, not wanting to attack him.

"Hey, calm down, man. What's going on?"

"What's going on is none of your *damn* business," Marcus said through gritted teeth.

Malakai took a long look at him. Marcus felt uncomfortable under his gaze as if he were being inspected under a microscope.

"Can't take a hint, Ridgewater?" he said as he placed another punching bag on the hook, replacing the one he'd torn to shreds.

"Huh," Malakai said silently, but loud enough for Marcus to have heard him.

"What?"

"I don't know what's going on, but if you're willing to open up, I might be able to help you."

"What makes you think I need *your* help?"

Malakai glanced to the pile of sand on the floor between them.

Marcus sighed. "I got a lot on my mind right now."

"Tell me about it," Malakai murmured to himself.

The men stood in silence, sizing each other up, both quiet and stubborn in their own way. Malakai stared him down, waiting there patiently, as Marcus finally caved in.

"Chloe's leaving."

The permanent stoic expression on Malakai's face transformed into one of genuine concern. "Leaving? I don't understand."

"You and me both." Marcus removed the wraps from around his hands and sat down on the bench, Malakai following suit.

"Did she say why? It's Chloe — there must be a logical reason behind her thinking."

"You really think logic plays a part in this?" Malakai nodded as Marcus cradled his face in the palms of his hands. "She's taking the girls with her, to the Order."

"The Order? Is that what she said?" He perked up at the sound of this new information, angling himself in Marcus's direction.

"What? Not you too. You know about the Order?"

"I'm mean, I've heard stories, but I never thought — "

"Neither did she. But Rowe and McPherson offered to take her and the girls in, to train them and protect them. She said she's was going to get stronger, more powerful."

"To protect you, I assume?"

"How'd y — ?"

Malakai stood and wiped the sand from his trousers. "It's Chloe, it's in her nature. You should know that better than anybody."

"I can't just let them leave. They're my family."

"And as such, don't you think Chloe would do anything in her power to keep you safe? She's sharp, she knows what she's doing. Trust her."

"Since when are you the expert on relationships?" Marcus scoffed.

Malakai glanced at something in the distance as he tried to gather his thoughts. He cleared his throat and then returned to the question at hand. "One learns more when they open their eyes to the truth."

"Meaning?"

"Keep an eye on those close to you."

And with that last tidbit, Malakai walked off with his hands in his pockets.

# Chapter 9

*Rae, Seattle, Present Day*

Rae sat on her bed, her feet propped on the covers as Zaraquel went to help Chloe pack. She looked up at the ceiling, her hair splayed out on her pillows. Taking a deep sigh, her body remained unsettled, as she could feel the acheri underneath her skin.

She itched and scratched, hoping the ache would subside. One scratch, then another — nothing. Nothing could take away the buzzing in her ears she felt each time the acheri yearned to surface. Rae squeezed her eyes shut and hummed the song she knew by heart, the one she heard in her dreams. She didn't know where she'd first heard it, but one thing was certain: it was one she would never forget, forever stuck in her mind. It was eery and soothing to her ears. She tapped her fingers on her leg to the beat of her humming.

She soon drifted off into a deep sleep, the humming still lingering in her mind. Rae found herself in a clearing in a forest she'd never been to. It wasn't the one behind her home in Yakima, nor the one near Michael's home. This one was different. It felt familiar, however.

*Where am I?* she thought as she walked through the forest.

Rae walked deeper and deeper into the shadowy depths of the woods until a sick feeling filled the pit of her stomach, rising up into her chest, and she stopped. Her breathing hitched, she couldn't move, and the panic grew. It was as if an invisible force stopped her. In the middle of the road was a giant goat standing on his hind legs, his horns raised high. He growled and turned to look at her, when—

A knock on the door interrupted her dream. Rae exhaled and opened her eyes. Groggily, she sat up and saw that it was Miss Arianna, standing in her usual long-sleeved dress with her hair in a bun, like an old-fashioned governess.

"Is everything all right, Rae?" Miss Arianna walked across the room, her brows pinched in the middle as she sat on the bed beside her.

Shaking in her skin, Rae was rattled from the nightmare that she'd witnessed. She couldn't believe what she'd seen. *A goat?*

Seeing the state she was in, Miss Arianna held onto Rae's shoulders, willing her to look into her eyes. Rae looked into Miss Arianna's eyes, blue and calming, and her breathing began to relax, nice and slow.

"Now, why don't you tell me what's bothering you, hmm?" She tentatively caressed Rae's cheek and placed a loose strand behind her ear.

Rae's voice shook—she was scared beyond belief. "I...I saw something. I'm not quite sure what it was, though. I'm so confused." She placed her hands on the sides of her head and gripped tight, massaging her temples.

"Now, now, Rae. You know you can trust me, right?"

Rae nodded as she intertwined their hands.

"Good. Just tell me what you saw. We can figure it out. Together."

She knew Miss Arianna, trusted her, and faintly remembered

her weeping by her side as she lay there in limbo not too long ago. So she told her what she'd seen in her sleep and how she felt. Miss Arianna embraced her, as she wished her mother had done rather than sending her away to Chloe, who she barely knew.

In retrospect, Rae realized that knowing Chloe was one of the best things that had happened to her. Nonetheless, the lingering sentiment of abandonment was ever-present. She was still young, a kid—a kid who needed her family. She might not know who her father was or if he was even alive, but she knew she had Mona and her mother. Rae just didn't have them *with* her. Missing them, she made a mental note to visit them, or at least let them know she was okay.

She peered up at Miss Arianna, who had begun rocking them back and forth as if Rae were a tiny babe in her arms. Liking that feeling of being cared for, Rae felt at home in Miss Arianna's arms. She was tender, soft, like a warm bath.

"Miss Arianna?"

"Yes, dear."

"Have you heard of the Order?"

They stilled as Miss Arianna stopped. Rae felt her heart beating furiously as her ear was pressed against Miss Arianna's chest. She dislodged herself from her arms and looked at her, questioning her.

"Miss Arianna? Are you okay?"

She looked at her beloved governess, her stare blank, her lips tight. She had never witnessed anything but a smile or the occasional furrowed brow when the girls were up to no good. But this? Rae was not familiar with this cold, odd stare. She felt a chill run up her spine, but she dismissed it.

As if a switch was flipped, Miss Arianna's face morphed into an almost robotic smile.

"The Order, you say?"

Rae nodded, slightly confused by her reaction. "Aunt Chloe, Z, and I will be leaving in a couple of hours. That's why she wants you to help me pack."

"I see. Well, whatever this Order is, I'm sure your aunt's just doing what she thinks is best."

"If you think so."

"I know so," Miss Arianna assured her.

Rae looked down, hesitant to confide her confession to Miss Arianna. "Uh, I...."

"Rae, you know you can tell me whatever is on your mind."

She smiled a small smile and confided in her friend. "I'm scared, Miss Arianna. What if I can't control the acheri? I'm barely holding on as it is. What...what if they can't find who did this to me? What if—?"

"No. No more ifs, Rae. Everything will turn out as it is supposed to."

Rae felt Miss Arianna run her hands through her hair, braiding it just like her mother had. She missed her mother as much as she missed her sister, Mona, if not more.

Her mind drifted to imagine how her life would have been if she'd stayed with them—if she was never born with the acheri in the first place. That was her secret fantasy, her forever dream: to be normal and with her family. She missed them terribly and wanted to see them.

~*~

*Thana, Seattle, Present Day*

Like the stylish vamp she was, Thana was dressed to the nines in a short fringe mini dress as she sipped champagne in a private room at a nightclub. She knew as a creature of the night she should have remained more obscure, more discrete, but that was far from her philosophy.

She liked to enjoy the lavish things life had to offer—expensive vacations and even more expensive clothing, and the models (men and women). When one could live forever, why not enjoy it? Having been alive for centuries, Thana had learned a long time ago that she couldn't wait for life to happen to her. She was alive, for all intents and purposes, and she was going to enjoy it.

Downing the drink, she gestured to the waiters for another, and immediately one went off to fetch it. She smiled as she bobbed her head to the raucous beat of the music.

"Humans are the lowest on the food chain," she said to no one in particular. She lifted her hand in the air, waiting, and a moment later, a drink was placed in her hand. Thana took a sip and closed her eyes.

Within her mind's eye, she saw her dear older brother Kabos standing across a lavish ballroom, dressed in the finest of clothing, his hair slicked back, his smile shining brightly—he looked every bit the prince. That was days before they became vampires. That's how she liked to remember him, happy, without the weight of the world on his shoulders.

Although they were not related by blood, they did share it. Kabos and Thana were bitten by the same vampire, and therefore, were related in every sense. And because of this, they shared a special bond, a magical one. If one were to think of the other, that would serve as a beacon, a sort of call that would beckon them to be there, no matter the obstacle—even death.

So when Thana thought of her brother, she knew he would be there. She felt a whoosh of air on her right side and smirked, pleased that her brother had come when she called.

"Kabos, dear. Although I cannot see you, I know you are here."

~*~

*Kabos, Seattle, Present Day*

And there he sat beside his sister. He looked at her, her lips around the rim as she drank the alcohol, knowing it wouldn't affect her whatsoever—it was purely for gluttonous reasons— *typical Thana*. Nothing had changed since the last time he saw her, soaking in every bit of her immortality like a selfish human. He'd never agreed with her carpe diem attitude in regard to their vampiric state.

When she called, he came—that's how it worked. Yet he hadn't received a call since she decided to join the Avalani. He had begged her to think with reason and not with her usual childish notion of superiority. Nonetheless, she said they aligned with her beliefs of maintaining the magical community's exclusivity. Despite him being an incorporeal personage, he knew she was aware that he was there, waiting and listening.

*But, for what?*

He wondered as he tried to drown out the obnoxious music.

~*~

*Thana, Seattle, Present Day*

Taking the toothpick full of olives, she took a giant bite of one and swallowed it. She slowly chewed it as she knew Kabos was there watching, hating the fact that she was probably wasting his time. But she wasn't. She merely enjoyed getting under his skin. He hid under the pretense of being all-knowing and wise, but he was anything but patient, so she milked it, taking her time to properly savor the olive in her mouth.

As if sensing his impatience, she felt the couch she was sitting on shake, and she smirked.

"Same old Kabos. Never one for subtlety, were you?" She chuckled and finished the remainder of her drink. Thana placed the glass down with a loud resounding thud as it hit the table. "Now, as to the reason you are here. I've been privy to some information regarding your particular family history. With the gypsies?"

She paused, purely for dramatic effect, knowing he could not respond.

"As I am sure you are aware, your precious Machiel has reverted to his old ways, bloodthirsty and such. Unlike the first time, where you were there to guide and assist him, that is not the case currently, is it? There is, however, a way, according to old gypsy lore, to get Michael back, if that's what you want. This curse can be reversed, just listen closely."

She felt the atmosphere around her thicken, making her skin tighten, and she knew that she had piqued Kabos's interest.

"Hidden within the depths of Malakai Ridgewater's reliquary is a book collected from the gypsies' homeland. You'll know it when you see it. The witches, witches you haven't seen before, are in search of something in that reliquary. But only a corporal being can access the vault, a precaution Ridgewater took. You need a witch to enter. Help them, and they will help you."

~*~

*Tall Dark Man, Hell, Present Day*

At the geographical center of the earth was a monumental cavern hidden within the depths. If one were to look at the exterior, one might even have believed it was a patch of dark soil, an uncared-for hole in the ground. Nonetheless, had they known what it truly was, they would shy far away, never to visit this barren plot of land in the middle of the earth.

Now, if one were reckless or brave, depending on the perspective, they could've touched it and felt the immense heat which radiated from that spot. But no one ever dared, so no one knew that within that pit lay the entrance to the Tall Dark Man's dwelling, which was every bit as hellish as its name implied. With excruciating heat emanating from every pore, only he could withstand the incalescence, as with every step he took, a distinct *sizzle* was heard.

The footfalls echoed in the long narrow hallway, as glimpses of his feet caught light—first, a pair of large, grotesque hooves, then a pair of human feet. A gigantically tall, lithe man caught a glimpse of his reflection in a mirror: first a shadow, nothing but black smoke, then consequently with a snap of his fingers, he began to morph into a man.

Dressed in a dark, impeccable suit that fit him to a "T," he walked around his minimalistic abode. It was obscure and lonely, as he was, just a throne-like chair with skulls that sat in the front of the dreary room.

The Tall Dark Man was not traditionally beautiful or handsome, his visage composed of harsh lines and edges—a sharp jawline, plump lips, the bridge of his nose straight, his cheekbones angular. He looked keen and dangerous. His hair was fashionably cut, short on the sides while a bit longer on top, and the dark curls hung over his sinful green, golden eyes.

He slowly sat down on his throne in the middle of the room and waved his hand, and a flimsy screen appeared. In an instant, the whole world, specifically the happenings of Seattle, filled the space. Zombies walked the earth; the vampire army was deep in training; Valentine was surveilling Marcus, and Machiel stared daggers into Amber's back. All was going according to plan.

He leaned forward when he spotted Rowe meditating in the garden. As if he sensed that someone was watching him, Rowe's eyes sprung open, looking directly at the Tall Dark Man.

Rowe muttered, *"Dissipati peribunt et abscondas me."* And just like that, Rowe disappeared from his sight. However, that didn't stop him from entering the Order's castle.

The attack on the palace had been a success. He couldn't care less for the students that had perished, but he'd gotten what he wanted: access. For he knew this to be true: once darkness entered, it never left, always leaving its residual print. Of that, he was certain.

~*~

He knew of Rowe's intentions to train both Chloe and Zaraquel, but he needed them distracted to complete his plan of opening the portal. Therefore, he fetched his ever-loyal pet and fallen angel

"Loquiel." His voice boomed in the empty room.

Poof! Loquiel appeared on his knees in the blink of an eye. "Yes, Master?"

He looked down at Loquiel, a glint in his eye as he smirked at his loyal servant. "Are you aware that Zaraquel will be going to the Order tonight?"

Crestfallen, Loquiel nodded sadly, grim at the thought that she was leaving him. "Yes."

"Are you also aware that as a creature of the darkness, you are not allowed on the premises? If you were, your death would be permanent."

Loquiel's eyes widened, the shock evident in his expression. "No, I wasn't. How is that possible?"

The Tall Dark Man looked out into the distance wistfully. "Magic is a wonderful thing. Dark and light, it knows no bounds." He cleared his throat as he was lost in thought. "Now, are you aware that because of this, you might not see Zaraquel, therefore preventing you from convincing her of your feelings?"

Loquiel blushed. "Uh, sir. I…. I di—"

"Didn't think I knew of your intentions towards the young Miss Tudor? Well, you're sadly mistaken. I. Know. Everything.

But you're in luck, dear friend, I have just the thing to help you with your problems."

"And what's that?"

The man extended his hand and laid it flat, and a potion appeared on his palm. Loquiel inched closer, curious as to what the vial held. "What *is* that?"

The Tall Dark Man chuckled. "You know what it is, don't you? You can sense it in your bones."

Loquiel licked his lips in anticipation. "A love potion."

"Specifically, your love potion for Zaraquel. The mixture of both your types of blood guarantees that she will fall madly in love with you."

"Master, I don't deserve this grand gift."

The Tall Dark Man stood from his chair to meet Loquiel at eye level. "Oh, but don't you see? You do." He began to walk around the room mindlessly as he spoke, Loquiel following his every move. He continued. "You deserve the world and more, Loquiel. And with this tiny vial, you will have her love. Isn't that what you want?"

"Very badly, sir."

The Tall Dark Man walked to him and placed the vial in his hand, closing his fingers around it, ensuring that he had it. "You will give this to her, no matter what. Nothing will stop you; do you understand?"

Loquiel stood straighter, more proud, ready for the task at hand. "Absolutely, Master. Whatever it takes." He turned to walk away but stopped at the sound of the man's voice.

"Loquiel?"

He stopped and faced him. "Yes?"

"Fetch Machiel, will you? It's time we had a proper introduction."

~*~

*Machiel, Hell, Present Day*

Given the visit from Loquiel, who he had never met before, Machiel was in the worst of moods. He had hoped his fight with Amber at the restaurant would put their relationship on a break; however, it had the opposite effect. For some reason, unknown to him, she tried harder to win his affection. And as part of his plan to shatter her heart, he had to follow through with the myriad of fake embraces and unbearable kisses.

He seethed at the thought of being near her. In any form—Illyris, Bircenna, or Amber—she reeked of the same desperation. It oozed out of her pores and into the atmosphere. Michiel had begun to lose his patience, so when the Tall Dark Man required his presence, he leapt at the chance of being away from her.

He stood in front of the master, neglecting to bow or kneel, for he thought it was beneath him to act in such a pompous manner. The Tall Dark man smiled at his stubbornness as he approached him, standing a foot taller than him.

"Machiel, I'm glad to have you back in all your glory."

"And I suppose I have you to thank for this 'awakening'?" He arched a brow in challenge.

"If not me, who then?" he countered. "Do not take this opportunity for granted, Machiel. I and only I have the power to revert you to that vegetative you were in."

Machiel glared at him, knowing it was The Tall Dark Man who held all the power. That was the reason Machiel despised people like him—he didn't like being controlled. It was Machiel who wanted to claim all the power, all the control.

He was more than strong enough, more than attractive enough. He could have all the woman, wealth, and blood he wanted. But the Tall Dark Man kept him from doing so. It simply wasn't part of his plan. Machiel was never one for following orders. But the master needn't know that. And so Machiel listened as he prattled on about a bracelet.

"You will proceed to give this cuff to Chloe." The master handed him the silver cuff with intricate detailing and continued. "Once on her wrist, she will no longer possess the ability of her sight, nor will she be aware of this."

"And where did you get this trinket?"

"An old friend," the Tall Dark Man snapped.

Machiel nodded as he took in a lengthy perusal of the empty room before him. Suddenly he felt a tightness in his throat, and he was violently thrown up and held against a wall. The Tall Dark Man held his hand in the air as if he were applying pressure, and he was. Machiel grunted in response to the thrashing.

He stepped in closer, invading Machiel's personal space so closely he could feel his breath on his neck. "You will not fuck this up for me, understand? Too many things have been set in motion for this *not* to go according to plan. You *will* do everything as instructed, Machiel. There is no question about that. Is that clear?"

Through gritted teeth, he said, "Crystal."

# Chapter 10

*Bradley McPherson, Seattle, Present Day*

He paced around the master library, the room filled to the brim with books. Beside him and all around him were opened books splayed on the desk and the floor. He felt the need to pull out his hair, given his frustration.

Bradley pounded his fists on the desk, and with a resounding whoosh, all the books closed. He took off his glasses and with a shaky hand and placed them on the desk.

"First the sigil, and now the goddamn pages that I cannot seem to find," he rambled to himself. "I have to find them."

Not knowing this information killed him. He had this need, this unquenchable desire, to know things, and if and when he didn't, he could always figure out how to get the information. Since he was a young warlock, he'd had this faculty for obtaining knowledge and safeguarding it within the crevices of his mind. He was like a walking, talking, breathing supernatural encyclopedia.

Thus, for that reason, he knew he had seen that mystical sigil, and for the life of him, he didn't know how he could've forgotten. He had a photographic memory—it was physically impossible for him to forget. Someone or something must have enchanted him somehow. But who? And when?

As he was lost in thought, he saw something move in the corner of his eye. It was wicked fast. He was tired of this, of feeling unprepared.

With a hushed whisper, he said, *"Prohibere. tardius moveri. Tardius."* What he saw before him was astounding. Never had he encountered a ghost. It was a man, looking wise beyond his years, his eyes all-knowing and kind.

Bradley approached the ghost with a curious fascination. "Who are you?" He stepped a little closer and waved his hands in front of him, He reached out a little further to touch him, but his hand fell through the translucent apparition.

The ghost chuckled and said, "You may not feel my flesh, but I assure you I am very real."

"I repeat, who are you?"

"I'm a friend during this perilous time. The name is Kabos."

"Tell me, Kabos, what makes you a friend?" Bradley eyed him suspiciously, not wanting to let his guard down.

Kabos raised his hands in defense. "I know what it is you seek, and I am willing to help you."

*How does he know of the pages?* Bradley questioned.

"Follow me, and I shall guide you."

Bradley was desperate, and so he trusted the ghost he'd never met.

~*~

*Bradley, The Reliquary, Present Day*

Bradley reached out to try to touch Kabos's hand — he'd always wanted to know if it was possible to touch a ghost and what it would feel like. The minute their fingers touched, he felt as if he was floating. With his eyes wide open, McPherson saw the world as he knew it spin before him. Kabos himself held an ethereal glow. The intensity grew, and he shone so brightly that

Bradley had to cover his eyes.

He heard a ringing in his ears, and then it stopped as quickly as it began. Feeling the ground beneath his feet, he wobbled, trying to gain his balance. McPherson rubbed his eyes and felt a hot heat around him.

"Easy now, you can open your eyes." And that he did, but what he found he couldn't believe: a reliquary filled with scrolls and books, artifacts, and precious stones.

He stood there, stunned. The academic in him was jumping with joy, but he was so shocked he didn't dare to reveal his true emotions. He thumbed through the spines of the books in amazement.

~*~

*Kabos, The Reliquary, Present Day*

Kabos looked at the warlock that Thana had advised him about. He looked enthralled with all the aspects of the tiny but filled reliquary. Seeing as he was occupied, Kabos took the opportunity to look for the book that would save his son.

The gypsies possessed ancient magic, and as he was part of the gypsy clan, he could feel it in his blood every time he neared something from his people. He floated about and willed himself to be invisible so he could look comfortably. With super speed, he shuffled through every object in the reliquary until he felt his body vibrate as he touched a tiny pocket book.

He held it in his hand and saw the old Romani scripture written on the cover. Before Bradley could notice his disappearance, Kabos pocketed the tiny book within his robes. He glowed, triumphant that he could save his son.

~*~

*Bradley, The Reliquary, Present Day*

He walked through the room in search of the unicursal hexagram, as he was sure the missing pages contained that particular symbol. McPherson looked at Kabos as he stood still as a statue in the corner of the room. The book in his hands was opening as he mindlessly flipped through the pages.

"How did you learn of this room, Kabos? I've never seen this in the estate."

Kabos chuckled. "That's because we aren't in the estate per se."

Bradley stopped examining his surroundings and looked up at the spirit. "And where are we exactly?"

"I believe this reliquary belongs to the one and only Malakai Ridgewater. In his pursuit of protecting magic, he collected some rarities along the way, including what you seek."

McPherson closed the book and walked up to the ghost, puzzled. "I don't understand. How did you know about this place?"

"You see, as a specter, I can be seen when I want to and not when I don't, and thus, it allows me the ability to be privy to certain information. So, whether you realize it or not, I know things that people would not like me to know."

Bradley shook his head at the unnecessary crypticness, and his gaze landed on Malakai's desk. He practically ran over when he saw a few loose pages stuck between the pages of a book. The unicursal hexagram was engraved on the corner of each page, and Bradley found himself laughing hysterically.

"This is it! This is actually it!" He looked up at Kabos, happiness evident on his face.

~*~

*Kabos, The Reliquary, Present Day*

It seemed that both men had found what they were looking

for. Kabos approached the ecstatic Bradley, his hands neatly folded in front of him. He could feel the giddiness emanating from the warlock's being.

"I believe it is time we return to our respective places."

"I don't know how to thank you, Kabos. You have done the magical community a great service, truly."

Kabos grinned, his smile spreading wide, the corners of his eyes crinkling. "No, young man, the pleasure was all mine."

They shook hands and traveled once more from whence they came.

~*~

*Zaraquel, Seattle, Present Day*

Zaraquel stood in the middle of her living room, surrounded by her friends and family. She saw her Aunt Amber embracing her mother, the two not willing to let go of each other. She scanned the room, not understanding the vast array of emotions.

*Yes, we are leaving, but isn't that a good thing?* she thought. *We're leaving to learn more about our abilities, to fight the good fight. That must count for something, mustn't it?*

She saw her mother, tears in her eyes, as she followed her gaze to her father, who stood at the entryway, his arms crossed over his chest. She couldn't place the look he had on his face—she had never seen it before. Since she was born, it had been all smiles and laughter, all the time—at least in front of her.

What could be wrong with her parents?

Cautiously she walked over to her father, and right before her eyes, she saw it—the forced smile on his lips, the hope in his eyes dimming. He was pretending that everything was fine for her sake, and she did not like it one bit.

Walking into his arms, she felt the warmth of his love as he embraced her. She sighed, sad that she would leave her father behind. She looked up and saw him, stern, not wanting to cry.

"It's okay to cry, y'know."

His chuckle vibrated through his chest, and she could feel it against her cheek. "I know," he said. "I'm just not sure if I start, I'll be able to stop."

At this confession, Zaraquel clung to him tighter. She had never been away from her father before.

"I'm coming back."

"I know," he replied.

"But I'll miss you too."

"I'll miss you more than you know."

His voice broke as he spoke those words. She wanted to ask if everything was all right with her mother—she sensed that something was off—yet she didn't wish to pry. She had faith that things would work out between them. Her parents were meant to be, after all—it was written in the stars.

She noticed Loquiel's wings turning the corner, and with one last squeeze in her father's arms, she ran off to go see her dear friend.

~*~

*Loquiel, Seattle, Present Day*

He saw her in the man's arms, and despite that, he was, in fact, her father and there was no ill will; he still felt sick. Not for one second did he like his Zaraquel in another's embrace, for she was his and only his.

With a slow gait and an ever-racing heart, he slowly turned as he came to face her, her face flush, her eyes brimming with emotion. He knew she didn't want to leave, but she felt like she had to as part of her duty. He knew this because he knew her, better than he knew himself

"Oh, Loquiel, I knew you'd come."

She ran up to him and buried her head in his chest. He leaned down to meet her, and in doing so, inhaled the scent of her hair, a mix of freesia and lavender. She smelled of sweetness and flowers.

"Of course, my beloved Zaraquel. There's no place I'd rather be than right here in your arms."

She looked at him with watery eyes and choked out the words that made his heart hurt. "Loquiel, I'm leaving. I don't know when I'll be back, but I just wanted to tell you that I will miss you. You're my very best friend. I don't know what I would do without you."

He held her closer. "Shh, darling. I know the sentiment." He sighed, his desperation mounting. "It is for this reason that I must give you something—it might be our only chance."

"What? What are you talking about?"

"Close your eyes, Zaraquel."

"Why?"

"Do you trust me?"

"With my life."

She proceeded to close her eyes as Loquiel gently poured the contents of the vial onto the palm of his hand. He took in her visage, so youthful and lovely. She was everything he'd always wanted, always needed. He inhaled and then blew the potion powder into her face. As he did, a luminous glow charged the air around them.

Before she could open her eyes, he took her face in his hands and kissed her. He felt the flutter of her lashes as she opened her eyes, only to close them once more. She hesitated for a second, but the second was over, and he felt her unwavering passion for him.

She clutched onto him as he to her, as if they were tethered by a string, neither one willing to part. He kissed her until he was sure she could feel his love for her. He felt warm in her touch, her heart beating furiously in her chest.

What Zaraquel didn't know was that this was his very first kiss. Never had he even dared to touch someone, let alone kiss someone before her. He didn't know if he was doing it right, but as if through instinct, his body took over. His hands firm on her waist, and her hands tangled in his hair, their tongues took part in an intoxicating and illicit dance.

It was moments before they parted, and when they did, their chests heaved in synchronicity. They were linked, one for the other.

Loquiel smiled. "Perfect."

Zaraquel stood there in a daze, a loopy smile on her face. "What?"

"You're perfect." He planted a kiss on the tip of her nose. She blushed as a giggle escaped her.

~*~

*Chloe, Seattle, Present Day*

Chloe walked up to her husband, the weight on her shoulders, holding her down like a bag of coal. It hurt. Leaving him hurt. But she knew this was the right thing to do. He turned away, as if looking at her caused him physical pain, and she knew it did because their bond affected her the same way. Despite their argument, she wrapped her arms around him. She could feel him wanting to resist, wanting to push her away, but he didn't, and for that, she was grateful.

"I wish you could come with me," she whispered into his ear, and he winced as if he were in pain.

"But that's not the case, is it?" He sneered as he backed away from her embrace. She stepped back as if she had been slapped. He took one last look at her, his nostrils flaring as he walked away from her.

"Marcus—"

She was interrupted from calling him back when Michael tapped her gently on the shoulder. She turned to see his head cocked to the side.

"Is everything all right, Chloe?"

Chloe craned her neck out into the hallway, only to see Marcus walking away further and further, until he opened the door at the end of the hallway and slammed it shut behind him.

"It isn't, but it will be," she sighed and fidgeted with her wedding ring on her finger. "It has to be."

"I know Marcus—he'll get over it. Just give him some time."

She gave him a sad smile. "Thanks, Michael. That means a lot coming from you."

Suddenly Chloe felt him grab her wrist with great speed and stealth and felt something cold and metallic. She looked down and saw she was wearing an intricate bracelet. The moment it was placed on her wrist, she felt there was something special about this piece of jewelry, but she just couldn't place it.

"What...where'd you get this, Michael?"

He looked at her straight in the eyes. "It belonged to Marcus—a family heirloom, if you will."

She admired the bracelet on her wrist. "It's beautiful."

He took a moment as if searching for the words. "He told me once that it was used for protection. I know he would want you to have it."

Misty-eyed, Chloe attacked Michael with a giant hug. "Thank you."

~*~

*Rowe, Seattle, Present Day*

Rowe looked on from the corner of the room. It was filled

with pure emotion—happiness, sadness, excitement, fear even—but he had an inkling that bringing Chloe, Zaraquel, and Rae along to the Order was exactly what they needed to defeat the darkness that invaded the castle grounds.

All he needed was the missing pages, which Bradley was searching for.

*Where is Bradley?*

He hadn't seen him in hours. Searching the estate with his telepathic powers, he looked for McPherson's heat signature, but he was nowhere to be found. Then he saw him in his mind's eye, standing behind him.

He turned to face a stunned Bradley, his hands shaking as he looked down at the missing pages. Rowe spotted the unicursal hexagram and glanced up at McPherson, surprised. Rowe pulled him to the side and held out his hand, and Bradley gave them to him. Pushing up his glasses on the bridge of his nose, he inspected the pages.

"Where did you find these?"

"Malakai's reliquary."

Rowe looked over to Malakai as he stood beside melancholy Amber, and a despondent Michael chatting away with Zaraquel. He chuckled in disbelief. "Well, thank goodness for that Ridgewater boy." He clapped Bradley on the back. "Very good job, Bradley." His eyes shone with pride, as he knew in his heart of hearts that they were going to succeed.

~*~

*Chloe, Seattle, Present Day*

With her new bracelet as a sign of her enduring love from her husband, along with the girls by her side, Chloe finally felt as if she was ready to take the next steps to protect her family. She scanned the room looking for Marcus but spotted a teary-eyed

Amber instead.

Their gazes connected, and Amber ran over to her and hugged her so tightly she could not breathe. Of course, she hugged her back, but that didn't stop the ache she felt when she didn't see Marcus there waving goodbye.

Amber sobbed into her shoulder. "I'm gonna miss you, Chloe."

Meanwhile, Chloe tried to laugh through the tears. "You know I'm coming back, right?"

"I know. It's just that.... Well, it's going to be weird without you."

"I know what you mean." She looked Amber in the eyes and smiled. "Everything is going to be okay."

Amber nodded and departed with one last hug. Chloe watched as she staggered back as Malakai reassuringly held her by the shoulders. She stood between her cousin and her daughter, gripping onto their small hands, and they looked up at her and smiled.

With a wave of Rowe's hand, the estate, as well as the people in it, began to dissipate before their eyes, as if they moved through time and space without ever really moving a physical inch. Chloe looked around her surroundings and found it was every bit as magical as she'd imagined—bright and glowing and shifting colors, like a prism hitting the light. She inhaled and closed her eyes.

The instant she let her breath out and opened her eyes, they stood inside the magnificent castle of the Order.

~*~

*Marcus, Seattle, Present Day*

The cold night air hit him like a rude awakening as he walked into the bar. He stumbled onto the bar and approached the bartender with bated breath.

"What will it be?" the barman asked, a small towel resting on his shoulder.

"Whiskey. And keep them coming."

The bartender arched his brow as he poured him a drink and handed it to him. "Bad night, pal?"

Marcus downed the whiskey. "Like hell." He plopped the glass down and motioned for another. He sat alone with his thoughts.

They were gone. He couldn't wrap his head around it. They were actually gone. Aside from Michael, he had no family, and the one he did have had left him, willingly. Yes, deep down, he knew they had to leave to grow their gifts. But an immortal such as himself was selfish. He'd lived his life long enough to know what he could and could not live without. He believed it within his bones that he certainly couldn't live without his girls.

In the midst of his loneliness, he found himself thinking about another period in his life where he'd felt—and truly was, in all honesty—alone. At a time when everything was frightening and new, his sire, Eliza, had abandoned him as a newborn so he could fulfill his role in the prophecy. He was angry, filled with rage, just as he was before when Kabos came to collect him after the death of Eliza.

"That's why it felt so familiar," he muttered to himself as he looked into the bottom of the glass. Marcus downed the remaining liquid, which burned in his throat. He knew deep in his gut that what Eliza did had to be done. Had she not left, he would never have met Chloe, and Zaraquel wouldn't have been born in the first place. But that didn't change the fact that these women that he cherished, that he loved, had abandoned him.

He was hurting. He felt his insides twist and turn as the anxiety of being alone once more settled in. Marcus hated that feeling, the ache. So, he did what he always did when he felt weak—he pushed the loneliness away and replaced it with a ravenous need to feed.

Hearing the heartbeats of each human in the room drove him mad. His blood boiled to control his bloodlust, but there was no one to police him. Those that he genuinely cared about had left.

*Why not?* he thought as he mentally prepared himself for the feast that awaited him.

He drank another and another, for he knew this had no effect on him. But the act itself, the burning of the liquid down his throat, was comforting. So he continued, so much so that he didn't notice there was someone lurking behind him, watching his every move.

# Chapter 11

*Amber, Seattle, Present Day*

If she was clouded by emotions with the event of Chloe leaving, or unsure of where she and Michael stood, she didn't know. But as she stood under the showerhead with the water running down over her face, her body, she couldn't contain her true emotions anymore.

With her head against the cold tile, she let out the pain that she felt. Chloe had left with Zaraquel and Rae. Michael, the man she thought was the love of her life, didn't want anything to do with her, or so it seemed. Amber had these powers, this magical life thrust upon her, and she felt incredibly lost. This sense of abandonment hadn't been felt since her time at the orphanage.

Instinct told her to scream, and she did. She screamed with all her might, and everything was silent. Once her eyes opened, Amber could see the the droplets of water freeze mid-air; the steam that once rose dissipated, and she felt light as air. So, in her rattled state, she looked down to catch her breath.

What she found surprised her even more—her amulet glowed and levitated above her chest. She caught it in the palm of her hand, and the light slowly dimmed until it faded to its original state. For some inexplicable reason, she knew that her power channeled through her amulet. Amber just needed to figure out how to access it.

~*~

Amber sat in front of her vanity, mindlessly untangling her wet hair. She looked at herself in the mirror and didn't recognize the woman she saw. Her green eyes were far darker than her usual color as if they, too, were sad. Her skin wasn't as bright or as dewy. It felt like she was dying inside — being hollowed out by the lack of love.

*What am I going to do? Chloe's gone, and Michael is too, in a way. Am I alone now? I mean, there's Malakai, but…. I just don't know what I'm doing right now. My powers are growing, I can feel them. They make me stronger, yes, but other than that, I feel…broken.*

She closed the clasp on her pink silk robe as she slipped into bed and closed her eyes, heavy as they begged her for sleep.

~*~

*Machiel, Seattle, Present Day*

Caught in the winding hallways of the estate, Machiel found himself upset with the idea that he let himself be controlled by none other than the Tall Dark Man. It was preposterous! Had he brought him back to his original self, one composed of insatiable lust and desires? Yes, but that did not give him the right to treat him like his own personal puppet.

For it was Machiel who invented the concept of free will!

Nonetheless, he'd gifted the bracelet to Chloe, just as the Tall Dark Man had asked. But as he walked to open the door to his bedroom, he stopped as another thought crossed his mind: *what else will he have me do?* He did not wish to burden himself with the ins and outs of the master's plans, for he had his own agenda to follow through with.

He stepped into his room and found Amber asleep in the

bed. As much as he hated her, and that he did, he also found her incredibly attractive. His body knew how to respond to her before his mind did. Kneeling, he traced her skin with the tips of his fingers and indulged himself. Her eyes fluttered open, and before she could question his actions, he kissed her. He rose to his feet, taking her with him as she latched her arms around his neck.

"Michael," she whispered, her voice filled with lust.

He abhorred that name and silenced her with his tongue. "Don't talk."

Despite wanting to put an end to this horrible facade, he had to make her believe the love they shared was real for his plan to work.

He was nothing if not dedicated.

~*~

*Amber*

With the feeling of his lips against hers, her doubts perished with every kiss he placed on her skin. He let out an animalistic growl as she unclasped her robe, and it pooled at her feet, leaving her naked. She smirked and began to unbutton his shirt slowly. Her body hummed with anticipation as she unwrapped him like a birthday present. He took over, not wanting to wait, and quickly removed his shirt and pants in one fluid motion. His hands moved so fast that she couldn't see them.

Amber tilted her head back as she laughed at his evident excitement. "Someone's in a hurry," she quipped.

He grunted as he wrapped a strong arm under her waist, and they fell onto the bed together. Burying his face into her neck, he bit her.

"Michael," she groaned, enjoying the rough nature of their foreplay.

He stared her straight in the eyes, coldly. "I said, don't talk." She gasped as he held her wrists above her head. "Got it?"

She nodded in response. This fervent passion allowed her to feel him in a new way. It was different, but so was he since he'd woken up. Amber didn't completely understand it, but she yearned to feel this close to him, so she welcomed it with open arms. She sighed as she felt a sudden release.

~*~

*Machiel*

She lay there beneath him at his disposal, and he grinned like a feral vulture waiting to devour her. From her collarbone to her breasts, his lips made a trail further down until he felt her grasp at the sheets beside his head. He felt her quiver underneath him, and he chuckled.

*Stupid girl, she doesn't know what's coming.*

The faster he moved his tongue, the louder her moans became, her pleasure mounting. She was enjoying this too much, and that didn't sit too well with him.

He stopped and looked at her, analyzing her like a test subject. Her chest heaved, her hair splayed on the mattress, and his mind began to drift. Machiel pictured his hands around her neck, choking the life out of her, her eyes rolling to the back of her head, his mouth on her flesh as he sank his teeth deep, making her bleed.

The blood spewed out of her body and filled his hands. She was gasping for breath, her life slipping away right before him. It felt so real he could almost smell it, almost taste it.

At this, he found *his* pleasure. His lust for blood was insurmountable. He made his way into her entrance and thrust into her, hard. She arched her back and met his hips with equal enthusiasm.

~*~

*Zaraquel, The Order, England*

Running down the spiral staircase, Zaraquel laughed as she was being chased by Rae.

"You'll never catch me, Rae!"

In the study hall, an open space for the students to practice their magic freely, Zaraquel ran ahead and hid amidst the bookcases lined against the walls. The room was dimly lit, only by candles that floated in the air, as if ghosts held them up.

She snuck a peek, waiting for Rae to find her, to no avail. She stayed hidden and admired the grandiose nature of the castle. Zaraquel simply couldn't believe she was training on the grounds of the Order.

Like her mother before her, she had heard tales of the mystique and magnificence of the Order. Witches and warlocks were bestowed with the utmost of power, and it was at the Order where they trained to harness it for good. The Circle, as it was once called, was a place where it was rumored Merlin roamed the halls. It was he who'd established this center for the magically gifted.

Despite leaving her father, Aunt Amber, and dear Loquiel — who she missed desperately — she was extremely excited. She wanted to learn everything she possibly could to defend her friends and family. Eager to start her new studies, she was ecstatic; however, the need to complete her first justified kill was something yet to be desired, as if she didn't have other things to worry about. She heard the footfalls in the long hallway and figured it was Rae catching up to her, so she took off running.

~*~

Zaraquel squealed in delight as she began to take flight. Rae, in turn, finally caught up to her, somewhat out of breath, and saw her flapping up in the air. She saw every crevice of the castle from this angle, and she felt like Princess Rapunzel up in her tower.

"That's not fair, Z, and you know it!"

Zaraquel playfully rolled her eyes at her friend's antics. "Whatever, Rae. C'mon, we've been here for three weeks. I know you know that levitation spell—try it."

She saw Rae stuff her hands in her pockets, completely unsure of herself. Zaraquel lowered herself, her feet hovering inches from the ground. She took Rae's hands in hers.

"Hey, Rae? You got this—you know that, right?"

"Right, right. Yeah, I know. I'm a Tudor witch—that has to mean something, right?"

"Duh. Now, do it." She shook her hands impatiently and waited for Rae to chant the words.

Rae closed her eyes and focused. *"Pluma quasi lumen, rigida in tabula. Air qui exaltas me. Air qui exaltas me."*

It took a while, but she felt the wind pick up beneath her feet as if the air were being sucked out of the room. The hairs on their arms stood up to attention, and that's when Zaraquel saw it. She gasped in amazement as Rae slowly but surely made her ascent. She quietly flapped her wings to meet her in the air.

"Rae, open your eyes."

When she did, Rae met Zaraquel's excited stare. However, when Rae saw that she was floating above the ground, her body shook terribly, her fear overcoming every emotion she felt.

Zaraquel chuckled and held onto Rae's hands, calming her down. "It's all right, Rae."

"I did it. I'm flying!"

"Technically, you're floating."

Rae squinted at her and shoved her to the side. "Semantics."

Zaraquel shrugged and looked at Rae mischievously as she took off with immense speed, waiting for Rae to chase her. "Catch me if you can!"

The girls laughed as they made their way through the high beams of the ceiling of the ancient castle. They grabbed onto each other's hands and spun in a circle, around and around and around.

~*~

Abruptly Zaraquel felt a burst of heat start from the tips of her toes to the very tip top of her head. She felt faint, and consequently let go of Rae's hands as she fell to the floor, fast and hard.

She knocked her head on the floor, and with eyes wide open, she saw quick successive bursts of images of her with Loquiel — all the time they'd spent together, the talks they'd shared, the strolls they'd taken — flashing before her.

All she saw and all she felt was Loquiel.

He filled her like no other, and she knew in her heart and in her gut that she needed him in her life more than ever before.

Rae drifted down to the floor, frantic that Zaraquel had somehow crashed. She felt Rae shake her by the shoulders, as Zaraquel had done when Rae fainted; it seemed she was returning the favor.

"Z…. Zaraquel? Z, are you okay?" Rae panted as she knelt beside her.

Slowly she sat up, and groggily she said, "Rae, relax. I…I'm fine."

"Fine? Fine? You're not fine, Z. You fainted, and you fell."

Rae grabbed her by the arms and helped her until they reached the couch and sat down together.

"Hey, Z, are you okay? What happened?"

Whipping her head from side to side, Zaraquel tried to shake off the residual feeling of Loquiel. Yet deep down inside, she could still feel him somehow.

"I'm not sure."

Dumbfounded, her mind was buzzing with uncontrollable thoughts. How on Earth did she fall if she had wings? If she was an angel? What was she feeling, and why? Why for Loquiel? She had never thought of him that way — until now.

She knew something was wrong, but she didn't know what. Zaraquel couldn't tell her mother — she already had too much to deal with — so she looked at Rae, and with a fake smile said, "Don't worry, I'm fine."

~*~

*Days Later….*

*Bradley, The Order, Present Day*

Bradley watched as Rowe taught Chloe and Zaraquel the proper hand gestures when they cast a spell. He stood behind Chloe and gently twisted her wrists at an angle, Zaraquel following suit. Chloe spoke, *"Bullarum,"* and a flurry of bubbles appeared out of thin air. Zaraquel giggled with amusement, as she was eager to try as well, hoping to successfully copy her mother.

Bradley was like Zaraquel in so many ways — always eager to learn something new, something out of the ordinary. He knew there was more to this earth than the fairy tales that littered the shelves of the libraries all over the world. What's more was that he'd had the suspicion that things of this spectacular nature were true — a feeling he'd had since he was a child, that magic was real. And he was right.

He smiled as memories flooded the forefront of his mind from when he was an eager student here within the walls of the castle. He remembered roaming the hallways looking to take part in the annual scavenger hunt, where the students gathered ingredients for the master spell that was revealed at the end of the hunt and performed by the prestigious professors.

Or the time when his fellow witches and warlocks had held an underground battle arena, a battle of the sexes, wherein students of the highest ranks within their specific fields — such as spell casting, necromancy, demonology, and so forth — fought to win bragging rights for the whole year. The fantasy took ahold of him as he reminisced on the happy and fun adventures of his young adulthood.

*Snap.*

He was shaken from his reverie when Rowe snapped his fingers in front of his face. "Keep your mind open to the future, Bradley, *not* the past."

The wise warlocks observed as Chloe helped Zaraquel with the pronunciation of a spell. They stood close in the corner, their elbows touching as they looked like they needed further assistance.

Bradley arched his brow as he noticed a slight edge to his teacher's voice. "What's wrong, Rowe? We have the pages, and we will—"

Rowe cut him off as he looked at him, his jaw tight. "That may be true—we possess the pages, yes. But we have yet to decipher them. We need to find a way to prevent what the Tall Dark Man wants to so badly complete."

He could hear it in his voice the moment he began to speak: the fear, the hesitation. In all his years under his tutelage, Bradley had never heard anything but confidence from the great Rowe. But now? Now, he knew something was gravely wrong, worse than before.

"What do you need me to do?"

Rowe rested his hand on Bradley's shoulder and gave him a tight squeeze. "I will focus on preparing the Tudors for battle and have them help me look for the guilty in regards to Rae. Meanwhile, you will decipher those pages. I would say take your time, but I'm afraid we don't have much."

~*~

*Weeks Later....*

Bradley had witnessed the rigorous training that Sebastian had bestowed on the Tudor witches. Each was excelling, their new specialties coming to light. Chloe, the master spell caster — which was fitting, since she'd always had a way with words — so reassured yet passionate, maintained the elegance of her great aunt and mother before her. The Tudor witches were of a great lineage, their line going back to the very first witches. Alongside the Hexhams, they were extremely powerful.

Now Zaraquel, as the child of the prophecy, had a gift for taking life, but also a knack for giving it. As the weeks passed, McPherson noticed how she became fond of the necromantic studies that Rowe went over. She was tasked with the responsibility of having her first justified kill to fulfill the remaining stipulations of the prophecy.

Rae, on the other hand, was also fascinated with the darker side of magic. As she was born with a demon inside of her, she took an interest in studying the dark arts of demonology. Bradley helped with the research aspect of the studies, as she yearned to know the ins and outs of why it was that demons existed, and what their purpose was within the confines of the magical community.

He was proud and amazed at the rigor and skill these women displayed throughout their time at the Order. They hadn't been there for long, but they surely made the most of it. He was thoroughly impressed, and that was far from an easy task.

~*~

Bradley sat there amid a pile of books as he worked to decipher the meaning of the pages. With tired eyes, he adjusted his glasses on the bridge of his nose and sighed. His frustration mounted with each passing day. He read it once more, but he did that just for the comfort of holding the pages in his hands since he had already committed them to memory.

*"Those marked with the unicursal hexagram will await a fate worse than death. First, their physical bodies will wither, then it is their souls that will remain. Alas, not under their own free will, but under his, the ruler of demons. His army will rise."*

And then he continued, more puzzled than before with the revelation of the new pages.

*"...There will be those, however, who will rise to end the curse of the unicursal hexagram. These selected few will possess the power to save humanity not only from darkness but from magic itself."*

He scratched his head. *How could this be?* He thought to himself time and time again, as he attempted to make sense of this quandary. The solution itself seemed almost impossible and exceedingly difficult to figure on his own. Leaping from his seat, he set forth to find Rowe. There had to be another way, a loophole that wouldn't result in the dissolution of magic.

~*~

*Amber, Seattle, Present Day*

Since the night they reconnected, Amber had never felt closer to Michael. They spent almost every waking (and sleeping) moment together. They were bonded once more, as they had been before he slipped into that tragic coma. She looked up at him and saw the man she fell in love with in the first place. The intensity, however, was different—that was something new. She couldn't quite place it. If it was residual anger or a newfound passion, she didn't know, but she welcomed it with open arms.

Standing beneath the streetlight of an alleyway, Amber was dressed to the nines in a short emerald green dress and silver heels for her night out with Michael. They'd been painting the town red since Chloe's departure, as Amber had been feeling kind of blue. She knew he sensed that, and she was grateful for the distraction.

She waited for him, leaning against the cold brick wall, and as soon as the back door opened and two women walked out, Michael was not too far behind. He cast a glance in her direction and signaled to her that it was time. She caught his gaze and nodded, the click of her heels catching up to him, and then past him and in front of the girls.

When Michael coughed into his hands, she knew that was her cue to trip and fall, blocking the girls' path.

One of the girls gasped, "Oh my god, are you okay?"

"Oh my."

They stopped in their tracks and bent down to help the distraught Amber. They took her hands and pulled her up; when she got back up to her feet, she revealed her growing white fangs. The girls, their victims, screamed for their lives. Instantly, blood-curdling screams filled the dark alleyway. The girls tried to run but instead found themselves boxed in by Michael. He, too, revealed his fangs. With the addition of his glowing eyes and claws, he was certainly a frightening sight to behold.

The girls screamed until they didn't.

The silence was all Amber heard, except for the quiet slurping from Michael. She saw him there, the girls limp in his grasp, one in each hand as he sank his fangs in one girl and then the other, alternating between the two. The blood spilled on the ground, but he didn't care — she could see that. She knew this wasn't her Michael, that something in between the time he woke up and the time they made love had shifted. She was changing, and she wasn't sure what to make of it.

Standing there, observing as he sucked them dry, a nasty ball in the pit of her stomach began to form. He looked up at her as if he were calling her over, demanding her to be by his side. She walked over to him, although almost every part of her body told her not to. She was in love, so she took a leap.

"You know you want to, Amber. Come here."

He held one girl and then handed the other to Amber. She looked into her eyes, and the instant she did, she wished she hadn't. The girl was confused and scared. Amber could smell the fear radiating off her hyperventilating body.

Amber followed the soothing timbre of his voice as it guided her lips to the necks of their innocent victims. She felt their soft skin as she ran her teeth against the soft surface. The faint pulse of their hearts — *thump, thump, thump* — vibrated through her being as she took her first bite.

Puncturing the girl's skin felt akin to that of the flesh of an orange, plump and ripe and for the taking. Deep within the depths of her soul, she knew this selfish act was wrong since they usually asked for permission from their victims. But this was different; this was her taking — taking something that wasn't hers.

She could feel Michael's stare burning holes into her head, so she stopped and caught him smirking as he could sense it was taboo as well. She stopped and wiped the blood from her mouth with the back of her hand.

"What are you doing? Why did you stop?" His voice was cold and hard. It sounded like a hammer hitting the ground.

"I'm not hungry anymore." She shrugged and avoided his stare.

He lifted her chin with the tip of his claw. "You want this, I know you do. You like it, even if you don't want to admit it — the feeling of their last breaths, of their hearts, beating so fast they feel like they might explode. You have a hunger for it."

She looked down, ashamed, not wanting to admit that what she was hearing was ringing some sort of truth.

"Feed."

So, she did.

And when they finished off their respective victims together, they dropped the bodies like dead birds that fell from the sky, like an apocalyptic warning.

In the heat of the moment, they stared at each other, focusing on the blood that dripped from their lips. They were consumed by an insatiable hunger for each other. Their lips met in haste, their hands desperate to free each other from their clothing.

~*~

*Loquiel, Hell, Present Day*

He could feel her.

He could feel her thinking about him.

He felt her skin as if it were his own; he could feel himself, slowly creeping into her mind, into her heart.

Despite not being able to physically see her, he, too, couldn't bear to keep the distance. He had to see her — the moment she left, it was as if a part of him had disappeared. To him, Zaraquel was like a phantom limb — not there but always felt.

And that's when he knew the potion the Tall Dark Man had gifted him was working. It was really working — he simply could not believe it. He stretched his wings and flexed them a bit as he prepared to take off.

He craned his neck and looked up to the heavens. Flapping his wings with incredible speed, he took flight. He knew the journey before him was a long one, but he smiled anyway, for he knew his love awaited him.

# Chapter 12

*Malakai, The Reliquary, Present Day*

He entered his treasured reliquary, as he did every month to keep an inventory of his precious trove. Walking around, as a vulture does when stalking its prey, Malakai inspected every aisle he'd so methodically organized. He noticed a few things were out of place, and scratched his head, perplexed, for he was the only one who had access.

"How the hell did this happen?"

Approaching his desk, he shuffled through the piles of books and noticed that the loose leaves of paper he had collected from the merchant during his time in Egypt were missing. He usually had a head for this sort of thing—organizing and keeping track of everything—but not as of late—not since Michael's awakening. Malakai wasn't sure, but he felt something was not quite right with Michael. Physically he appeared to be fine, but it was the way he looked at Amber. It wasn't his loving or lustful gaze as it was before. Now...now it felt forced like he was trying to hide his true emotions from surfacing.

Malakai brushed that off as mere jealousy on his part. He had more critical matters to take care of—the pages: the pages were missing. Malakai knew someone with great magic had to have taken them, for he had the reliquary sealed for precaution, for circumstances such as this. He sat down, his thoughts racing.

He'd begun this journey of collecting artifacts for selfish reasons, to find some fact behind his history with Amber. To fortify his feelings for her, there needed to be a rationale, and he made it his mission to find it. But then he got to thinking, what if he found something that was of great worth to someone else? Could it be that it was they who broke into his mind palace? He desperately needed to find out. But to do so, he needed to return to Michael's estate.

~*~

*Malakai, Seattle, Present Day*

Dusting the dirt that had fallen from the ceiling off his shoulders, he was too distracted to notice Amber coming in his direction. He unknowingly bumped into her in one of the many hallways of the estate.

"Oh, shit." So stocky was his build, he nearly knocked her down. With quick reflexes, he grabbed her by the shoulders. "I'm sorry, Amber. I was—"

"Distracted?" She smiled that smile, the one that made her whole face light up. Her face was flushed, her hair beautifully braided to the side. He had to stop himself from looking at her like some lovesick fool.

"Pretty much."

She chuckled. "Got a lot on your mind, Mal?"

*Mal.* He loved it when she called him that—it warmed his insides like nothing else. She made him feel special, but he knew that wasn't the case, as she was just as nice and sweet to everyone else she met.

She tucked her hair behind her ear and shifted her weight from one foot to the other. He knew she wanted to ask him something, he just didn't know what. And when she avoided his gaze, he knew it was something important. She was nervous — that in and of itself was nerve-racking for him, but he was the picture of cool and calm. He didn't want her to worry more than she already was.

With a calm and even voice, he said, "So, what's up?"

She looked at him, brows furrowed as she if were trying to solve a difficult puzzle. "How do you do that?" A smile slowly slipped onto her face.

His smile mirrored hers. "Do what? What are you talking about?"

"I don't know, you always seem to know what to say."

He shrugged his shoulders nonchalantly. "It's a gift, I guess."

She playfully shoved her shoulder against his. "Shut up." Both began laughing as if they were children hiding a secret. "So...."

"So? C'mon, Amber, I know you want to ask me something, so just ask it."

Malakai could see her taking in a deep breath. "Michael and I...."

He did everything in his power to muster a look of interest. "Yes?"

"Well, we were wondering if you wanted to go on a double date with us."

No sooner had the words left her mouth than he was left reeling with the odd request. "Double date? With you and Michael? Me?"

She gave him a sideways glance. "Why are you repeating everything I just said? Yes, a double date."

"And who would I possibly go out with?" *Someone that's not you?* he thought to himself, although it did him no good, for he knew the answer all too well.

She rolled her eyes and crossed her arms across her chest. "Really, Malakai, you don't have to lie to me."

"I don't understand."

"I know you're seeing someone."

His eyes widened in surprise, and he belted out a hearty laugh. "That's impossible."

She looked up at him with genuine confusion. "Wait, wait. Now I'm confused."

Wanting to ease her qualms, he softly touched her forearm. "Amber, I give you my word…." He paused to let her know he was serious. "I am not seeing anyone."

"Oh." Her lips puckered in surprise. "Then, um, who's M?"

*How did she hear of her?* His eyes slightly widened in surprise. "M. I don't recall mentioning anyone by that name, let alone that letter. Where did you hear that?"

"I, uh, overheard you talking on the phone a couple of times."

"Is that so?" He arched a brow, admonishing her to a degree, but more curious than anything. He leaned in a little closer and could see her pupils dilate. "You just happened to be there when I was talking on the phone?"

The blush started at her neck and then slowly climbed onto her cheeks. "Purely coincidental, yeah, that's right."

He chuckled, for it sounded like she wanted to convince herself more than him.

And then he remembered who they were talking about. M. His blood froze, and his heart skipped a beat, and then it started once more, rapidly. *M. M. How could I forget?* He could feel his skin grow cold, and Amber noticed.

"Malakai, are you okay? What's wrong?"

He sat down on the bench that sat against the wall; she quickly followed. He found his hands shaking as he prepared to tell her what he'd kept from her for years. Feeling her small, warm hands slip into his, he looked at her appreciatively and let out the breath he didn't know he was holding.

"We have to talk."

~*~

*Miriam, Delaware, 1990*

Miriam ran further and further away as she tried to muffle her sobs. She didn't see the death of her husband, but she knew the instant he died. She felt it. And when Malakai ran out of the clearing with Amber wrapped in his arms, she knew what she felt was true.

"Go, go now, Miriam. Amber is safe with me."

Her eyes filled with water as she looked from Malakai to Amber, to the blood that pooled in the snow not too far ahead.

That was all she could look at—the blood, dark against the stark white snowy ground, the last remnants of her husband. Memories of their time, albeit short, were all that filled her mind. She saw him when he'd first rescued her—Miriam wrapped in his arms as she felt his warmth against her nude, cold flesh. The crinkles near the edges of his eyes there every time he smiled down at her. That look of pride the moment he cradled their baby in his arms, and the look of understanding and compassion he had when she told him the dark truth of her past. She loved him with every fiber of her being, and now what? What was left? Malakai was taking her daughter, the last reminder she had of Nikoli. The realization hit her: she was alone.

All. Alone.

It seemed as if she was standing there for hours, her feet glued, it seemed, to the ground beneath her. She couldn't move, not that she wanted to anyway. Miriam honestly tried, she did. With one final look, Malakai parted ways, with baby Amber tucked safely in his arms.

Miriam met her daughter's green eyes. They were sad as if she knew what had transpired moments before: the death of her father.

*Mother, you may not understand this now, but I have lost many — lovers, friends, family — and you will get through this. It is my belief — for you must, as I do, carry both your blood and his — that you will surpass this. You have to. If not for you, or me, then for the fate of the entire magical community.*

She couldn't be more proud of the fearlessness her infant daughter possessed. Miriam knew she was right. But she always knew that it wasn't as easy as her daughter made it out to be.

She nodded and waved a tearful goodbye, and with that, they left.

There she was, amidst the piercing white snow, alone, tears falling down her face. Her daughter had left because she had to — it was written in the stars. But her husband? He'd been taken from her. And in that instant, she knew what she had to do.

Miriam wanted to get revenge. She could feel the heat starting at the tips of her toes and traveling up her body until it reached her fingers. The snow melted and transformed into a pool of water, the steam rising as if it were a natural hot spring.

The power of the darkness simmered underneath her skin, her blood boiling with anger, with loss. She could no longer control the darkness she kept under wraps. All the Tall Dark Man had taught, what he trained her for, was kicking in.

With a magnificent, soul-searing scream, Miriam looked up to the heavens and let out all the pain and anger she felt. The witch-fire lit her whole body, and with her arms stretched out before her, she set the forest ablaze as if an atomic bomb had exploded, the circumference of Miriam's upset was so grand.

Suddenly she stood in a barren circle of burnt soil and grass, crisp to the touch.

She was ready to avenge the circumstances of the ones that left her behind.

~*~

*Alexander the Great, Egypt, 332 BC*

It had been a dream of Alexander's to visit the mystical land of Egypt, entrenched with a rich history of the gods, which influenced his mother Olympia's storytelling, for which she fondly called him the "son of Zeus." With a steady diet of long and adventurous tales, he was brought up on the tellings of Egyptian rituals and customs — specifically their values in regard to their worship of the gods. Alexander came to believe that he himself was a god — worthy of becoming one at the very least.

It was with a great sense of nostalgia that he stepped onto the golden sands of that ancient land. Yes, he was there to provide his military wisdom. However, he became entranced with the idea of the divine, the celestial. Liberating the people from those that held them in their clutches, he was seen as savior and liberator, which pleased him a great deal. However, what he sought more than this particular praise was the knowledge that something transmundane existed. He knew that humans were superior to the animals that walked the earth, but he often wondered if there was something, or someone, more supreme than he, Alexander the Great.

He crossed the lands in search of this knowledge. With the astounding pyramids quite the accomplishment, and the religion itself so intricate, it amazed him to no end. So perfect was their construction that he was even more convinced that a supernatural force had a hand in the formation of such a feat. In time he befriended the most respected priests, and they, in turn, confided in him regarding sacred rituals. A religious man, Alexander, then proceeded to begin each day with a sacrifice to the gods.

He followed the teachings of Psammon, which taught, "all men are ruled by a god because in every case that element which imposes itself and achieves mastery is divine." He did as he usually did since the weeks following his arrival—he walked into the temple, vast and cold, a bird squirming in his hands. He stepped up in front of the altar and placed the bird on the flat surface, feeling the rapid heartbeat underneath his thumb.

*Crack.*

He snapped the bird's neck quickly, and the blood sprayed his cheeks.

"For the gods, to be a god."

Alexander chanted this time and time again to fulfill what he deemed his destiny. The stars and the fates had pointed him to this destination. His mother's tales prepared him for such an obligation, a deity to the people.

~*~

Another night, another sacrifice, yet this time was different, substantially. Tonight, as he held the bird by his neck and wrung it, the sound of the crack amplified and echoed throughout the four walls. The room illuminated with a bright light that erupted from the skies. A gust of powerful wind moved Alexander from the place in which he stood

"Heavens, what is that?!" He looked up but covered his eyes at the sight. It was all too luminous. And in a thunderous roar, a voice spoke from above.

"You there. Is it you who has claimed to be the son of Zeus?"

"Yes, it is I, Alexander, the living god. Who is it that speaks to me from the skies?"

"Amun-Ra."

Not much surprised Alexander, but hearing this name sure did. "The Hidden One."

"You have heard of me, yes?" Alexander nodded, too dumbstruck to trust himself into verbalizing actual words. "I have created all, and my breath is life."

He fell to his knees, his hands outstretched, before chanting, "Amun-Ra, the Great One."

"Enough, my son of sons, that is enough. I ask this of you, a special task at my request."

"Anything, Amun-Ra, absolutely anything."

And so Amun-Ra spoke loud and clear the words Alexander never forgot. "There will come a time, one in many lifetimes, in which a woman—a woman of my creation—will roam the earth with the sole purpose of unifying the races for the good of mankind. You must aid her when all seems lost. She holds the key. She *is* the key."

~*~

*Rae, The Order, Present*

During their weeks at the Order's castle, Rae felt a sense of ease, of comfort—a feeling she hadn't felt since she first left home in Yakima. There was something about the castle that reminded Rae of her and her sister Mona. Was it the two towers that were at opposite ends of the building, only bonded by the bridge that held them together? It had to be that.

Since her arrival at the Order, she often found herself sitting atop the hill that overlooked the castle—not too far off, but still on the grounds that protected them. Rae enjoyed the change of scenery immensely. Michael's estate was filled with too many intense and frightening memories of her comatose state. She'd sit firmly on the grass and dig her fingers deep into the earth, and this act made her feel more connected with Mother Nature itself. All her senses came alive. She heard the water from the river bend a few feet away splashing against the rocks, the little ants that climbed atop her blanket trailing off into the grass, and the flowers smelled sweeter, more potent.

As she rose to her feet, she made her way back to the castle.

Rae thought to herself, *How did I get so lucky to have a family willing to take care of me this way, with the Order? The actual Oder? Wow, I can't wait to get back to train with Z and Aunt Chloe! This is going to be so much fun!* She clapped her hands, giddy for her upcoming classes with Rowe.

Each day she felt stronger, more powerful. Rae found she was specifically succeeding in spellcasting. With help from Rowe and McPherson, Rae felt more confident with her abilities than she ever had before. Her mother had always praised her for her pronunciation and her enthusiasm with her hand movements, in terms of the delivery of her spells, and now she felt up to the task. She was ecstatic that something in her life was working out for the better, rather than all the chaos that surrounded her and her family.

Despite this multitude of sensations, she could feel her acheri side wanting to surface. It was different than before, however. The pull to unleash her was stronger as if the acheri had gotten a taste of life without Rae, and now it wanted to draw her in, further into the dark side. For this reason, it was different, but it also varied from before, mostly for the fact that Rae was intrigued by this darkness.

She had known what it was like, albeit for a brief time, to live without the acheri inside of her. And yes, she'd liked it, enjoyed it even. But she also knew she didn't feel complete without the acheri. She didn't feel whole, and that's what scared her the most. Rae had missed the acheri—she just didn't realize how much until she was gone.

~*~

Rae arrived somewhat refreshed and ready to face the day

ahead of her. Suddenly she felt someone gently grab ahold of her hand, and she turned to come face to face with Rowe himself. She looked up at him and smiled, and he returned the gesture as he guided her into the library.

"What's up, Rowe?"

"Why don't you have a seat, Rae?"

She did so and eyed him, a bit confused. Restless, she tapped her fingers against the chair's armrest. "Is something wrong?"

"No, not at all." He sat on top of his desk directly across from her as he adjusted his sweater, straightening it. "It has come to my attention that you have been excelling in the spell-casting courses that McPherson has been teaching these past few weeks. Is that true?"

She nodded, proud of her success.

"Good. Then hopefully you can assist me with this mystery I am facing. Can you help me?"

Rae jumped up at the notion, excited by the fact that *he* was asking *her* for help. "Of course, Mr. Rowe. Anything."

He reached beside him to prop open a book, thick and worn as if by many years of use. Rowe thumbed through the pages as Rae walked over to stand beside him, curious to see what he was looking for.

Stopping when he found the page he was looking for, he read it aloud for Rae to hear. "This spell must be read aloud by that who the curse was inflicted on. Only then will the nature of the incantation be revealed."

"What does that mean?" Rae implored, her tiny palms sweaty from the sudden onset of nerves.

He looked at her, the lines on his face reminding her of the rings of a tree, fine and overlapping. Rowe possessed all the wisdom in the world. Somehow she knew this, and she believed he wanted the best for her. And right now? He needed her to be an active participant in looking for her attacker.

She looked down at the book in his hands, her eyes following every word as she read silently.

*All will be revealed,*
*The truth, either dark or light.*
*The soul will be healed*
*And the whole would be right.*

She looked up at him, still unsure, and with a nod, Rowe took her hand in his and urged her on. Rae squeezed tightly and remembered that she wanted to discover the truth.

*"Omnia in futuro revelanda est,*
*Ténebris lumen veritatis neque.*
*Et sanabitur anima mea*
*Totum ius esset."*

In an instant, following the moment she repeated the spell, Rae felt as if she were being punched in the gut, as if her breath was taken out of her. And just as it was over, a burning sensation appeared behind her ear. She yelped in pain.

Rowe's eyes widened in surprise as he saw the witch's signature appear once more, as it had before. It looked like it was tattooed onto her skin, a now permanent feature — a mark of her own. Except it wasn't, not really.

Slowly raising her hand, Rae reached up to the burn mark, and as soon as she did, the Tudor gift of sight kicked in, fast and hard.

*A young man, a gifted strong warlock, walked on the castle grounds — a clearing? — years ago. He was spellcasting, a spell she couldn't quite decipher — it was all muffled — but he was clearly passionate. A rift in the sky opened, first red then black, and the warlock's eyes glazed over, black and dark. And in another instant, her mother, also young, was seen laughing, having the time of her life with him. Another snapshot was of Pandora and the warlock in a passionate embrace. Rae saw her mother mouth the name, "Briar." Could it be? Was that man her father, her and Mona's father?*

Her breathing slowed, and she was back in the present, with a concerned Rowe overlooking her.

"My, is everything all right, child?"

She knew she should trust him, but she also knew deep in her gut that what she had learned, she had to keep to herself. At least until she could dig a little deeper. Wasn't that why she was there in the first place, to educate herself?

So she did what she knew very well how to do — she pretended everything was fine. "I saw something."

"What did you see? Describe it as best as you can, please."

She nodded and continued. "There was something in the sky. Something big and dark — like a hole. Yeah, a hole in the sky."

Rae couldn't be sure, but she thought she heard Rowe gasp.

*That couldn't be good.*

~*~

*Valentine, Seattle, Present*

It had been a few weeks since he began following Marcus. He knew his schedule like the back of his hand: a morning run, the a.m. feed, the bar, the p.m. feed, and then the bar once again. It was tiresome, and frankly getting on Valentine's nerves.

He knew what Machiel had tasked him to do, and he was all too ready to execute his wishes. Today was the day. Marcus was weakened from weeks of not feeding but drinking alcohol heavily. Valentine knew from his interactions with the godforsaken animals that a vampire needed more than a bit of blood and wine to keep up his strength. And from what he had witnessed the past weeks, Marcus was losing it. He was weak.

The night was dark as Marcus stumbled out the bar. He teetered as he walked down the empty street, his senses not at capacity. With a quick and cautious gait, Valentine stalked behind him. Valentine's hand rose high, firm with a stake in his hand. Swiftly he plunged the stake into Marcus's neck, catching him off guard.

Marcus yelled in pain, his hand tending to the pain. "What the fuck?" he roared, his claws and fangs making an appearance.

Violently he yanked the wooden stick out and dropped it as he felt a hot heat all over the palm of his hand. A geyser of blood sprayed Valentine on his face. Marcus, with slow-moving reflexes, turned to face his enemy, only to see Valentine with a smirk on his face as he wiped the blood off his face with his forearm.

"Valentine," he growled, low and cold.

Valentine whipped out two more stakes, tinier than before, one in each hand. "It's time you die. You don't belong here."

Marcus sneered as he placed pressure on his wound. He looked at his hand, stunned that he continued to bleed and would not heal. The more he touched it, the worse it got.

Valentine laughed — his plan was working. "It's no use, you dreg. The stakes were laced with holy water."

"What?"

That's when Valentine could see it, the anguish that Marcus was in. He writhed as he fell to his knees. From all his years as a hunter, Valentine knew very well that the holy water acted as a deadly poison. He walked over and stood above him as Marcus tried to heal his body.

But once, twice, Valentine hit him with the stakes once more, one in the stomach, the other in his left leg. He wouldn't get far if he tried. If the poison settled in as Valentine timed it, Marcus would be dead in less than five minutes.

"There's nothing more pathetic than dying alone."

He crouched down and whispered in his ear as Marcus tried to crawl away, leaving a trail of blood behind him. He stepped on him as he plunged the stake deeper into his leg. Meanwhile, Marcus wept in pain. Valentine was filled with the memory of his wife and daughter dying by the hand of a monstrous vampire.

"You *deserve* to die, every one of you. I'll make sure of it."

Valentine gave one last look before spitting on him and walking away.

~*~

*Marcus, Seattle, Present*

As he heard the footsteps move down the street, he was blinded by searing pain, an inescapable discomfort unlike he had ever felt before. It started at the entrance points — the leg, his chest, his neck. Marcus attempted to remove the stakes, but his hands quivered from the weakness he felt.

The holy water that entered his veins felt thick as it moved through his blood like viscous sludge. But what had hurt him, even more, was the fact that Chloe had left, never knowing that he forgave her. Yes, for weeks, he'd tried to numb the pain with boundless amounts of alcohol and refusing to feed, but deep down, he knew his wife was right. That she'd left in hopes of doing the right thing, of protecting her family. He knew that.

All he wanted now was to tell his daughter and his wife how much he genuinely loved them. As he gasped his last breaths, the darkness came and overwhelmed him.

~*~

*Chloe, The Order, Present*

It started suddenly and out of nowhere, the pain—sharp and unrelenting. She was in the middle of training alongside Rae and Zaraquel, under the supervision of both Rowe and McPherson. It was as if her legs had given out, and she fell to the floor on the battling mat.

"Mom!" Zaraquel flew over to her mother's side as the others quickly followed.

Chloe checked her chest, her neck, and legs to see if there were any visual markings of the pain. There weren't any. Nothing.

*How could this be?*

She could feel it as if she were hurt—why couldn't she see the evidence?

"Mom. Mom, are you okay? What happened?" Zaraquel attempted to help her up.

Chloe sat straight and looked up at all the worried faces above her. Then it hit her: Marcus. Something was terribly wrong with her husband.

"It's Marcus. I have to go."

# Chapter 13

*Briar, England, 1991*

It was his last year as part of the Circle. Briar had succeeded in becoming the class's top warlock—Mick came in second. He stood in the classroom, prepping for his final exam.

He ground the arrowroot in the mortar and pestle hard, into fine dust, and then sprinkled it into the brewing pot. Instantly the smoke changed to a deep burgundy color, and the class of aspiring witches came near, surrounding Briar's station.

This was what Briar was good at—mixing and testing, creating and perfecting. It was like a spark was lit, and he knew what he was meant to be doing with the rest of his life. The problem was, he wanted to know *all* magic—light and dark. There had to be some way he could access all the information in regard to the magic within the world. He had to find a way—there had to a purpose for his gift other than to be a part of *his* plan, as his advisor liked to remind him. Whoever "he" was.

And so began his quest for the tree of knowledge.

~*~

Sleepless nights were spent in the library, so much so that it was a rarity for anyone to see him out of the room filled with an endless number of books. His hunt for the tree of knowledge was relentless. He scoured the books with a spell the ancient witches used to cast. *"Imple verba mea, clarifica me."*

With a raised hand and books in front of him, the pages speedily flipped through on their own, the ink-welled words jumping at his fingertips and into his skin. Within seconds he was filled with every word in the books. He spent days like that, frozen with his hands suspended above the pages, soaking in all the information he could.

"Mate, mate, that's enough." Mick patted him on the shoulder only to have Briar turn to face him, his eyes bloodshot. "For fuck's sake, Briar!" Mick grabbed him by the hands and shook some sense into him until the books stopped flipping on their own—everything stopped.

Briar heaved as he grew tired and fell into the seat behind him. He sighed, frustrated. "What the hell, Mick? I was onto something—I almost found it."

Mick ran a hand through his hair. "Man, you've been here for weeks. You've practically been through every shelf. What more do you think you're gonna find?"

Briar slowly stood, his hands shaky, his breath wavering. "I was almost there."

Mick cautiously approached him. "What you're doing, what you're looking for, is extremely dangerous. You have to be careful."

"The time for being careful has passed, Mick. This is much bigger than all of us."

"That's exactly why you have to stop."

Waving him off, Briar gripped tighter onto the desk before him, the residual words still vibrating on his skin. They hadn't faded away when he stopped chanting the spell—they were simply just there as if that was the place they belonged.

"Fuck off, Mick. I mean it." He stormed off, leaving Mick in his wake.

~*~

There was something about the clearing in the woods. Yes, he continued to have that dream about the goat and the two girls, but that didn't scare him anymore. If anything, it intrigued him even more. If he could find the tree of knowledge, he could also decipher the strange dream. No longer would he have to wonder — he'd know with certainty.

Briar walked straight into the woods and waited at the exact spot in the clearing, hoping it would trigger an epiphany. Wanting to forge some kind of connection with the earth, he knelt on the ground. On the soft dirt, he used his index finger to draw the sign he'd seen so many times forged in the forbidden texts — the unicursal hexagram. He didn't know he was drawing it at the time, but his fingers moved of their own volition, and the symbol appeared on the ground.

*"Surge tenebris, dabitur mihi potestas."*

He felt the wind pick up, and his heart began to race, nearly wanting to jump out of his chest. When he heard the distinct sound of hooves hitting the ground, Briar slowly turned to come face to face with the large goat, who transformed into the figure of a man.

"It's you. The man from my dreams," he stuttered, in complete awe. Briar wanted to stand, but the Tall Dark Man held his hand in the air above him, and Briar could not move — he was frozen in place. "What...? What's happening?"

"Stay. Kneel before me, son."

"You're him. You're the man she's told me about, aren't you?"

"Ah, yes, my dear Elizabeth. Always the helpful one, isn't she? Nevertheless, I can help you find what it is you desperately seek."

Eyeing him cautiously, still not believing what it was before him, Briar asked, "Why? Why would you help me? I'm just a warlock."

"A special warlock that has been stemmed from my very own seed. Yes, you are very special, indeed. You see, I've waited a long time for someone like you, someone with the drive, and most importantly, the thirst. You feel it, don't you? The need?"

Briar couldn't help but admit the truth, and so he nodded. "Yes, I can't sleep, I can't eat. All I think about is...."

The Tall Dark Man leaned into him, his eyes gleaming with mischief. "The power?"

"Yes," Briar whispered in confession.

"I'll help you, only if you help me in return." He outstretched his hand to the young man. "Deal?"

Briar shook his hand with a firm shake. "Deal."

What he didn't know was that he had made a deal with the dark lord, a deal that was sealed with his life. He didn't know the stipulations of the pact that he made. He didn't physically sign his name away, but he had a feeling he'd signed away something far more precious.

~*~

*Chloe, The Order, England, Present Day*

"Marcus," she croaked weakly as McPherson helped her to her feet. Zaraquel took her by the hand, exasperated.

"Mom, is something wrong with Dad? What's wrong?"

Chloe wanted nothing more than to soothe her daughter's worries and tell her that everything was fine, but she didn't want to lie to her. She knew she could handle the truth—Zaraquel was strong.

"Listen, sweetie. I have to go check on Daddy for a bit to make sure everything is okay, all right?"

Zaraquel hugged her tight, not wanting to let go. "He's okay, though, isn't he?"

Chloe was warmed by her daughter's love for her father. She was a daddy's girl, so her worry was natural, but Chloe knew deep inside that what she'd felt moments before was serious. She was, in fact, worried, but she didn't want to alarm the girls. Or McPherson and Rowe for that matter.

She and Marcus were bonded, meaning that she felt what he felt. He was in pain, and she had to leave now. There was no question about it.

With a firm nod, Zaraquel indicated she understood. Knowing she'd read her mind, Chloe let go and faced Rowe and Bradley.

"I have to go."

Rowe placed his hand on her shoulder, "I know, do what you must. But I must caution you that we still have a way to go in regards to your developing powers."

"I understand." She turned to her trusted friend, Bradley. "Take care of the girls. Keep them safe, please."

He embraced her in a quick hug. "I'll guard them with my life, I assure you."

Chloe wrapped Rae and Zaraquel in her arms, giving them each a kiss on their foreheads. She let them go and stood in the center of the room.

*"Bonded we are, bonded we shall be, take me to thee."*

Her palms face up, she floated in the air, only to disappear before their eyes.

~*~

*Chloe, Seattle, Present Day*

She landed inches away from him and saw his bloodied and bruised body on the ground. The streets were empty—no one was in sight.

"Oh Marcus." She crouched to her knees and cradled his face in her hands.

His eyes flickered open to look at her. "Chloe?" His voice was weak, deflating like the air escaping a balloon, barely above a whisper.

"Hey, baby, it's me," she said, her eyes tearful. It hurt her to see him hurting.

"I...I'm sorry, Chloe. I—"

"Shh. It's okay. I'm gonna fix you?"

~*~

*Marcus, Seattle, Present Day*

When Marcus awoke, he was in his bed in Michael's estate. He tried to check to see if the stakes were still there, where he had left them, but they were nowhere to be found. All he felt was numb.

Surveying the room, he saw that Chloe sat beside him, in deep sleep. When he looked in front of him, he saw Amber sipping on some tea.

"You're awake, that's a good sign." Her voice was an angelic whisper.

"What happened? Is Chloe actually here?" His voice, still raw, was foreign to him.

He saw Amber stare lovingly in Chloe's direction and smile. "Yup, that's her, our little miracle worker. She came into the estate, and Michael and Malakai helped carry you in. As for what happened to you? We were hoping you could tell us."

In that moment, he didn't really care why Valentine had attacked him. All that mattered was that Chloe was there beside him.

"She came back," he said to himself, not knowing if Amber

could hear him. He reached over to gently brush the hair from Chloe's face.

"Of course she did. Was there ever a doubt?"

"I was a dick."

"Well, you're not wrong."

He glared at her but knew she was right. She was just like Chloe, always right. How did they do that? Marcus looked away, ashamed.

"You were brutally attacked, Marcus. By whom?"

When the memories of that night's events hit him, he was enraged all over again. "It was Valentine."

"What?"

"The stakes were poisoned with holy water. I couldn't move—I could barely breathe. But I'm sitting here, and all I feel is numb. How?"

Amber turned her gaze to Chloe. "It was all her. It seems her time at the Order has really strengthened her powers. She removed the holy water from your system—think of it as a magical blood transfusion."

He looked over at his wife with great love. "She's amazing, isn't she?" Marcus sighed, "When she left with the girls, we didn't leave things in the best of terms. I didn't think she ever wanted to see me again. I mean, it's been weeks, Amber, and this was the first time we've made contact."

Amber lamented and looked on, taking in what he was saying. "I know it's hard, and I won't pretend I know what it is you guys are going through. But I know this—that's what love is. Especially the once in a lifetime variety."

He saw Malakai approach the doorway and stop in his tracks as Amber's voice filled the room. Marcus chuckled as she continued.

"It's difficult, and it's tiring, but if the love is true, then it's definitely worth fighting for."

The men smiled at Amber's penchant for sentimentality.

"What do you think, Malakai. Is that true?" Marcus saw Amber still at the sound of Malakai's name. Her smile was stiff, the warmness in her eyes from moments ago now snuffed out.

*How odd.*

Malakai cleared his throat and stepped into the room. He greeted Marcus with a smile and then looked straight at Amber. "If love is true, *anything* could be forgiven, if done with the best of intentions, no matter how misplaced."

Amber closed her eyes shut, but when she opened them, they were glowing. She quickly shut them, and her breath quaked as if she was trying to gain control.

Concerned, Marcus sat up, careful not to stir Chloe beside him. "Amber, are you okay?"

She stood abruptly with a curt nod. "I'm fine, just need to get some air."

Malakai looked after her when she left, and then back to Marcus with a pained expression on his face. "Feel better, Marcus. Excuse me."

He left quickly, to follow Amber, no doubt.

~*~

*Nimue, Camelot, 1276*

It had been a couple of days since she first met the infamous and all-powerful Merlin. And she knew that he was falling for her plan. He may be magical and powerful, but he was also a man. There was one thing a man could never resist — her feminine wiles. A smile here, a twirl of her hair there, and the trap was set. All she had to do was stand there, and he came to her.

Men were helpless against her sexual prowess, and she knew it.

So, there she was, in the middle of the woods, following Merlin to wherever he was going. She stepped with caution to not cause awareness of her being there. He did not know of her presence, although he was waiting for her. For someone filled with great magic, he wasn't the most careful — which was to her advantage. Another benefit, in her favor, was that he was of the attractive sort.

It was as if the fates paired them together, both practicing in secret. At the height of the century, the act of practicing magic was forbidden, the dragons were slaughtered, and every other magical creature was imprisoned — or worse, put to death.

Nimue, however, had heard rumors of a man capable of exceptional enchantment. She traveled near and far, from the lake to the land, in search of this man. And it was her luck that she encountered him in Camelot. She'd seen it in his eyes, in his delicate movements as he walked throughout the market a little more than a year ago, when they first met.

It didn't hurt that she'd seen him perform magic in front of her, turning a mere stone into a piece of gold and giving it to the impoverished vagabonds that lined the street. Only the man that the people spoke of could've done such a thing.

She had to get to know him. Most importantly, she had to gain his trust and learn from him. Nimue was not the type of woman to let a man control her or to be his plaything. Of a different mindset for the time, she yearned for power and control of her own.

It was time to make her presence known. She took a few steps and cleared her throat. He turned and threw a flirtatious smile in her direction.

"I was beginning to think you were going to leave me here, stranded and alone."

She threw her head back and laughed as she swatted him

on the shoulder. "How could I? When last we met, you said you were going to show me a surprise. Or was that just a ruse?"

He took her hand in his and pressed it against his heart. "Milady, how could a thought such as that cross your mind? Do I have the painting of a liar?"

Feigning to inspect him, she smirked. "No, I dare say you do not."

"Good. Now, let me show you what you came for."

~*~

They stepped into the tree, and within, Nimue found herself in a labyrinth that led into a small den-like room, rimmed with books and vials and trinkets — all things that were concerned with magic.

She took a turn around the room and thumbed through the spines of all the books. "Wow, this is magnificent. How wondrous."

Merlin chuckled at her excitement. "I'm glad you think so." He snapped his fingers, and in seconds the size of the room lengthened. She looked out and realized it seemed to have expanded for miles on end. She looked at him, speechless — she could not believe what she was witnessing.

"What is this place?"

"Within these walls are every bit of magic that his been expelled from this land, and many lands like it. It is my frail attempt at restoring — or shall I say maintaining — *the order* of magic within the realm."

Her eyes scanned the room — what a marvelous sight! "Everything here is magic, you say?"

"Every single thing," he said proudly as he walked over to a shelf and pulled out the grimoire, *Baloc ræftum*. She walked up beside him and leaned over to see a necklace, a beautiful amulet. Her eyes widened at the prospect of holding it in her hands.

"This amulet contains the source of power needed to keep this 'living library' afloat."

"Does it now?" Her interest was piqued, and she knew the next step in her plan.

~*~

*Sabre, The Covenant, Present Day*

It was the little things that caught him off guard—the way that Michael seemed repulsed seconds before Amber would approach him; or how he almost seemed displeased with the fact that Chloe was able to save Marcus.

Michael had been different since he woke up, and Sabre was the only one that noticed that. Perhaps it was the fact that he was the oldest wolf among them and was prone to being alone, and in turn, more observant, or, he was the only one living with his eyes wide open at all times. He did not turn a blind eye to the truth, even if it could signify a harsh dose of reality.

And as Sabre continued to gather evidence against Michael, he became more and more convinced that he should contact the Covenant. It was his obligation as a loyal wolf to alert the Covenant in order to protect the magical community; and, in doing so, protecting his pack and friends.

~*~

*Chloe, Seattle, Present Day*

Her body still felt drained despite having a full night of sleep. What she didn't realize was that she was wrapped in Marcus's arms. As the realization hit her, she snuggled closer to him, her arms wrapped around his waist. Her eyes fluttered open to find he was smiling down at her.

"Morning, sunshine."

She chuckled as he planted a kiss on her forehead. "How are

you feeling?"

"Much better—y' know, since you saved me." Marcus smirked, and she buried her face deeper into the crook of his arm.

"Anytime."

She reached up to place a peck on his cheek, but he turned, so their lips met. Her eyes burst open when he deepened the kiss, and she moaned into his embrace. All healed and filled with a furious passion, Marcus hovered over her as he planted kisses on her neck.

"If this is payment for saving you, I should do it more often."

He playfully nipped at her jaw. "Shut up."

She arched her back in response. Chloe felt a fire light within the pit of her stomach and felt the power surge into her. Her eyes glowed, and with a flick of her hands, she threw him against the wall and smiled. His hands were raised above his head in submission as she rose to her feet to meet him.

He smirked. "I see those lessons have been paying off." She nodded as she unbuttoned his shirt and ran her hands over his chest. He groaned in pleasure. "It's hot, Chloe."

"Yeah?" She looked at him with an impish smile on her face.

"Definitely."

~*~

*Chloe, Seattle, Present Day*

Moments later, they lay naked, wrapped up in their sheets, whispering sweet nothings into each other's ears. She laid her head on his chest and sighed. He was okay, and he was alive, and the time had come for her to leave and return to the Order, as promised.

Her head propped up on her elbow, she played with his hair with her other hand, wrapping it around her finger.

"I love you; you know that."

"And I love you, more than you could imagine."

She smiled in response. "I have to go back."

"I know. And as much as I don't want you to go, I know that you must. I see that now. They need you over there. Zaraquel needs you—*I* need you to learn as much as you possibly can."

Chloe chuckled. "God, you really are amazing, aren't you?"

"I wouldn't go that far."

"I won't let you down. I won't let any of you down."

"I know."

They kissed once more for good measure.

~\*~

*Zaraquel, The Order, Present Day*

Zaraquel grew more anxious, given the time her mother was away. She began to pace around the bedroom she shared with Rae, provided by McPherson and Rowe. They were situated at the tip-top of the tower that overlooked the grounds, which was helpful when Zaraquel wanted to fly and stretch her wings. The inside of the room was fortified by the dome shape and appeared as if the woodland sprites had helped decorate it. Vines and flowers hung from the ceiling, and two plush beds were placed side by side with quilted duvets. It was a dream.

But right now? She felt trapped. Looking over to Rae as she lay on her stomach reading a book, Zaraquel felt a bit jealous at her obvious complacency. She and Rae had been getting stronger with the frequent practice sessions, but something kept nagging at her—she just couldn't pinpoint what.

"You're going to run a hole in the carpet, Z. What's up?" Rae now sat up and watched her friend in distress.

Meanwhile, Zaraquel plopped down and sat on the floor, looking up at Rae. "I...I don't know. I just know something isn't right."

"Wow, how incredibly descriptive."

Zaraquel took a pillow and chucked it at Rae, who failed to dodge it and screeched in surprise.

"Hey!"

Zaraquel rolled her eyes in response, stood up once more, and began pacing again. Rae got up and stood in front of her, blocking her path. "Hey, your dad's gonna be okay. Whatever it is, your mom's there now."

Sighing, she knew Rae was only trying to help, but her words didn't diffuse her worry. "I know. Maybe it's just.... You know what? I'm gonna go on the roof, meditate for a bit — maybe that'll help."

"That sounds good. I'll be in here if you need anything."

And with that, Zaraquel jumped off the windowsill with a smile and flew to the rooftop.

~*~

She sat on the rusted shingles as she felt the wind brush upon her face. She closed her eyes and took in the feeling: *How wonderful.*

Like a soft caress, Zaraquel enjoyed the air as it hit her face — perhaps that was why she took pleasure in flying. But then she remembered why it was that she was up there in the first place.

For someone so young with a great responsibility thrust upon them, Zaraquel became riddled with anxiety. Much like her auntie Amber, her life was decided not by herself, or even by her parents, but by others. The stars, the fates, whatever she wanted to call them, had other plans for them. They were the children of the prophecies — only they knew how the other felt. Their destinies were intertwined long before their births were conceived. That was just the way it was, and there was nothing she or Auntie Amber could do about it.

They had to roll with the punches. She was ready. She could

feel it in her bones, in her soul, that the path chosen for her was the right one. And yes, she also knew she was running out of time to find a justified kill. But she was preoccupied with growing her magical powers. She needed to shift focus.

However, as the young adolescent she was growing into, she wanted to at least feel like she had her own choice in the matter. That's where Loquiel came into the picture. Ever since she'd left to go to the Order, she couldn't help but feel something more, something deeper for him.

Thoughts of him—of his laughter, his smile, his body, his everything—filled her mind as the days passed. It had come to the point where she'd fly to the estate to see him if she had to. Every time she closed her eyes, he was there to greet her with a kiss on her cheek, and sometimes her lips.

She smiled at the thought of seeing him. Her parents didn't know about his existence—no one did—and that made their relationship all the sweeter. He was *her* choice. She chose to keep him a secret. He was hers and no one else's.

She didn't just want him, she had to have him—she needed him. There was only one word that came to mind when she thought of him: *insatiable*.

# Chapter 14

Amber quickly made her way out into the garden, running her hands through her hair in frustration, and sat down on the lounge chair in the corner. She took a few calming breaths, but she could feel the magic trickling down to her fingertips. She was hit with the memory of her conversation with Malakai, so brutally fast that she had to sit down on the bed to catch her breath.

~*~

"We have to talk." As he said those words, she knew nothing good could come of it.

He placed his hand at the small of her back as he guided her to sit down beside him. She could tell by the tightness of his jaw that something was bothering him a great deal.

"Whatever you have to say, Malakai, you can tell me." She placed a hand on his knee and squeezed. He winced at the gesture, and she quickly retracted her hand.

"I have always kept you safe. It's my duty, my role in the prophecy. But I found that wasn't the only reason I found myself protecting you so adamantly."

A blush reached her cheeks as she fully understood what he implied. *He feels it too.*

"I care about you, more than I should admit. But you have to know this to understand why I took the actions I did."

"Malakai, what's going on? I don't understand."

He took her hands in his and looked at her with pleading eyes, then whispered under his breath, "I'm sorry."

She quirked a brow in confusion and tilted her head. "Sorry. What?"

"I wasn't completely honest when I told you I wasn't seeing anyone, at least not in the way that you think."

"I don't understand." She really didn't. Amber truly had no idea what Malakai was talking about. It was as if the words he was saying were gibberish. "Malakai, what on earth are you talking about?"

"It's your mother."

She tried to measure her words carefully as if she couldn't believe what it was she was hearing. "What about my mother?"

Amber heard him take in a breath, his hands stilling in her hers. "She's alive."

~*~

"She's alive."

His words vibrated through her again and again. They rattled in her brain, and she couldn't shake them loose. A hot heat filled her being, a sensation she'd never felt before like she was standing close to the sun and couldn't move away.

"Amber." His breath was ragged.

She heard him before she saw him, and she did *not* want to see him right now, maybe not for a couple of years.

"Amber, *please* look at me." His voice dripped with ache.

She whipped around to face him. "No, you do not have the right to do that. You cannot ask me to do something for you. How could you keep something like that from me, Malakai?"

"I'm sorry, Amber. I swear to God, I did it only to protect

you."

"That's rich, when all you did was *hurt* me instead."

He flinched as if she had slapped him. "That was the last thing I wanted to do."

"You know, everyone says they want to protect me, but it's like they forget who I am." With every word she spoke, she could feel herself burning brighter. Her feet began to rise from the ground till she was a good two feet above Malakai. "I am the queen."

"Amber…." His voice was weary.

"I. Don't. Want. To. Talk. *Especially* to you." She ground her teeth, angry that her friend could betray her in such a way. Her body was on fire, but it didn't seem to hurt her. It fueled her to continue.

He raised his hands in defense. "You need to calm down."

"Calm down? Me?" The fire around her grew in strength and brightness.

"You could hurt those around you, even yourself."

"What?"

"It's rare, but I've seen it once."

"Rare? What the hell are you talking about now?"

"Witch fire. Your mother has that gift too."

The fire began to dim at the mention of her mother. She took a few calming breaths and landed on the ground, her feet firmly planted. She looked at him with a new determination in her eyes.

"Tell me everything you know about her. No lies this time."

He took a moment to respond like he was trying to convince himself of something that he was second-guessing.

"I can do you one better."

She arched a brow in response, waiting for his answer.

"How would you like to meet your mother?"

~*~

*Moments Later....*

Her mind was foggy with the overload of information Malakai had revealed to her. She took her time walking through the estate, hoping to gain some peace of mind. But the walk did nothing. She was furious — how could he lie to her that way? She could not comprehend how her sweet Malakai was capable of such cruelty.

He had betrayed her under the guise of "protecting" her, and that didn't sit right with her, not one bit. She was now, as in her many lives, strong and capable and independent. She didn't need someone, let alone a man, to take care of her. It was her destiny to take care of others and save them.

What she wanted, however, was to have someone comfort her, that someone being Michael. She knew in her heart of hearts that Michael would make her feel better. Their love for one another was stronger, given their recent time together. But that was the thing about their relationship — she didn't need him in her life, she wanted him in it.

So, when she opened the door to the bedroom they shared, she expected to see him there waiting for her with a smile on his face.

~*~

*Machiel, Seattle, Present Day*

He saw the horror on her face as Amber opened the door. Machiel knew what she was seeing, and swore that he could hear her heart breaking. There he was lying naked on the bed with a beautiful woman on top of him. He didn't know her name or what she did for a living, and he didn't care. All he cared about was what he had been plotting since he was reborn: to break the queen just as she'd broken him, millennia before. He smirked when he saw her eyes well up with tears.

His companion turned to face Amber and asked, "Who's the girl?"

Machiel looked straight into Amber's eyes, now red from the tears that fell from her eyes. He waited, savoring this moment — a moment he'd planned to a "T" — as he remembered overhearing the conversation she'd shared with Malakai hours before.

*Her mother, the deceit...how heartbreaking.*

Thus, today was the day to enact his little project. He had to kick her while she was already down.

Looking into her eyes, he said, "No one. She's no one."

Like the sound of a crack from the whip hitting the air, a guttural moan escaped Amber's lips. With a quick movement of her arms, she flung the girl off Machiel and onto the floor. He laughed at her display of unnecessary passion.

She glared at him and walked out, slamming the door shut.

*Perfect.* She was gone, and he'd ruined her life. Everything was going according to his plan. Now he just needed to meet with the Avalani to see if everything else was in order. Knowing that Valentine had failed, Machiel had to see that Marcus was done away with another way.

~*~

*Malakai, Seattle, Present Day*

He stood in the shower, the cold water hitting his back. Malakai closed his eyes as if he were in physical pain. And he was. When Amber hurt, he hurt. It killed him to know he was the one that caused her anguish.

*Why? Why did I have to hurt her like that?*

As the water fell from above and hit his face, he let out a horrendous scream. All the emotion he kept hidden beneath his calm, and collected veneer escaped. He began to transform — his nose into a snout, his teeth sharper than knives, his ears pointed and on the top of his head. Fur sprouted and began to cover his body as he stood on all fours. For the first time in years, he could not control his transmutation into a wolf.

He howled, made his way out of the shower, and leaped out the window. Faster and faster, he ran off the estate grounds and into the woods, where he felt more at home. Despite that feeling of comfort, it was only temporary. What worried him more was that he was losing control. He had to get out of there, to solve his issues before they posed a problem for the people he cared about — *especially* Amber.

~*~

*Miriam, New Orleans, Present Day*

It had been years since she had heard Malakai's voice until a couple of months ago when he first called her. He had always kept her up to date on Amber's wellbeing, and for that, she was eternally grateful.

She had a box of photographs and keepsakes dating back through Amber's childhood. Miriam smiled as she flipped through the photographs: Amber, five-years-old, dressed as a witch for Halloween; her at twelve, winning the science fair; her with her foster parents at the park, laughing; at twenty, surveying an archeological dig.

Miriam looked at her daughter's life in pictures as she continued to pack her bags. For the first time in twenty-four years, she was going to see her daughter. Ecstatic that she was going to have a piece of her family together again, Miriam could not wait to jump on the plane and head to Seattle.

That's when she felt it: the rise in temperature. She knew that feeling all too well — the witch-fire. Except it wasn't hers that was activated, it was Amber's. Quickly shoving her belongings into the suitcase, she knew she had to go see her daughter fast before things got worse. She did not want the Tall Dark Man to find her, especially since Amber was the child of the Blood Prophecy. It was a mother's obligation to keep her daughter safe.

~*~

*Mona, Yakima, Present Day*

It had been a year since Rae's departure from the coven, and the absence of her sister couldn't be felt greater than it was now. She sat there in a black dress in a room she'd shared with Rae — still outfitted with twin beds, side by side as if Rae had never left in the first place. There was something about sisters, but more specifically about twins — they shared a bond like no other. They knew exactly what the other was thinking, before voicing it aloud. Or if one of them was feeling blue, the other could sense it. For this reason, Mona found it even more distressing that she could sense that the acheri was growing stronger within Rae.

She'd always wondered why the acheri had chosen her sister and *not* her. What was wrong with her? Was she not special, or worthy? What did Rae possess that she did not?

Each was magically gifted in their own ways. As Rae had grown more powerful — despite their distance, she could feel that she had — so had Mona. They were twins, and so they were connected. They were connected in more ways than one, or so she found out when she was clearing out her mother's room.

Underneath her mother's bed, she discovered a box — a box with a unicursal hexagram embossed on the top. As Mona was the bookworm of the two, she knew through her vast research that a sigil of that caliber had a dark past. Not only did she recognize it from her dreams, but as her gift of sight was more finely tuned than Rae's, she could see the significance of the sigil. With the tips of her fingers, she touched the ridges of the mark and froze, her eyes glazing black as she gave in to the sight.

Given its dark past, she couldn't go as far back as its origin, but she could access the history of which warlock used it the most. It was as if the mark itself was controlling what she was seeing.

*She saw her young mother, with a man who she could only assume was her father, given their close embrace. Her mother kissed him with passion as he took a cuff bracelet off her wrist. She'd seen it before in photographs — always of her mother, and never with someone beside her.*

*She looked at the man and recognized him, but she couldn't quite place him. Mona lingered on his face for a moment longer.*

*And then in another flash was the same man shaking hands with a dark being that disguised himself from her. A puff of smoke was all she could see when she tried to dig deeper. And then again, as if the channel changed on television, so did her vision.*

*The sigil was drawn on the ground and on the walls of various murderous happenings within the magical community. Years ago, before her time, occurred a massacre of thousands of witches and other magical creatures worldwide, and no one ever knew who or what caused it. But the unicursal hexagram was present at each murder scene.*

It was too much. It was all too much. Mona felt something wet drip on the front of her hand, which caused her to wake from her vision. Her eyes returned to normal, but it took a while for them to adjust. Never in her years of practice had she had a vision such as the one she'd just witnessed — her nose even bled.

She tried to access the vision once more and home in on the man she believed was her father. That's when she realized he was the same man that visited her right after Rae left Yakima. He came to her in secret and revealed himself to be a friend from her mother's past. But given the nature of the vision that just transpired, she knew he was, in fact, her father. She knew it. *Why didn't he tell me? Did he not trust me?*

He taught her spells and enchantments, made her stronger. Where Mona knew Rae had constant help from their cousin Chloe, she had him to lean on, to guide her — her teacher, her father. The moment she met him, she was drawn to him, and trusted him immediately, no questions asked. However, with this revelation, she didn't know how to feel. So, ever the academic, she focused on the vision to dissect it.

The vision itself seemed to steer her away from the events she wanted to prod into. It was unlike anything she'd ever experienced, and she was more intrigued than afraid. Mona couldn't wait to investigate, but what she was dealing with now was personally more pressing. She had to contact Rae. She'd been trying for months, but she couldn't reach her. Not only did she miss talking to her, but she had to tell her something that happened a couple of days ago. She couldn't handle it on her own, not anymore.

Mona had to tell Rae that their mother had died — she just didn't know how.

# Chapter 15

*Sabre, The Covenant, Present Day*

Sabre, in his dire wolf form, searched near and far for the Covenant's secret meeting place. He scavenged the land, attempting to track their scent, as the Covenant was known for switching their meeting place as least two times a day as a precaution, given the troublesome times they faced.

Their sole purpose was to protect the secret of the magical community, for the humans were not to know of their existence within the world. However, that was getting harder and harder to keep under wraps, with talk of sightings of zombies roaming Seattle and God knows where else. The Covenant was certainly busy.

Now Sabre sat on his hind legs as he tried to track their scents, as each was distinct—a wolf, a witch, and a vampire, all in collusion to protect magic at all costs. He breathed in their respective pheromones and homed in on a location. Howling, proud that he had found them, he took in a couple of more breaths and lunged forward, gaining ground. It was as if the ground disappeared underneath his paws as he was running furiously with immense speed. It seemed he took flight.

~*~

Finally, Sabre reached a cave deep within the forests of Seattle. He stilled, the cave immense in size and depth. He took one more sniff and was certain this was the place. Sabre let out a warning howl, alerting them of his presence.

Amid the darkness was a speck of light that only grew in intensity as Sabre stepped closer into the cave.

"Who goes there?" A deep throaty woman's voice was heard within the depths. Illuminated by the light, Sabre was able to see that the woman who spoke was a wise ancient sorceress with flimsy, cotton-like hair. Beside her stood a tall, lanky, almost skeletal vampire and another dire wolf, his grey fur virtually a shimmering silver. They all stood there in their natural state — in their magical prowess. Sabre was slightly stunned.

He communicated via mindspeak, as he knew the witch and vampire could not understand his native tongue as his fellow dire wolf could.

*My name is Sabre, a warrior wolf involved in the great battle of the Blood Prophecy.*

*Come closer, we won't bite — much,* said the vampire as he egged him on.

Sabre ignored him and continued with his urgent message. *I believe the queen's consort is not who he appears to be, at least not anymore.*

*Explain,* the silver dire wolf implored.

*Since he awoke, it seems he has reverted to his old animalistic instincts. You see, I met him before his sleeping spell, and he was completely different. Reserved, yes, but always polite — a true gentleman if you will.*

*And now?* The witch leaned in closer, more intrigued now than before.

Sabre tried to collect his thoughts and continued. *The way he looks at the queen, it's not a look of adoration, of love, as before. Now it seems he's filled with the desire to kill her.*

The Covenant let out a collective gasp as they took in the news.

*No, this will not do. This will not do at all. This could be the end.* The witch said aloud what all the men were thinking.

Sabre's worst fear was that the witch was right—this would put an end to the prophecy. What could possibly happen without the unification of the creatures? Amber was their saving grace—they *all* needed her. Something must be done, but what?

~*~

*Kabos, Seattle, Present Day*

Kabos had been following Michael for days without him noticing. As a spirit, he could make himself known when he wanted to and stay hidden when he didn't—which he used for his advantage, of course. What he saw disturbed him, and he only knew one simple fact to be true: the man before him was *not* Michael. Once more, he was Machiel.

The time came for Kabos to reveal himself as he followed Machiel into the library.

"Son?"

Machiel whipped around to face the ghostly spirit of Kabos. "It's you, Michael's old man." He chuckled. "He's not here."

Kabos sneered. "I know."

"What do you want?" Machiel spat out as he walked through Kabos as if he weren't there in the first place.

Kabos huffed as he reached into the pocket of his robes and pulled out the tiny book from the gypsies that he'd found in Malakai's reliquary. He shuffled through the pages until he found what he was looking for. He didn't have to look for the page to know what the words said, for they played on an endless loop in his head:

*The inner self will come to light when he who gains the truth and the might. Yet, it must be wanted and yearned; until then, can it be earned.*

Kabos floated over to him and thrust it into Machiel's chest.

"What the hell is this?" He took the book in his hands and gave a gander as he let out of haughty chuckle.

Raising his hands and placing them on Machiel's temples, Kabos used his celestial gifts and showed him memories of Michael's life. In an instant, it hit him in a rush, the images from his past: Countless plane rides alongside Marcus and Kabos; sipping wine and dining with Marcus; the moment he saw Amber and his life changed; their first kiss, the first time they made love. He saw everything as if for the first time.

Machiel let out an animalistic growl and pushed Kabos away with so much force that when he hit the wall, books cascaded down onto the floor. Kabos, uninjured, got up with gusto and approached him.

"See what you're missing? If you just read the book, you can have it all back, just as it was before." Kabos pleaded with his son. "Please, Michael. Just read the chant, I beg of you."

Machiel shoved him off once more, revealing his fangs and angry red eyes. "It's Machiel, *not* Michael. Michael's dead."

Kabos looked up at his son in horror as the truth settled in. His son didn't want to be saved, for he was no longer there. Kabos had believed that if he showed him his past life as Michael, he'd want to return to his prior self. Unfortunately, that was not the case. The stipulations of that gypsy spell were clear as day: the curse would only be reversed if the recipient wanted to be saved. And the fact was that Machiel did not.

Taking one last look at the man that used to be his son, Kabos was beside himself. He felt that every metaphysical cell of his ghostly form was expanding. He looked at his hands and found he was fading right before his eyes. Machiel didn't wish to see him, and that need was more powerful than what Kabos could control.

The air around him grew thinner, the space surrounding him somewhat denser, confining. Kabos was trapped, as the moment he blinked and opened his eyes, he found himself out of the estate. He tried to phase in and enter the house once more but couldn't. Machiel's will was so strong that Kabos couldn't break through. And in all honesty, he didn't know if he wanted to. The truth of the matter was that although Kabos had made Machiel, he was no longer his son.

~*~

*Machiel, Underground Seattle, Present Day*

Machiel could care less what Kabos wanted for his life. It wasn't his life to live or control, for that matter. All he wanted was to follow through with the plan he had concocted. Yes, he'd broken Amber's heart, but that was only a part of the whole. He'd always had a knack for these kinds of things: chaos. It seemed it was in his nature, that inherit darkness. It was always present, but he'd never done anything about it until he was turned.

Since he was first created, he'd known there was more to his life than the riches and fine dining that his family had provided for him. There was blood, and there was lust, a power that was unappeasable. The hunger that was deprived by the human tendencies of being sociable and respectable, civil. Yet, Machiel was sick and tired of civility.

Being a vampire was the greatest gift anyone could have bestowed on him, even if it was the always virtuous Kabos. Machiel felt free to act as he pleased. *What a glorious time it was.* He sighed as he let the memories take hold of him. But that was the past, and he was here in the present, stuck with all his current problems.

Cracking his knuckles, he took cautious steps, as in he was in no hurry. Machiel smirked at the thought of making them wait. But alas, he had to succeed where Valentine had failed. If not him, then who?

Nevertheless, as he walked through the narrow hallways of their hidden castle, it was time to put the next phase into action. Machiel walked into the room and found that Thana, Valentine, and Krieg sat around the table, waiting for him.

Thana placed her high-heeled feet on the table and sat further back into her seat. "Took you long enough."

Krieg grimaced and shot a menacing growl in her direction. Meanwhile, Valentine rolled his eyes at their antics. Machiel sat down at the head of the table and folded his hands on the top of his lap.

"Krieg?"

At the sound of his name, Krieg perked up. "Yes, Master?"

"The time has come to gather the troops. I have it under perfectly good assurance that we have an ally in our midst. Enter." Machiel leaned forward, pleased with himself.

Soon footfalls were heard echoing from the hallway nearby, and in came Mozart, with a violin in one hand and a dead corpse in the other. He let the corpse fall onto the floor with a loud thud. It was a mess of mangled bones and flesh, looking nothing like the human it once represented. The group, save for Machiel, looked as puzzled as ever.

Valentine quirked a brow in confusion. "What the hell? Is that Mozart?"

Always one for theatrics, Mozart chuckled and adjusted the violin onto his shoulders. He cleared his throat and closed his eyes as he began to play a haunting melody. Thana was genuinely impressed as she listened, but it was Kreig and Valentine that seemed to be losing their patience.

"What is the point of all this?" Kreig whispered.

The music began to pick up speed, and a distinct cracking was heard. The bones were popping back into place and twisting into their former glory. And just like that, the woman's eyes burst open, and she began to pick herself up — clumsily, and almost drunkenly she stood. The room let out a collective gasp.

Kreig shrugged, unimpressed. "So he wakes up the dead — so what?"

Having enough of his unforgiving attitude, Machiel stood and approached him, his eyes red, his teeth sharp. "How many vampires do you have ready, Krieg?"

Krieg avoided his heavy stare. "Enough."

Getting in his face, Machiel snarled, "Your little band of vampires and their fifty-plus friends is *not* enough. Mozart here is doing us the favor of lending us a hand in building our army. Isn't that right, Mozart?"

He nodded in response. "The dark lord said I am at your disposal."

The room was silent at the mention of the Tall Dark Man's well-known moniker.

Machiel clapped his hands. "Well, let's get this started, shall we?"

~*~

*Rae, The Order, Present Day*

Laying on her stomach in the bedroom that she and Zaraquel shared, Rae saw as Zaraquel danced across the hallway, singing loudly and off tune.

*What is up with her? She's been weird all week — singing, dancing, sneaking out. I don't get it. Does Aunt Chloe know? Should I tell her?*

Suddenly, through the corner of her eye, she spotted

something moving in the corner. Sitting up in the middle of the bed, Rae took in her surroundings. Everything was as she and Zaraquel had left it — the books on the shelves, their studying materials on their respective desks. And that's when she saw it: the Ouija board was moving all on its own. She leapt to her feet and climbed off the bed and ran to the board, hoping to catch the message.

She looked around, wondering if she could spot some paranormal force tricking her, but there was nothing in sight. Rae was, in fact, alone in the room, except for the unknown "thing" attempting to contact her. Grabbing a small notepad and a pen, she began to jot down the letters as they appeared before her. Just as soon as the message started, it stopped.

Rae looked down at her lap to read the message aloud. "Rae, it's about Mom. Come quick, Mona."

Her blood ran cold as she dropped the notebook on the floor. With her mind racing, Rae didn't know what to think. Memories of her mother, as well as all the times they'd missed because Rae had run from the coven, flooded her mind. Her mother, Pandora Tudor, a woman of many secrets and many problems. She was erratic but loving all the same. She and her sister didn't know much about her past, but they knew it was dark, something she'd never talked about. And with what Rae had seen with the spell she cast, she knew why. Her father was just as mysterious as her mother, if not more.

But the more she thought about the fact that she didn't really know her parents, Rae began to panic. She was losing control of her life, her human side submissive to the acheri that had begun to surface. Rae's neck swung unnaturally backwards, so much so that it should've been a fatal injury. Her eyes clouded black as a sinister smile slipped onto her face. The room began to violently shake as objects flew across the room, back and forth, back and forth.

Chloe and Zaraquel, as well as Rowe and McPherson, burst into the room at the sound of the ruckus. Rae saw them in the distance and dug deep within the crevices of her soul to hopefully reach out and contact them. Her eyes were still black, but when she opened her mouth, a bright light spewed out, practically blinding her onlookers. A tiny voice was heard amidst the harsh light — it was Rae.

"It's my mom, she's gone. She's gone. Mona told me." She was sobbing and in pain, her voice wavering. The room vibrated with her sadness.

Chloe stepped into the light approaching her cousin, tears streaming down her face. "Rae, I know it hurts, and I know you're a little lost right now, but sweetie? You must calm down so we can help you. Okay?"

Rae sniffled, her head now upright as she kept her back to them. The air around them felt heavy with all the emotions running high — it was understandable.

"I can take you home, Rae. You and me," Chloe pleaded with her.

Rae could hear as she took tentative steps towards her, placing her hand on her shoulder. With the assurance that Chloe would be taking her home, everything in the room calmed down — the temperature settled, as did the objects flying across the room. Everything and everyone was eerily still. She turned back and saw everyone's stunned reactions, to which she simply shrugged her shoulders.

~*~

*Chloe, The Order, Present Day*

As Chloe waited for Rae to pack her things, she sat in the castle's greenhouse. For some reason, since she arrived, she found that room specifically eased all her qualms. And she needed some peace and tranquility given what she and everyone had witnessed moments before. She had never witnessed such a thing. But then again, her life was anything but normal—spells and curses; demons and wolves; prophecies and destinies.

She tended to a few plants to pacify her mind, and in doing so, Chloe thought about how poor Rae must've felt when she found out her mother had passed.

*Poor Rae.*

Chloe had only met her Aunt Pandora once, and she didn't even know it was her in the first place until her mother revealed why she was crying immediately after she had left. She would never forget her though, the frightening and immensely sad woman that rung the doorbell. Aunt Pandora was thin and haggard, her skin almost pale, translucent. It was like she saw her as a ghost before she even became one.

"I'm ready, Chloe."

Shaken from her thoughts, Chloe turned to face Rae with her bag in hand. She nodded and picked up her bag from the ground and walked hand in hand with Rae into the drawing room. The girls entered to bid their goodbyes to Rowe, McPherson, and Zaraquel.

Zaraquel ran into her mother's arms and communicated via mindspeak. *Take care of her, Mom.*

*Always. Now be good and listen to McPherson and Rowe. Keep working to find your justified kill. I have a feeling it'll be soon.*

*You know, your gift of sight is really annoying sometimes,* Zaraquel confessed.

Chloe smiled, but once they separated, she had a feeling because, for the longest time, she hadn't had any sort of premonition—ever since she joined the Order. Did they have something to do with it? *Weird.*

She turned back, and they all waved goodbye. Well, one problem at a time. What she needed to do now was focus on the task at hand. Chloe began the teleportation spell. She did just as Rowe and McPherson had taught her: she thought so clearly and thoroughly with the intent that she didn't have to recite a spell, and only waved her hand in front of her in a circular motion.

The wind picked up in the room as Chloe held her hand in front of her, and before she knew it, a luminous portal opened to showcase the Yakima house's front door. She felt Rae clutch her hand a little tighter and saw that she was nervous. Chloe gave a warm smile as they walked into the portal, and moments later, they stood at the front door of their former home.

~*~

*Rae, Yakima, Present Day*

Chloe, with a snap of her fingers, changed their day clothing to something more appropriate for a funeral service.

Rae was not feeling well and thought the nerves were getting to her since this was the first time she'd stepped into the house, as well as seeing her mother and sister since she left. Her emotions were all on a fritz, going everywhere and nowhere all at once.

Suddenly the door opened before them as if the house itself knew they were arriving. With a deep breath, Rae stepped inside, unsure if the coven was going to welcome her back. She was bombarded by figures all in black, some of their stares full of menace, the others pity.

Then, just as soon as she placed her bag down, she felt Mona run into her arms, sobbing uncontrollably.

"You made it."

At the sound of her sister's voice, Rae broke down and cried a river of tears that never seemed to end.

~*~

With her sister by her side and Chloe on the other, alongside the other witches of the coven, they formed a circle as they held unlit candles in their hands. Her mother's body, however, was laid on top of the altar, a delicate sheet of silver sheathing her entire body from prying eyes.

Chloe's mother, Marlene, was the high priestess of their coven, and therefore led the ceremony. She stood at the forefront of the room, commanding every bit of attention despite the sadness evident in her eyes. She cleared her throat and lit the candles as she whispered, "*Candelis accensis.*" Rae felt the hot heat of her candle's flame warming her hands, and consequently, her face.

She held hands with her sister as they placed a photo of them with their mother on the altar. Soon after, the rest of the coven members placed mementos of Pandora's life, along with calla lilies, on top of her corpse. Each retreated to their respective spots as they joined hands and began to hum an eerie tune.

"*Ignis,*" said Marlene, and the candles that were once held floated up in the middle of the room. She continued, "*Aer,*" and a gust of wind swirled the levitating candles around the room. "*Aqua,*" she softly breathed, and water materialized out of thin air, joining the rest of the elements. And lastly, "*Terra.*" Dirt and soot from the hearth merged into the mix until it was an amalgamation of earthly fundamentals.

The humming crescendo at an all-time high from the witches sounded like a haunting and disoriented church choir. Their voices mounted, and then just as soon as it started, it stopped abruptly, and Marlene began her final blessing, holding back the tears.

*"Bone of my bone,*
*Flesh of my flesh,*

*Blood of my blood....*
*Dear sister, you are gone, but never forgotten*
*May your spirit finally rest*
*Forever present in spring as you are in autumn*
*None of the love that we have shared, gone unexpressed."*

Rae looked at her aunt, her lips slightly curved into a smile of sadness and a hint of gratitude. Surveying the room filled with the women of her coven, Rae felt some resentment, but she also felt grateful that they were there to take care of her mother and sister when she herself couldn't.

The only person she felt was missing, who had felt like a mother to her during her time away from home, was Miss Arianna. She needed to find some way to make contact. Perhaps she could alleviate some of the grief that Rae was feeling— although she knew that wasn't necessarily true, as no one could replace her mother, she had to try. Rae did not like to feel the anguish that coursed through her body. As if sensing the pain she was in, Mona squeezed her hand a little tighter, accompanied by a hopeful look in her eyes.

# Chapter 16

Amber, Seattle, Present Day

Distraught from the betrayal that she faced from the two seemingly most important men in her life, Amber was feeling her emotions run through her. All her thoughts were consumed by the cataclysmic events that had transpired: one, her mother was, in fact, alive and Malakai lied about it; two, rather than mending it, Michael had broken her heart by cheating on her. Suffice it to say, this wasn't her week.

It was past midnight, and Amber was doing what she always did when she was stressed—baking. Pots and pans clattered against the metal oven as she tried to find the perfect one to make the bundt cake she made every time she got her heart broken. She'd started this tradition back when she was in high school, and her first official boyfriend, Wyatt Sharp, had shattered her heart into tiny, itty bitty pieces.

She was all kinds of heartbroken, and for all intents and purposes, Amber was all alone. Hearing the latest news of the Tudor family's fallen witch, she knew that Chloe had gone home with Rae. As for Amber's mother, she didn't know who she was or if she was coming. So there she was, gathering all the ingredients necessary for her Dark Chocolate, Dark Heart chocolate bundt cake.

"What's going on in here?" Marcus leaned across the door frame in his pajamas as he ran a hand through his hair.

Amber grabbed a piece of chocolate and popped it in her mouth. "Nothing."

With a brow raised, Marcus gestured to the vast array of baking utensils and ingredients. "This is nothing?"

As she mixed the ingredients in the bowl, she said, "You know, I had a little craving for something sweet. And I thought, instead of going out to buy something, I could just make it, y' know? A little chocolate never hurt anybody."

"You're rambling."

"Well, isn't someone astute this fine morning — I mean night."

He walked over and sat across the island from her. "Hey, Amber? Are you all right?"

"Define 'all right.'"

"I see." He got up, dug through the liquor cabinet, got some glasses, and sat back down as he poured the tequila into two separate glasses. She eyed him suspiciously as she continued to pour the batter into the buttered mold.

Marcus handed her a glass as she placed the pan into the hot oven. When she chugged it down, Marcus's eyes widened in apparent surprise. She slid the glass in his direction, and he caught it as if he were a professional bartender.

"Hit me," she said, as the tequila felt warm and fuzzy in her throat. He poured her another drink. As she raised the glass to touch her lips, Jerome stepped into the kitchen, wearing his fluffy robe, trying to stifle a yawn.

"Jer, I'm sorry. Were we making too much noise?"

"No, no." He waved his hand in the air, dismissing them. "Not at all, Miss Amber."

"Jer, it's just Amber, you know that," she said with a smile.

He returned the smile, but quickly returned to the business at hand. "You have a guest waiting for you in the foyer."

She looked at Marcus, and his confused expression matched hers. They all quickly retreated and walked into the foyer. Amber came to a halt when she saw the woman with red hair, a color that matched Amber's.

Her voice quivered. "M...mom?"

The woman turned to face Amber, a small, insecure smile painted on her lips.

~*~

*Miriam, Seattle, Present Day*

She could see Amber was still rattled as she sat down on a bench outside. Miriam saw her chest rise and fall as her daughter tried to calm her breathing just as the sun started to rise. She approached her and sat calmly beside her with a glass of water in hand.

"Here you go."

Amber took the water and nodded thanks, and took a long sip before looking at her once more. "You're here. You're actually here."

Miriam chuckled. "Here I am, thinking the very same thing." The women shared an awkward laugh as they tried to piece together the life they'd missed—a mother and a daughter, each alone, but now reunited. Soon after, Amber's laughed transformed into a sad sob.

Miriam reached over to caress her daughter's hand and felt Amber freeze beneath her touch, their shared gift of sight kicking in.

~*~

*Miriam and Amber*

The women sat frozen in their seats and flung back as if a powerful wind had a hand in gluing them to their seats. Their red hair blew in the wind as they gripped tighter onto each other's hands. Their eyes open, no longer green but a bright white, their vision was clouded by their gift, and their minds and memories merged as one.

All the memories they'd experienced in their individual lives were seen through the other woman's perspective, like a movie playing in their heads.

*Amber, as an infant in Malakai's arms, as she watched her mother stand, the snow beneath her feet. She could see her father through her mother's eyes, as those memories remained fresh in her mind since his passing. And how her mother was captured and tortured by the Tall Dark Man. That was the first time Amber laid eyes on him, although not really since he appeared as a puff of smoke, blocking her sight from digging any further. Now, Miriam saw Amber's childhood – her triumphs, her losses. It was as if she was there beside her, living her life with her. Amber gasped when she saw the imprint that happened between her and Malakai when they first met when she was but a baby.*

~*~

*Miriam*

The sudden surge of power drained their bodies and their minds, yet they were caught up as if their link was never severed in the first place. They faced each other with tears in their eyes and hugged, making up for years of embracing and affection.

"Oh, Amber. I'm so sorry about *everything*, sweetie." Miriam wept into her daughter's shoulder.

"Mom, you did what you had to do. I was a wise baby if I remember correctly." Amber laughed through the tears, and her mother smiled.

Lovingly Miriam looked at her daughter as Amber stared at

the beautiful sunset before them. She remembered what she'd seen when their minds merged into one—the fight with Malakai and the fall with Michael. Her poor daughter's heart was aching if it wasn't already shattered.

"Amber?"

She turned to face her, the sadness evident in her disposition—her slumped shoulders, her eyes red from the tears shed. "Yes?"

"I know you're feeling down right now, but just as you told me all those years ago, you are strong and independent, and I know you have the power within you to pick yourself up and accomplish what you are destined to do. You cannot give up—you have to keep fighting."

Miriam saw as Amber choked back her tears and smiled through the pain. They hugged each other once more, and Amber whispered in her ear, "Thank you. I always wanted to know what it would be like to have you in my life." They parted, and she sniffled, "And now I do."

Miriam herself began to cry as she placed a few strands of her daughter's silky hair behind her ear. Amber looked into her mother's eyes and opened her mouth to ask something, but Miriam quickly responded before Amber could say anything.

"Now, sweetie, Malakai did what he thought was best for you. All he ever wanted and still wants to do is protect you."

She looked at her, stunned. "How did you...?"

"A mother always knows, honey."

They shared a moment, and Amber chuckled. "So, he imprinted on me?"

"No, no. I don't think you understand. It was you who imprinted on him. You chose him. You knew before any of us that he was the one you needed."

~*~

*Loquiel, Hell, Present Day*

It had been weeks since Zaraquel became his, and when he said "his," he meant it. He could feel their connection growing stronger. It had been quite some time since he had gone out and spread his wings; however, for the love potion to take effect, some distance was required.

He was going as crazy for her as she was for him — of that he was positive. He could feel her heartbeat as if they were one. He flew up from the depths of hell onto the earth's bounds and flew across the skies to reach her. With his wings soaring and his muscles burning, Loquiel could feel himself going out of breath, but that did not stop him — nothing would stop him from getting to Zaraquel. He had always loved her, and it was about time she realized it too.

And now, thanks to his master, the Tall Dark Man, his deepest desire was coming true. For that, he was forever grateful and would remain his faithful servant till the end.

~*~

*Loquiel, England, Present Day*

That was when he saw her — Zaraquel, sitting perched atop the roof of the castle, the sun setting as the light hit her long hair cascading down her back. He stopped mid-flight, and she looked even more beautiful than he remembered. She sat there, angelic as ever, her chin resting against her hands.

He flew to her fast, the last stretch, and their eyes met, hers so full of glee she jumped up to her feet and unfurled her wings excitedly.

"Loquiel," she squealed.

Finally, he was inches away from her, but when he reached over to place her hands in his, he was repelled by an unseen shield.

"What the hell?" He bounced back, in shock.

"Loquiel, what's wrong?" She stood there, confused.

He approached again but was pushed back. He scratched his head and got to thinking about the reason why Zaraquel's mother couldn't bring her husband to the Order. There was darkness in him — in all vampires, really. What if Loquiel had spent so much time in hell that the darkness penetrated his soul? He was a fallen angel, after all.

"Loquiel?" He heard her soft voice tinged with worry.

"Don't worry, Zaraquel. I'll figure something out."

*Why?* Why was this happening to him? She was finally within reach, and they were still separated.

"Wait, I think I know what to do. Don't move." She closed her eyes and raised her hands against the shield. A few moments later, she was able to bypass the barrier, and her hands reached his. She pulled him in with such great force that he fell on top of her.

Close. So close the tips of their noses touched. He could feel her hot breath on his face, her heart racing in her chest.

"Hi," she mouthed.

He smirked and mouthed, "Hi."

Her eyes sparkled with mischief as she bit her lips. Meanwhile, his gaze traveled from her glittering eyes to her rosy cheeks, and finally to her lips.

*This is it.*

~*~

*Zaraquel, England, Present Day*

*This is it.*

Her palms sweated in anticipation, and her stomach was filled to the brim with fluttering butterflies.

*This is it, he's going to kiss me! Loquiel — oh, I'm so happy it's going to be with him. Why didn't I realize he was so, so dreamy? Do people still say that? I hope it is like our first kiss, only better. Wait, do I tilt my head to the side? What if I bump into him and our teeth clash? What do I do with my tongue?*

"Shh." He cupped her face and stilled her racing thoughts as if he knew exactly what to do. She smiled in response.

She had never experienced this before: her body felt warm, and her insides like Jell-O. All foreign sensations, but she didn't mind, not at all.

He moved in closer, and she stilled, holding her breath, not wanting to ruin the moment. Loquiel nestled his face in her neck and inhaled her scent.

"Mmm…." She couldn't control the sounds that erupted from her body.

He chuckled, and she could feel his smile on her skin. He peppered her with a trail of kisses—her collarbone, neck, cheek, and her lips. He hovered over her lips for what seemed like a long time. She laced her hands behind his neck and pulled him to her.

*Not so fast, little one,* he said via mindspeak.

*Shut up and kiss me.*

And that he did…repeatedly.

~*~

She lay beside him, her head upon his chest. Sighing, she admired the stars up in the heavens. They sparkled even brighter tonight as if God himself approved of the angelic coupling. Zaraquel felt him looking at her, and she glanced up to meet his eyes.

"What?" She giggled so much that her cheeks reddened.

"Go out with me."

She sat up. "What? Like, like a…a date?"

He followed her and smiled at her innocent question. "Yes."

She turned at the sound of McPherson yelling her name

inside. She bit her lips nervously. "I don't know, Loquiel. I have to study, and I can't ask my mom 'cause she's not here."

"That's exactly why you should go—you won't have a curfew. We can spend all night together."

"Loquiel, I—" She stopped as he silenced her with his kisses. She breathed him in and sighed. He lifted her up and placed her on his lap as he clasped his arms firmly behind her; meanwhile, she toyed with his hair in her fingers.

He whispered as she continued to kiss him. "Tomorrow night. Say yes."

"Yes," she sighed, overtaken by the flurry of emotions and the excitement of teenage rebellion.

~*~

*Malakai, The Woods, Present Day*

Feeling the dirt beneath his paws, Malakai looked from the woods that surrounded the estate, where he could see all, hear all within the mansion's walls. His abilities as a werewolf were heightened since he was in his natural state as a full wolf.

With his strengthened vision, he could see Amber and Miriam in the kitchen making breakfast as Jerome and Marcus set the table.

*At least she is happy,* he thought. That's all he'd ever wanted.

He surveyed the rest of the building, but Michael was nowhere in sight. *How odd.*

*What's the matter, Malakai?* Sabre approached him, tall and elegant as ever. Sabre's steps were always so soft and subtle, he could never hear him—although that talent had its advantages when he really thought about it.

*Michael. I can't sense him.*

*You've noticed it as well, haven't you?* Sabre inquired.

*I don't understand.*

*Michael is not the same since he awoke from his deep sleep. Surely you know that.*

*I tossed it up to an adjustment period. Is that not the case?*

Sabre growled in discontent. *I have been charged with the task of keeping an eye on Michael, and have been given orders to deal with him by any means necessary.*

*By whom.*

*The Covenant.*

The Covenant. Malakai knew those were tall orders indeed, and should not be disobeyed at any costs. But at the cost of Amber's heart? He couldn't bear for her to risk any further hurt.

*But —*

*But nothing.* Sabre cut him off and narrowed his eyes, sneering. *He cannot, for whatever reason, ruin the prophecy.*

All Malakai thought about was Amber. He stood up to Sabre, meeting his dignified stance, and growled. Sabre bared his teeth, sharp like razors.

*It affects us all. Understood?*

Malakai stepped back, embarrassed by his uproarious behavior.

*Perhaps that is where your issue lies. You prioritize her above all else, even the prophecy. Perhaps that is why you find yourself unable to transform properly.*

Malakai's eyes widened at Sabre's accuracy.

Sabre continued. *When you are ready to perform as it was written, look for me. Maybe then, in finding your true purpose, you'll be able to balance the wolf with the human.*

With a parting nod, Sabre ran off as Malakai simply stood there in shock. The remaining dire wolves played a game of catch and release, their howls vibrating through the atmosphere. However, with a supernaturally loud growl on Sabre's part, the wolves quieted and quickly followed him.

That's when he felt it: the hot hum of Amber's stare in the back of his furry skull. He didn't have to turn to know she was aware of his presence.

*What are you doing here?* Though she communicated telepathically, her voice was still angry and chilled him to the bone.

*Amber, please listen. I —*

*No.* She silenced him. *My mother explained your reasons, and my head understands the logic, and I appreciate that you tried to protect me. But my heart? My heart…. Mal, you helped break it.*

Those words shattered *his* heart.

*I think….* Her voice broke as if she was trying to keep her composure. *I think we both need some time apart.*

She was right. But then again, she was always right. And so, with one last look towards the estate, he ran to follow Sabre and the dire wolves. Perhaps he could assist to figure out what was really going on with Michael, and of course, he'd have a chance to get his priorities in check.

~*~

*Tall Dark Man, Hell, Present Day*

He sat there in his tailored black suit atop his throne with his hands folded across his lap. With a snap of his fingers, a puff of smoke appeared in the air and materialized to televise the happenings that occurred above.

"Perfect." Rae was embraced by the sudden arrival of Miss Arianna. "Everything is as it should be."

He saw them there together: Mona, Rae and….

Tilting his head, he smiled as he saw her look directly at him as if she knew he was watching. And she knew very well — she had worked with him for centuries.

Miss Arianna, or as he referred to her, his dear Elizabeth,

caressed Rae in her arms and met his sinister smile with one of her own.

*Snap.*

And they were gone. He was alone once more.

He crossed his leg over the other, and a book materialized in his hands. He traced the words on the cover with his thumb. *The Alchemy of Three,* it read. He chuckled as he remembered crafting it moments before he met Elizabeth. She was his witch of the past, and of course, was vital to his design.

*Three sorcerers from different points in time who were conceived of mortal flesh and of wicked seed will open the mouth to the world's most impure and dark. Only then can the world begin anew.*

The stars were almost aligned to set the last act in motion.

~*~

*Briar, England, Late 1995*

It had been years since he graduated as an elite member of the Circle. Briar was now a professor of the dark arts, alongside Mick. The Order simply couldn't part ways with two of their most gifted witches.

Thanks to the Tall Dark Man, he now had a purpose to find the tree of knowledge. That was what he was doing deep within the depths of the Order.

Hidden within one of the books he had scavenged through, he'd found a map protected by a spell. However, being as talented as he was, Briar snapped, and the map appeared before his eyes. He held it in his palms as he navigated through the bottom floors of the castle. No one knew where they were located, or even that they existed, except for him, and God knows who.

Down there, it played with his senses. Briar didn't know if he was still inside the castle's bounds. He could feel a crisp breeze as if he were outside, but as he walked down, he could see the walls, so he knew he was still enclosed. Feeling discombobulated, he looked down to his map to see if he was heading in the right direction.

Everything was charted to a "T," save for a noticeably empty spot in the corner, between what was labeled, "Unspoken Spell Directory" and "Herbs for Ineffable Acts." The more he looked around this treasure trove, the more he became interested in what the Order did. It seemed as if they had an impressive collection of all things magical. Who or what did this collection belong to, exactly?

"What the fuck is this place?" he said to himself.

He walked a little further until he reached that empty divot. He touched the wall—nothing. No knob, no handle, not a single thing. However, he did feel there was a slight temperature change from the rest of the room. *"Ipsum revelare,"* Briar whispered, and a knob with a vine-like design appeared to be etched on the wall, but it didn't surface.

*How odd,* he thought.

Despite this setback, he needed to report back to the Tall Dark Man.

~*~

*Hours Later....*

Within the safety of the wood's clearing, Briar recounted the night's events to the master. The Tall Dark man tapped his chin, intrigued by the aspect of a door with the unopenable handle.

"Fascinating, isn't it, Elizabeth?"

He turned, and she appeared right in front of Briar. He stepped back and looked at the woman that had been guiding him for years. The disembodied voice had a face—a simple but beautiful one. She was short amongst the men, but she held her ground.

"Why, I must say it is." She agreed with him as she smiled in Briar's direction, a sort of affection evident in her eyes.

"That clever son of a bitch." The Tall Dark Man began to pace, the leaves crunching beneath his feet. He took a moment and collected his thoughts.

"A spell such as that must be tied with the old magic, blood magic," Elizabeth remarked.

The master uncharacteristically clapped his hands, but then quickly gained his composure. "Very good, dear. Very good."

Briar's brows cinched in confusion. "I don't understand."

Chuckling, the Tall Dark Man looked at Elizabeth and smiled. "To be that young, huh, Elizabeth? And trivial." Briar saw that Elizabeth shook her head in disapproval of that specific witticism. Nevertheless, the Tall Dark Man dismissed her and continued. "But alas, Elizabeth here is correct. That enchantment is one of blood, so it requires blood to open it."

After a wave of the master's hand, Briar looked down and felt a burning sensation on the front of his hands. He yelled in pain as he looked up to the skies. "What the hell?!"

Placing his fingers on the newly branded burn, he traced the sigil—the unicursal hexagram.

"With this sigil, you will notice a remarkable surge in your powers. But to maintain that surge, you must vanquish other witches. In doing so, you will gain access to the tree of knowledge, and therefore know how to open the portal to a new and illuminating world, without rules, without boundaries."

Other witches, people who had finally accepted him, must die for him to open that door? Was he willing to risk this? Put people in danger? Mick? Pandora? Himself? How he loved Pandora, more than he'd thought he could feel for another person. But this was the master. Briar had a debt to pay, and he didn't want Pandora in the middle of it. So he did what he had to do.

"Will you fulfill your duty, young Briar Hexham, and commit the most heinous of sins and kill other witches? For power? For the tree of knowledge? For the New World?" asked the Tall Dark Man.

With determination, he nodded and accepted the challenge. "Yes. Under one condition."

The Tall Dark Man raised a brow in surprise at Briar's gall. "Go on, what is it?"

"You must, by any means necessary, protect Mick and Pandora."

~*~

*Days Later....*

Briar knew this: to open the door to get to the tree, he had to kill his people, the witches. And he had. For days since he was instructed, he'd committed the murders in secret. Witches from all over the world, from different covens, were slaughtered by his hand. The act of spilling blood didn't bother him as long as he protected the two people he was closest to.

He'd entered the kitchen to wash the blood off his hands when he felt Pandora's arms wrap around his stomach. He turned and leaned into her touch.

"Hey, I didn't know you were back."

"Yeah," she said, her face blank.

"What's wrong, babe?"

"My sister didn't want to help. She said she was done."

"Look, if it's about the money, I know my professor's salary isn't much, but—"

"It's not just that, Briar. It's...." It was as if her body gave out and she fell into his arms. "She's gone. My mother's dead, and I was too high to remember that my sister called me about it."

She sobbed in his arms, and he held her, wanting to take

away all the pain she felt.

"Baby, I'm so sorry."

He pitied her, he did. But all would be better when he completed his mission. Just a couple more sacrifices would give him access to the source of all power. With that knowledge in the dark man's arsenal, only then could he succeed in opening the portal to the new world.

~*~

*Mick, England, 1995*

Mick had known Briar since they met at the Circle years ago, and to teach alongside him had been a dream. But lately, he'd noticed that Briar was more distracted and erratic than usual. Perhaps he was also frightened about the sigil massacre? The panic had settled within the witch community. Not since Salem had there been such a violent witch hunt—all were on high alert.

Since Briar met Pandora, he'd calmed down somewhat. She was nice—a little naive and too trusting, but sweet all the same. They needed each other. Mick had never in his life witnessed a partnership such as theirs, so dependent on each other. Briar had settled down, even bought a flat, but there was something about him that had shifted. Something darker.

Therefore, Mick took it upon himself to cast an invisibility spell on himself, as well as an attachment charm, meaning wherever Briar went, Mick followed, stuck to him like glue without Briar knowing. But the spell was only temporary—only twelve hours to gather the necessary information.

What he saw shocked him to the core.

It was him. Briar was the one responsible for all the carnage. Why? With every kill, Mick yearned to stop them. But the attachment spell had a caveat, as did every spell, for magic comes with a price. This spell was of the voyeuristic nature. The caster could attach themselves to the desired individual, but only for observing. They were forbidden to act on their own volition.

So, when Briar traveled from coven to coven killing witches, Mick could only stand there and watch. His vision stained red from all the bloodshed — he was in a state of shock.

When they returned to the Order, he didn't realize it at first, which was natural considering he had never been to or known that there was a bottom level to the castle. There they were in a labyrinth-like reliquary when they stopped at a wall with an intricately drawn sketch of an ornate door. Mick saw that when Briar placed his hand, which seemed normal to the untrained eye but quickly revealed a sigil — the unicursal hexagram — the drawing on the door became more life-like, it's edges and grooves protruding from the wall. It looked real, but not close enough for it to be legitimate.

"Damn it," Briar sneered. He sighed as he pinched the bridge of his nose in frustration. Mick knew him well enough to know he was just about to reach his breaking point. There had to be a reason why Briar was committing such treason. Mick just had to figure out what.

Briar slammed his fist against the almost-door, causing Mick to shake in his boots.

"Guess I'll have to keep going."

If that meant killing more witches, Mick could no longer stand there and watch. He had to tell someone — he had to tell Rowe. If not for the witches' lives at stake, then for Briar.

~*~

With a snap of his fingers, both Briar and Mick were transported into Briar's flat. Briar fell to lie back on his couch and took a couple of cleansing breaths. Meanwhile, Mick shook his head, pissed off.

Pandora slowly walked out of the bathroom, holding

something in her hands. Briar saw her worrying disposition and quickly stood to meet her halfway.

"Babe, what's wrong?"

She jumped when she saw him there in front of her.

"Uh, hey, um…Briar? When did you get here?"

"Just a moment ago. What's going on?"

Mick inched closer, intrigued at what could have caused Pandora such distress.

Briar held her face in his hands. "Talk to me, baby."

She looked up at him with tears in her eyes. "That's exactly it. I…I'm pregnant."

When Mick looked up and saw their faces, he couldn't tell if they were excited or were terrified.

Maybe, both?

# Chapter 17

*Merlin and Nimue, Camelot, 1278*

He closed his eyes to listen to the wind that rustled through the leaves, the water that crashed against the rocks as he sat there by the riverbed. There were only hours now until the unleashing of magic that he had been working towards finally came to fruition.

Merlin smiled as he looked over to Nimue, whose long hair tastefully covered her breasts as she floated in the water. It had been two years since he took Nimue under his wing, teaching her the wonders that magic could offer, and he had to admit the romantic relationship they shared wasn't too bad either. She swam to him, and as she walked out of the water to him, she appeared as a mythical creature herself, a siren.

"What are you smiling about?" she asked slyly as she sat on his lap.

He wrapped his arms around her and kissed her passionately. "I'm lucky, that's all."

She swung her head back, laughing. "'That's all'? Care to elaborate?"

"Tonight at the stroke of twelve, magic will be reunited with all creatures small and tall alike. And well, of course, then there's you."

A blush rose to her cheeks, and then she looked around to take in her surroundings, not quite meeting his gaze. "This is a big night indeed."

~*~

*That Night....*

He found himself alone, waiting for her to come, but she had yet to arrive. *Where could she be?* Merlin stood there in his reliquary, and it was exactly midnight on the dot. He sighed, hating to start without her.

This moment had been in motion since the disbandment of magic. He had been planning meticulously. The herbs he used, the measurement, the correct phrasing, the intention, his state of mind when he recited the spell—it all had to be completed with precision.

With his arms at his sides, his hands shook slightly as he couldn't contain his nerves—this was a big moment. Closing his eyes and clearing his mind, he centered himself. The wind around him picked up as he floated up into the center of the room as if being picked up by the gods themselves.

His heart slowed down, and he was ready.

> *"Magic hear me,*
> *Magic feel me,*
> *Reveal yourself, you are universal.*
> *Please come back, come full circle."*

Boiling in his blood, he felt the magic that surged in him pour out in plenty. Through his eyes and mouth, his fingertips and chest, an eminent light beamed from his being. Merlin felt his insides being pulled apart, so much so that he failed to see

Nimue enter, witnessing this magical transfusion.

~*~

She stood there in complete awe of what she was seeing. He looked like a deity, or perhaps an offer to the gods. She wasn't sure what it was, but Nimue had a task in mind, and she aimed to follow through. Despite her recent romantic attachment with Merlin, she had one thing that was her number one priority — the necklace. She had to get it.

As he floated and chanted, she looked through the bookcase he had shown her before, but it wasn't there. *Damn it.*

She had to hurry — the wind was starting to settle, and the spell was coming to an end.

~*~

The spell was complete — he could feel it in his bones. Magic was once again vibrating through the air. He opened his eyes and was surprised to see Nimue rummaging through his shelves. She stopped and gasped as she held the amulet in her hands.

Disappointment made its way into his heart as he returned to the ground, the floor beneath his feet. *How could she? After everything we've shared? The magic? The love?* He gathered his heartbroken sentiments and clenched his jaw with a new sense of determination. She could not just betray him like that. But, most importantly, because he'd taught her, she posed a danger not just to those around her, but to magic itself.

She had to go.

He saw her eyes gleaming triumphantly as she looked at the necklace in her hands. He focused all his energy and was able to read her thoughts.

*Stupid bastard. I can finally have all this power to myself. Become the world's queen.*

That was enough.

With a wave of his finger, the amulet flew from her grasp

and hovered above his hand until he snapped, and the necklace disappeared into thin air. She looked around and caught Merlin's downcast gaze as she tried to regain her composure.

"Uh, Merlin. Hi, love. H…how did the spell go?"

He walked up to her, took her hand in his, and whispered, "*Sterilis.*" Suddenly her hands felt cold, and the freshness of her skin dimmed.

She backed away from him, terrified. "What did you do to me?"

"I took from you what you tried to take from me."

"What on earth are you talking about?"

"The amulet. I know what you are thinking, who you really are."

Her hopeless expression slowly transformed into that of a vixen, and she chuckled. "What are you going to do about it?" She flicked her hand in the air, wanting to fling him against the wall. She tried once more and again, but she couldn't.

Nimue looked at her hands, shaking. "I…I…."

"They're gone—your powers."

She looked at him, tears in her eyes, and ran towards him, yelling, "And now so are you!"

With a wave of his hand, she disappeared before she could hit him.

~*~

*Nimue*

Nimue found herself in the middle of nowhere. She knelt on the ground, the hot heat scorching her skin. Yelling at the top of her lungs, Nimue didn't hear the distinct sound of hooves nearing until the gargantuan goat stood right before her eyes.

The goat crouched down, their eyes staring deep into each other's.

"Don't fret, dear child. I can take all your troubles away — if you give *me* a hand, that is."

She nodded in agreement.

~*~

*Rowe, England, 1995*

Rowe once more faced disappointment from those close to him. There he stood in his office, his hand on Mick's forehead, chanting an ancient spell to reveal what the person had witnessed in the last twenty-four hours. He saw everything as it had transpired moments before, his jaw ajar in shock. He could not believe what he was seeing.

Briar, his beloved student and then professor, was capable of such atrocious acts? Rowe simply could not fathom it. Briar was responsible for the sigil massacre. But he also knew about that door.

*Now how did he know that?*

Removing his hand from Mick's face, he let him sit down and catch his breath. Rowe began to look through the books in his office. When he opened the *Balocræftum,* he discovered the map was nowhere to be found.

"Damn it!" Rowe saw that Mick looked at him, his esteemed professor, flabbergasted by his sudden outburst. "Apologies, Mick. The room you followed Briar to was supposed to be unknown by *everyone.*"

"Everyone but Briar, apparently."

"Exactly. Both you and I know Briar very well, and we know he is intelligent beyond his years. But he couldn't have gone this far on his own."

"So, you're saying someone helped him?" Mick inquired.

"Yes. It's essential that we keep him from killing witches, as well as opening that door."

"What exactly is behind that door?"

"Behind that door is what holds the entire Order together—the castle, the magic, everything. It is the fabric that allows access to all the world's existence. The portal takes many forms—the sun, an apple, a tree…."

"Are you saying the portal is the tree of knowledge itself?"

"Yes, yes, I am."

~*~

*Chloe, Yakima, Present Day*

The day after the funeral, Chloe sat with her mother, Marlene. They looked out the window, sipping their coffees as the leaves fell to the ground outside. Chloe had missed being home more than she realized. She reached over and grabbed her mother's hand, clasping it in hers.

"I missed you."

"I…." Marlene looked down at Chloe's wrist and stopped. "Uh, Chloe, where did you get that bracelet?"

She smiled, looking at the gift her husband had given her. "Marcus. Well, it was Michael. It's like a family heirloom Michael thought I would want to have from Marcus."

"Really?"

"Mom, you're acting weird. What's going on?"

"Oh nothing, honey. It's just that I thought your aunt had one exactly like that years ago. But it must be my mind playing tricks on me. Y'know, I'm not a spring chicken anymore."

Chloe laughed at her mother's odd sense of humor.

~*~

Chloe loved using her magic—it made her feel special—but sometimes she liked to do things normally, like washing dishes. Yes, it was quite a mundane and menial task, but she found it soothing for some reason. So as she washed the dishes, she glanced outside the window, and something caught her eye.

It was Mona.

Mona was in deep talks with someone, someone Chloe could not see. Mona's back was to Chloe, so she didn't know she had an audience.

"*Revelare,*" Chloe whispered. She wanted to see who or what her little cousin was talking to. However, the enchantment didn't work. Chloe couldn't see anything besides Mona. And as if sensing someone was looking in her direction, Mona turned, her eyes black.

Dropping a dish, Chloe gasped when it shattered on the floor. She pricked her finger and looked down for a second to see the blood begin to pool. Once more, she looked out to see Mona, but she wasn't there anymore, as if she'd disappeared into thin air.

~*~

*Machiel, Seattle, Present Day*

Machiel found himself quite chuffed at the success of breaking Amber's heart. He kept replaying her reaction over and over in his head, a constant loop of shock and tears. Despite the victory of that certain feat, however, there was still one thing that irked him, one thing that put a pin in his plan. Marcus. Marcus was still breathing and alive, for all intents and purposes.

Given that Machiel was the vampire king, he was privy to ancient rituals and customs. And right now? He needed Valentine.

~*~

*Machiel, Underground Seattle, Present Day*

Valentine met him in his throne room as Machiel sat nonchalantly draped across his cathedra. He looked at him menacingly with a knowing smirk on his face.

Meanwhile, Valentine rolled his eyes with a huff. "What do

you want, Machiel?"

He rose from his seat and met Valentine until he was face to face with him, staring him directly in the eyes. "Valentine, Valentine." He walked around him, circling him until Valentine shifted his weight on his feet. "You were the only one who did not complete the task he was given."

"I don't understand."

"As I understand, Marcus is still alive, when he's supposed to be what…?" Machiel placed his hand behind his ear as if to feign that he was listening.

Valentine looked down, ashamed. "Dead."

Machiel stopped and growled. "Exactly." He placed a hand on Valentine's shoulder and forced him down on his knees as he yelped in pain. Machiel dug his nails into his skin until Valentine bled. He looked firmly into his eyes, both of their pupils dilated—Valentine was caught in a trance while Machiel spoke hypnotically. "Linked by blood, linked by flesh, you will do as I tell you to do."

He let him go, and Valentine fell to the floor, weakened by the hypnosis. Licking his fingers to taste the blood, Machiel was satisfied.

~*~

*Valentine, Seattle, Present Day*

Valentine stumbled across the lawn, dragging his feet and arms as if he were a ragdoll. He couldn't control his movements — his actions were not his own, but Machiel's. The tyrant vampire king had possessed him, the vampire hunter.

Looking translucent as he shone in the sun, he saw Marcus hunched over on the ground tending to the estate's garden, unaware of Valentine's presence. He lunged at him like a wild animal, hanging off his back. Removing the holy water drenched dagger from his pocket, he proceeded to stab Marcus on his side. Marcus howled in anguish but managed to throw Valentine off his back.

With Marcus now hovering above him, his fangs made an appearance, and he looked like a feral animal. Valentine looked at him in disgust, further fueling his desire to get this over with. Marcus tried to claw at him but was stopped short because of the poisonous nature of the holy water.

Quickly Valentine rolled him over to his back, and now he was on top, a stake in his hand. He cackled, noticing the fear in Marcus's eyes.

~*~

*Machiel and Kabos, Underground Seattle, Present Day*

Laughing maniacally, Machiel sat in his chair with the real human version of Valentine on his knees beside him. His fingers were plunged into his neck, not wanting to sever the link. He cackled at the mischief brewing within his mind.

Behind them, Kabos looked on in horror, aghast that this monster could kill his own child that he was so close to; Zaraquel's father, no less. He had to warn her at once.

~*~

*Zaraquel, England, Present Day*

She smiled a stupid silly smile as she looked down at their held hands—hers and Loquiel's—as they landed on the rooftop. This was their fifth date, and she was having the time of her life. She couldn't believe she had a boyfriend, especially an angel! She felt like jumping from the excitement.

He chuckled as he looked at her, and she quirked her brow in confusion. "What?"

"So, I'm your boyfriend now?" he smirked.

"How did yo—?" She smacked him on the arm. "Hey, no mind reading, Lo!"

"Z, we're connected. Anything you feel..." he touched her wings with his, "I feel." She closed her eyes, soaking in the feeling. He continued. "Anything you're thinking, I can hear. And vice versa."

She could feel his breath on her neck. "We're meant to be together."

Zaraquel couldn't take it anymore, and when she opened her eyes, she kissed him. She never realized she would like the act of their lips touching until she met him. It was crazy—she felt a little unhinged.

Suddenly she heard someone clear their throat, and she spun on her feet to come face to face with Kabos. A furious blush filled her cheeks, and she too cleared her throat.

"Uh, Kabos. Hi. I...I didn't see you there."

Loquiel whispered in her ear, "Who is that?"

She waved a hand in the air dismissively and walked towards Kabos. "Is everything all right?"

"I'm afraid not," Kabos said as he straightened his robe. "It's your father. He's been hurt."

Zaraquel felt like hell froze over, and her heart stopped. "What?"

"He's not doing too well. Please, you must come with me immediately."

As she was about to take Kabos's hand, she felt Loquiel holding onto her. "Please, Zaraquel, he's at the estate. Plenty of people can help him. Stay."

"He's my father. I have to go."

She heard him, his inner thoughts rattling in her brain. *Fuck! She's supposed to stay. He promised she would love me. Did the spell not work?* She gasped, and he realized his mistake. "Zaraquel...."

Reality hit her like a bucket of cold water—none of what she felt was real. And she had to leave, *NOW*. She stood beside Kabos, and with tears in her eyes and in an exceptionally low voice, she spoke to Loquiel. "Don't *ever* come looking for me. I *never* want to see you again."

Kabos put his arm around her, enveloping her in a warm hug as they disappeared into the atmosphere, traveling through space and time.

~*~

*Zaraquel, Seattle, Present Day*

Zaraquel stood there with Kabos at Michael's estate. She nodded in gratitude as he faded away into the abyss.

She saw her father there on the ground, his hand on the gash that continued to bleed. Valentine sat on top of him with the stake in his hand right above her father's heart. At that same instant, her father opened his eyes and made eye contact, tears springing from his eyes until finally, he closed them.

"No!" She saw the translucent image of Valentine and called upon her inner power. Zaraquel knew she had to do something to separate the two. With her power, she chanted a spell she remembered learning, and the next thing she knew, Valentine was sent flying in the air. He rolled into the grassy patch a few feet away from them. Zaraquel tried to sit her father up against a brick wall. She brushed his hair from his face. "Daddy? Daddy, are you okay?"

He grunted, but his eyes were still closed, and she placed her finger near his neck. He had a pulse—good. She heard the rustling of leaves and remembered that Valentine was also breathing. She stood, and all the Order's training came to her as he staggered to stand. Grimacing at his appearance—bloodshot eyes, dry, flaky skin—she took a deep breath and focused herself.

He'd hurt her father—she would not stand for that. Valentine ran towards her, and she knew she had to do something but wasn't sure what. How was she supposed to fight something, not entirely there? Zaraquel focused her power and threw a kick in his direction, hitting him in the gut. But he didn't react, nothing.

She tilted her head to the side. "What the fuck?"

He couldn't feel anything. She let out all her aggression—the hurt that plagued her, the betrayal—and finally, she knocked him down. Zaraquel continued to punch him until he was a bloody mess. He stopped moving, rendered immobile, still translucent, but she was able to fight him. She could feel his breath laboring beneath her fists. He kept murmuring, but she couldn't hear him, so she crouched down. All she heard was a faint, "Machiel."

Valentine's invisible form turned solid. Zaraquel gathered up that same anger as before and grabbed his neck, squeezing. A few staggered breaths later, he was dead.

Her wings unfurled, and she turned to see that they were, in fact, red. Her first justified kill—a vampire hunter.

# Chapter 18

*Mona and Rae, Yakima, Present Day*

Mona saw her sister in the arms of a woman she referred to as Miss Arianna. She didn't know why, but she immediately felt as if she were a kindred spirit. She caught her gaze from across the room and met her with a smile. Rae turned to her and unwrapped herself as she ran to her.

Rae buried her face into the nook of her neck, still sobbing. With a blank expression, Mona patted her twin sister's head. "Hey, you wanna go upstairs for a bit?" Blotchy and red-eyed, Rae nodded as Mona led them to the room they'd shared not too long ago.

She patted the empty space next to her, and Rae quickly sat down, placing her head on Mona's shoulder. It had been a couple of days since the funeral, and Rae was still down in the dumps.

"How ya doin? Huh, you okay?"

Rae sniffled. "I feel like I'm stuck in a hole and can't get out."

Mona turned to face her, and Rae looked up. "Hey, you know you are not alone in this. You got me."

Rae wiped her snot with her sleeve. "You don't really seem sad, Mona."

"I suffer in silence," Mona deadpanned.

Rae scoffed and paused as something caught her eye.

*Perfect. She saw it. Maybe she could help me finally open it.*

Rae leaned over and grabbed the box.

"I…I found that under Mom's bed a few days after…."

Rae dropped it as if the mere touch of it burned her. Her eyes widened. "This was hers?"

Mona proceeded to tell her about the vision in regards to her father, but she left out the bit about the massacre. She decided Rae was not ready for that.

"And you can't open it?"

Mona shook her head, placed her hand on the box, and feigned a few tears. "I just wanted to feel closer to her."

Rae planted her hand on top of hers, and like a *Whoosh!* of air was sucked out of them, the gift of sight kicked in, and their eyes went black.

*Rae and Mona found themselves in a dark lonely place as if they were stuck in a void. Briar, now older, with salt and pepper hair and a hint of a beard, walked toward them. Mona ran up to hug him, and he chuckled. Meanwhile, Rae looked at them in apparent puzzlement.*

*She finally walked up to them, taking in the full view of the man in front of her.* "Dad?"

*He nodded and looked down at her, smiling.* "There you are, my Rae of sunshine. I've been waiting for you." *He crouched down to meet her eyes.*

"You have?" *She startled him when she embraced him in a hug, and Mona smiled at the pretty family picture they had formed.*

"Where are you? When can we actually see you?"

"Whoa, slow down, Rae."

"She can't. It's a problem, really," *Mona smirked.*

"I'm in the middle of something very important, but I wanted to see you girls given the circumstances. Hey, listen, your mom? Your mom really loved you. She always said you were the best parts of her."

*"She did?" The twins said simultaneously.*

*He nodded and gave them both a hug.*

*Rae looked up at him curiously. "Dad?"*

*"Yes?"*

*"Is there something we can do?"*

*He shared a look with Mona, and then looked back to Rae. "I don't understand."*

*"You said you were doing something important. Can we help?" Rae looked to her sister for back up, and Mona quickly nodded.*

*"Actually you can, but...."*

*"But what?" Rae perked up. "I'll do anything to help. Anything."*

*"You can, but you have to leave the Order. It's the only way."*

*Without hesitation, Rae said, "I'll do it. I just have to pack my things."*

~*~

Chloe, Yakima, Present Day

Sitting down, she couldn't help but feel a lump in her throat. Her whole life froze when she answered her best friend's phone call.

"Chloe? Chloe, are you there?"

She heard Amber calling her name through the phone and cleared her throat. "Uh, yeah, I'm right here."

"Look, honey, I'm so sorry. I...I was out with my mom, and... and...." Amber started to cry.

"Hey," Chloe stopped her. "None of this is your fault, okay? I'm just glad Zaraquel was there." *The question is, why was she there? How did she know?* "Um, where is she?"

"Z?"

"Yeah, can I talk to her?"

"She's asleep right now. I guess the whole justified killing thing got the best of her."

Chloe stood from her chair and leapt to her feet. "She what?"

"She killed Valentine to save Marcus. I didn't mention that?"

She huffed in response to her friend's aloofness. "No, I...I just.... Can you have her call me when she wakes up, please?"

"Sure thing."

And with that, Chloe, dumbstruck, hung up the phone and sat back down. Her mother walked in to see her in such a state.

"How's Marcus, sweetie?"

She sighed, looking more confused than ever. "He's alive, thanks to Zaraquel."

"That's good, though, isn't it?"

"Yeah."

Her mother sat on the table and took Chloe's hands in her. "So why the long face, huh?"

Tears welled in her eyes. "I didn't feel anything this time. I didn't know he was hurting. He could've died, Mom!"

"Sweetie, that's normal. You weren't there."

Chloe began to feel a hot heat overwhelm her, but she didn't care. "You don't get it. Me and Marcus, we're connected. We're linked. Everything that happens to him, I feel. And I didn't feel anything!"

"Chloe...."

Her mother was no longer looking at her but down at the bracelet on her wrist, which was now glowing. Chloe jumped and backed away from her.

"Mom, what's going on?"

Marlene shook her head. "I knew I'd seen that bracelet before. It was Pandora's."

Scoffing, Chloe tried to pull the bracelet off but couldn't. "That's impossible. It's from Marcus—Michael gave it to me."

"No, no. It was Pandora's. She hadn't worn it in a long time, but it was hers. She never told me where she got it. But later, I learned it was making her sick, dimming her powers the longer she wore it."

"What?!" *Why would Michael give me such a thing?*

"Luckily, your mother knows a thing or two, and we can remove it in a jiff."

"No, it's okay. Now that I know the bracelet is culpable, I can just...." She closed her eyes and focused on her desire to be complete once more, to be linked to her husband, to go see him. She felt a surge of power course through her veins, and then *snap!* "Do it myself." The bracelet broke in half and fell to the floor. She looked at her mother and smirked as she snapped her fingers, and the bracelet was lit aflame.

Marlene let out a surprised chuckle. "Did I ever tell you I'm proud to be your mother?"

Chloe joined her mother, laughing. "Not enough."

"Go on. Go with Z and Marcus — they need you."

"But what about Rae?"

"I'll make sure she makes it back to the Order."

Chloe didn't have to be told twice and took her leave.

~*~

*Tall Dark Man, Hell, Present Day*

He chuckled as he walked into the dark abyss he called home. The air was humid, almost like if he walked there long enough, he would suffocate. But that's the way he liked it. The pain reminded him he was still alive.

He fixed the cufflinks on his sleeve and stopped to look in the mirror. His green eyes sparkled and met his reflection. No longer did he look like himself, but none other than Briar Hexham.

~*~

*Malakai, The Woods, Present Day*

Malakai, in his wolf form, glanced over the cliff that overlooked the waterfall in the densely packed forest. He knew that Sabre and the dire wolves meant well when they invited him for a run. He needed to clear his head, free himself from his emotions and obligations, and free himself from Amber. He knew what he felt for her was real, but given the circumstances, they both needed space no matter how much it hurt him. He was so lost in his thoughts; he didn't hear Sabre approach him.

*Distance is what's best for right now,* Sabre said.

Even though he knew Sabre was right, he didn't have to like it. But he did have a point. Malakai needed to figure out his purpose as an individual without Amber. However, that was part of the problem—he didn't remember his life before her. He was always alone. But the moment they met, he was given an instant family. With his dying words, Nikoli had wanted to keep his daughter safe, and Malakai had promised Nikoli he would do so. He hadn't failed him, and he wasn't going to.

But that's when it hit him. His sentiments towards Amber were what fueled him to fiercely protect her. Yes, it was written in the prophecy, but it had surpassed that a long time ago. Despite the fact he knew she was with Michael, he knew with as much certainty as he knew his own name that the feelings he had for her would never fade.

Sabre was right, though—they needed distance. Malakai knew very well what Amber was capable of—she was strong and independent. But she also had a heart of gold, and he'd hurt her even though it was done with the best of intentions. The secret he'd kept from her had caused some serious damage. She wanted space, and he'd respect her wishes. When the time came, he would be ready to be by her side once more.

~*~

*Bradley McPherson, The Order, Present Day*

With Zaraquel back at home taking care of Marcus, Bradley decided to look and see how Rae was doing since her mother's passing. He quietly stepped inside their room and found that Rae was sleeping, her hair splayed out on her pillow. That's when he saw them, her packed bags in the corner of the room.

*What?*

He drew closer and saw her exposed neck, the mark of the sigil on her flesh clear as day. He didn't know why, but for some reason, he had the urge to touch the mark. McPherson was drawn to it like a moth to a flame. Maybe it could spark an idea.

As he inched closer, the nerves began to rise from his stomach to his throat. With his index finger, he gently touched the sigil. He barely grazed it, but that was all it took. That one touch sent him spiralling deep into those memories he thought he had lost. He fell to his knees and felt like his brain was quite literally on fire.

He saw it all, remembered it all....

*He was a student at the Circle, a loner really, until he met Briar. They would practice in the woods, laughing, joking, and getting knackered. He remembered his voice. It had been a long time since he heard his voice, but it was his, nonetheless, in happier times.*

*"Knock it off, Mick!" he said with a laugh as Mick tried to levitate Briar, but he was barely floating above the ground.*

*It was good, until it wasn't. The memories of following Briar that one night and discovering he was the reason for the sigil massacres in the '90s broke McPherson once more. He could feel the pain as if it were yesterday. And, then just like that, in another flash, he saw himself sitting beside Pandora with Rowe's hands on their heads.*

*He chanted,*

*"Memories precious memories fine.*

*Erase them and return them when it is time."*

*Rowe had successfully erased the memory of Briar and anything that pertained to him.*

*The sigil.*

*The portal.*

McPherson fell to the floor with a loud thud, loud enough that he heard Rae get up from her bed. The last thing he saw before he closed his eyes was her, worried and confused. But then again, so was he. Why would Briar place a curse on his own daughter?

~*~

*Briar, England, 1995*

Flustered with the news that Pandora was expecting, Briar didn't know what to do with himself. He returned to the flat with a box of chocolates and ice cream in hand — mint chocolate chip, her favorite. But when he opened the door, he found that all her things were gone.

"What the fuck?" He dropped the things from his hand, and the chocolates rolled on the floor.

He searched the entire apartment — the room, the bathroom, the kitchen, the little patio outside — but she was nowhere to be found. Briar attempted a locator spell, and the sigil on his hand glowed, but it was as if she didn't exist anymore.

"Elizabeth! Elizabeth, where are you?" He yelled out to the empty room, wanting to see his protector. In the blink of an eye, she appeared.

~*~

*Elizabeth, England, 1995*

She could see he was hurting, that he was in pain. She knew of his attachment with Pandora, how close they were. And she also knew he wouldn't stop until he found her.

That wasn't part of the plan, however — she didn't want him

to deviate. So, she did what she thought was best: she lied.

She looked him straight in the eyes as she sat him down before her. "She left."

Much like his demeanor, his voice broke. "What?"

"I saw her pack her things. She was speaking to someone on the telephone, and said she never wanted to see you again." She looked at him as he took the news.

He stood, throwing his hands up in the air, and began to pace. "Why?"

"You didn't tell me she was so powerful."

He stopped in his tracks. "What do you mean?"

"She performed a sort of ritual, a very dark one."

Angrily he grabbed Elizabeth by the shoulders and shook her. "You were watching, and you didn't do anything?!"

"Unhand me, Briar—*now*." He released her begrudgingly. "I couldn't possibly reveal myself. It's not part of the master's plan."

"Fuck the plan!"

Elizabeth sneered—she would not stand for that type of language. "Bite your tongue, young man."

He rolled his eyes, then pleaded with her as he held onto her hands. "You know how I feel about her, and you just let her leave? You let her perform dark magic?"

"She wanted to forget."

"Forget what? You're not making any sense."

"Forget everything—her life…you."

He froze, unable to keep himself from crying. He fell to the ground, and she caught him, wrapping him in her arms. They sat there on the floor, the minutes ticking by.

"Why? Why does everybody leave me?"

She patted him on his head. "Hush now, boy. You are not alone, nor you never will be. You hear me?"

He nodded, and she couldn't help but feel a bit sorry for all the pain he had suffered in such a short life. Elizabeth didn't want to admit it to herself, but she thought of Briar as a son. And as much as she didn't like to see him cry, they had a mission to complete, no matter the cost.

She took his face in her hands until he was looking at her. "Now you listen to me. You're gonna prove that girl wrong. You're going to show her the kind of man you are, the kind that could, that *will* bring the new world alight."

He nodded, a fire of determination in his eyes.

"Take your broken heart and heal the world, Briar."

# Chapter 19

*Rowe, England, 1995*

Rowe rubbed his hands together as if he were getting rid of some invisible dust. He looked down and saw one of his esteemed students turned trusted college professors lying on the couch, sound asleep. The memory wiping spell had taken a toll on him, although he'd never know the true cause of such a deep sleep until the time was right. He let McPherson sleep and headed down to the Pit.

He simply could not fathom that Briar Hexham was responsible for such a disturbing exploit. Of course, Rowe had always sensed there was some sort of darkness in him, but he assumed that was because his parents had abandoned him. That sort of childhood trauma darkened the soul, no doubt. Rowe attempted to clear his mind with each descending step into the depths of the castle's grounds, but then he heard the distinct sound of a doorknob rattling in the distance.

Instantly he rushed down and saw Briar trying to open the door to the portal. "You," Rowe growled, "don't belong here anymore."

Briar turned to face him, and Rowe saw the slow smile slip onto his face, a dark glint in his eyes. "Oh, so the old man finally caught on, huh?"

Having had enough of his insolent behavior, Rowe, with a flick of his hand across the air, slammed Briar against the wall. Briar wiped the blood from his lips and laughed as if that hadn't hurt him at all.

Rowe stood there, stunned. "Wh....? What?"

"What, you thought *you* could hurt me?" With his hands at his side, Briar lifted all the sharp objects in the room and pointed them in Rowe's direction.

Rowe looked around him, astounded that this event could occur in the first place. *How and where did he accumulate all of this magic?* He could not have come this far on his own. And then he thought back to the sigil. The sigil was of the darkest of origins, of the most ancient. Rowe suddenly realized who — or what, more accurately — was helping Briar in this mission to open the portal. Only that could explain it.

It was him: The Tall Dark Man, the root of all evil.

Rowe knew what he had to do. He had to commit the most treacherous of sins one could commit within the magical community: to kill one of their own. He had to, for the good of the people. If he didn't, the ramifications could be dire.

Briar snapped his fingers, and the sharp objects began to move toward Rowe rapidly. He could feel the rush of the wind from the weapons, and Rowe closed his eyes — not because he was afraid, but because he didn't want to change his mind. With the weapons inches away from piercing his flesh, Rowe whispered, "Morietur." The weapons fell to the floor with a loud crash at the exact moment Briar's body hit the ground.

Rowe walked over to him as Briar's body seized, rigor mortis setting in, his bones twisting abnormally around his body, his eyes glazing over black. Sighing, Rowe waited as the body disintegrated before his eyes. He needed assurance that this sort of treason would not happen again.

He prayed to the heavens that it wouldn't.

~*~

*Rae, The Order, Present Day*

With all her bags packed, Rae knew that her sister and father would be expecting her soon. *Her father!* She was caught in disbelief, for after losing a parent, it seemed she'd gained another not long after. *What a miracle!*

She practically danced down the steps and was almost out the door, but quickly stopped when she found herself in front of two stern looking men with their arms crossed in front of their chests: McPherson and Rowe.

Arching her brow in resistance, she stood her ground. "Can I help you?"

"Rae, where do you think you're going?" McPherson asked.

She didn't flinch at the question, which she was fully prepared to answer since she was anxious to leave to meet her father and sister. "It's time for me to leave."

"Is that so? According to whom?" asked Rowe, perplexed by her shift in attitude.

Hearing the leaves ruffle behind her, she turned and, in the middle of the forest, saw who she was waiting for. A collective gasp was heard—she could only assume it was from both Rowe and McPherson. And she faced them only to find that she was correct—they'd paled in comparison to moments before.

*Why? Why do they wear those expressions of fear and shock?* she thought.

"B...Briar?" McPherson's voice quivered. Rae looked at him, confused that her tutor knew her father.

"You know my father? How?" Rae asked, no more time for pleasantries.

Bradley addressed her question with his eyes trained on Briar at all times. "We were friends…a long time ago."

"Were?" Rae echoed. "What happened?"

He narrowed his eyes and refused to provide her with a valid answer. At this, she stomped her foot on the ground in a childish manner.

"How?"

"Rae, enough," Briar snapped.

She turned towards him, head down, slightly ashamed. "Sorry."

She turned to gaze at the magnanimous Rowe to gauge his reaction, and he looked as if he'd seen a ghost. And then he spoke the words that changed her mind about him. It was a low whisper, but she heard him loud and clear.

"I killed you."

Rae looked back at her father to meet the smirk that slowly touched his lips. But then the words that Rowe said registered in her mind. He had killed him, or he thought so.

Then she felt it: the acheri unleashing, making herself known. She dropped her suitcase and shifted into her darker, more violent self.

"You what?" the acheri practically growled. She lunged towards Rowe, but Bradley quickly stepped in front and warded her off. He placed his hands in the air, and when he did that, Rae could not move her feet from the ground. She could *not* move.

*Tsk. Tsk.*

Briar shook his head in disapproval and flung Bradley away, sending his body flying and crashing in the distance. The acheri cackled and was soon joined by her sister, Mona, who stood on the other side of their father. They looked at each other and grinned.

Rae felt her father's hand in hers and looked at her sister, to see that he was doing the same with her. With their hands linked, so were their minds.

*"Close your eyes and focus."*

The girls did as instructed and felt a rush of power run through their bodies. They felt a hot heat and anger, overwhelming and all-too powerful. Unstoppable.

As if on instinct, all three raised their hands in Rowe's direction and sent a surge of dark smoke magic towards him. Rowe was too slow to react and fell back, the darkness knocking him out. And with that, the Hexham's took their leave.

~*~

*Nimue, The Order, Present Day*

She chuckled at the sight of Rowe splayed out on the floor. *A present, for me?* she thought. She tiptoed around him and crouched down to take a closer look. She grunted as she looked at the fine lines on his face, the crinkles around his eyes, his soft hair.

"It appears time was not kind to you." She grinned as she played with her own silky hair. Making a deal with the Tall Dark Man had its perks. Eternal youth, for example. A glimmer caught her eye: a chain around his neck. Her eyes glittered in anticipation as her hand slivered under his shirt. She felt the heavy weight of the stone in her palm as she pulled it out and into the light. With a forceful yank, she retrieved the amulet.

"Finally," she whispered in yearning.

Now she had to keep her word to the dark master and remove Rowe from the premises. For what, she did not know—nor did she care, if she was being honest. All Nimue wanted was to give Merlin a taste of his own medicine.

~*~

*Later that night....*

*Merlin, Underground Cellar, Present Day*

Before he even opened his eyes, he had a distinct feeling that he was no longer in the Order. The air was brisk but suffocating. *Odd.* Merlin urged himself to open his eyes, to see where he was, to have the confirmation that he was correct. He did, and he was...not inside the Order. He looked around the small damp room with a small window propped open in the upright corner. The moonlight peeked through, but that was all that illuminated the room. Other than that, he couldn't see much — it was too dark.

He relied on his sense of touch rather than that of sight. That's when the thought occurred to him that he was a magical being. He could enchant his way out. But when he opened his mouth to say something, he couldn't speak. This couldn't be — someone would have to possess great magic to subdue *him*. But who?

*Click. Clack. Click. Clack.*

The sound of heels hitting the concrete floor filled his ears, and that's when he saw her — Nimue. His blood curdled in fury — he'd assumed she had perished. He opened his mouth to speak again but remembered he couldn't, and found that fact made him even more upset.

He saw her snicker at his reaction, then she laughed. "What's wrong, Merlin? Cat got your tongue?"

Merlin merely grunted in response, seeing as that was all he was capable of at the moment. Nimue looked exactly the same as when he'd left her. He still felt that pang of betrayal deep in his chest when he looked into her eyes. But now, as he sat there with his arms and legs bound to a chair, all he saw was darkness.

She had the amulet in her hands, and he gasped. *How?*

"It seems after all this time I got what I wanted. Life's funny that way, isn't it?" She swung it from side to side in front of him, as if trying to hypnotize him. Nimue held it, but then let it go, suspended in the air, mocking him. He looked at it, hard, until *poof!* It was gone.

She walked around him, slowly and deliberately, teasing him. "Now, you may be asking yourself: how on earth did Nimue accrue all this power?" She lifted her chin, and a dark matter swirled above it. "You see, when you banished me...." She neared him, so close he saw the freckles smattered across her nose. Nimue continued. "When you *stripped* me, I was lost and alone...empty." Her voice dropped an octave, low, venomous. "You did that."

He felt a twang of remorse, but it quickly faded when he remembered what she had done, what she had succeeded in doing now.

"Alas, I was found. He gave me life. He gave me a purpose. He gave me magic. And now, I must repay him in kind."

*How?*

She answered him as if she knew exactly what he was thinking. "Forget the Order—it's no longer your concern, it's gone. And you? You're here to stay, with me, however I deem fit."

~*~

*Amber, Seattle, Present Day*

For the second time that week, Amber was left reeling. Her heart was broken with the loss of Malakai and Michael, but now, with the revelation that Chloe disclosed—Michael giving her a bracelet that dampened her powers—Amber was confused, angry. She didn't know what to think.

So, to ease the chaos from her mind, she decided to do the only thing that made sense to her: confront him. She blew the doors open and walked into the library. Amber found him sitting by the desk, reading a book. He was not startled or surprised at her outburst. He didn't even react when she came in, guns a blazing.

"Can I help you?" she heard him ask.

In a fury, she whipped her hands in the air and up the desk went, crashing into the wall, the books falling down like rain. Amber grew more agitated with the fact that she saw him smiling at the ruckus she was causing.

"What's with the theatrics, huh?"

She closed her eyes and tried to contain her anger, but found that she couldn't. The tears rushed out and down her cheeks. Amber wiped them away. She didn't have time to cry—she had already spent too many hours crying over him.

Enough was enough.

She took a breath, and a gush of air lifted her inches from the ground. "I've had enough of your lies," she gritted her teeth, "*Machiel.*"

She stilled when he didn't even try to deny it. *It's true.*

Amber had known in her heart that he was different when he woke up, but her love for him ultimately blinded her. What a fool she was. To think she was risking the lives of others in her quest for love. How selfish.

She saw him, how his comportment shifted, and she could finally see him for who he was. His eyes grew red, his talons grew, and his fangs revealed themselves. He looked like a monster. Yes, she was slightly afraid, but more than that, she was furious. Furious at him for lying to her, but more so at herself for believing him.

With a quick gesture of her hand, she snapped his neck. She knew very well that he didn't die, but the act of seeing him fall to the floor like a limp ragdoll was in and of itself satisfying. She had to gather her friends and get out. She needed to get out *now.*

~*~

*Later....*

*Amber, Seattle, Present Day*

With her friends and family in tow, they walked into a seemingly abandoned building. Zaraquel and Chloe held onto Marcus as he limped to a stop in the middle of the room. Meanwhile, Jerome and Miriam followed closely behind.

Chloe snapped her fingers, and all their suitcases and belongings sat in the corner of the room, neatly stacked.

It was art deco at its finest. The size of the building was built up, immense, with tiny little lights lining the hallways. High ceilings and intricate wall design with illustrious shapes graced the decor. Teal and gold pillars lined the walls, while long red velvet curtains dressed the windows. It was like a retro dream. She didn't know why, but for some reason, Amber felt right at home.

She followed her mother into the grand hall with a domed ceiling of stained glass. The beautiful light that shone through danced around the room.

Amber looked around, amazed. "Wow, Mom. How did you know about this place?"

Miriam chuckled as she walked over to her daughter, pulling her in closer. "I made a call to a friend."

"That's quite a friend," Zaraquel remarked, brows raised. Her parents gave her an admonishing look. She simply shrugged and walked off to look at the paintings that hung on the walls.

"No, she's right. Who is it, Mom?"

Miriam didn't doddle and looked Amber straight in the eyes. "It's Malakai, sweetie."

"What?" After the way she'd acted — how she'd pushed him away — he still cared enough to give them a place to stay? She was all wrong about him.

~*~

Amber was lost in thought when she was unpacking. She didn't hear Chloe knocking, much less see her when she walked in.

"Earth to Amber." Chloe waved her hand in front of Amber's face.

She snapped out of it. "Sorry. I don't know where my head's at."

Chloe sat down on the bed and crossed her legs. "I mean, I get it. It's been a lot to take in this past twenty-four hours."

Amber plopped right next to her and let out a sigh of relief. "Right? I mean, that *thing* was Machiel. He…he's evil. What he did to you…. I can't believe he tried to manipulate us like that. I feel so stupid."

She felt tears start to pool in her eyes—she squeezed them closed to keep them from falling. Chloe gently wiped them away, her cold fingers on Amber's warm cheek.

"You are *not* stupid. We all believed him, he played us all." Chloe took Amber's hand in hers. "It is not your fault, okay?"

She couldn't help herself from blubbering, so she did anyway. "And then there's Malakai. Y'know I'm still pissed and all that he lied, but my mom was right. He did it only to protect me. And he lets us stay here, no questions asked, and I can't even find him to say thank you. God, I'm such a bitch."

"Hey, no. You are not a bitch. A witch, a vampire, a wolf, and a queen, but not a bitch."

Amber chuckled at the impressive yet real list her friend had compiled. She composed herself and placed her hair behind her ears.

"You know we can always do a locator spell, right?"

Amber perked up. "Really?"

Chloe nodded excitedly. "C'mon, let's find him."

As Chloe stepped out to retrieve some crystals, Amber felt the holes in her heart grow slightly smaller. There was hope, and his name was Malakai.

Chloe returned with a map in her hand and a couple of crystals. She laid them flat and held her hand out. Amber took it in earnest.

"Now, all you have to do is clear your mind and think of him, and only him. That way, we'll get a clear location."

She nodded as Chloe held the chain that held the crystal above the map. Her hand was incredibly still as she scryed. Suddenly, the air felt thin, and the crystal began to move frantically, never really settling in one location.

Amber looked up at her friend. "Is that normal?"

Meanwhile, Chloe gazed at the stone, confused by its actions. "Umm, let's give another shot. Maybe—"

Letting go of Chloe's hand, Amber abruptly stood. "Maybe he doesn't want to be found. I mean, I get it, after the way I treated him—and I did say I needed space. I can't blame him for giving me what I asked for, right?"

~*~

*Bradley, The Order, Present Day*

Hunched over his desk, Bradley frustratingly pushed all the papers from his desk and let out a bloodcurdling scream. He was sick and tired of the mess that had occurred—gaining back his memories and remembering the truth, the little known fact that Briar was alive, and that Rae left with him.

What else could go wrong?

Before he could think of all the horrible things that could happen, he sought clarity, peace of mind. And to do that, he needed to dig deeper into the second half of the unicursal hexagram. He rose and began to collect the papers he'd knocked off the desk in his fit.

His hands shook as he picked up the paper and read it once more.

"*...There will be those, however, who will rise to end the curse of the unicursal hexagram. These selected few will possess the power to save humanity not only from darkness but from magic itself.*"

He started to wrack his brain as to who those chosen were. His mind was muddled, with all the past events still in clear view. Everything was fresh and raw, like an open wound. Then a thought occurred to him—if he couldn't figure out who these people were, there had to be some other way to discover the hidden truth, a magical way. After all, he was a magic spellcaster—he had to use that to his advantage. He thought back to his years of study and practice and frantically wrote on a scrap piece of paper.

*Reveal what cannot be seen.*
*Light the way to expose the chosen.*
*Is it the witch, the wolf, or the queen?*
*And with these few words, let the curse be broken.*

He read them and re-read them until finally, he was satisfied. Then he read them aloud until the missing page floated up in the middle of the air. It shook violently, and the waves of energy reverberated across the room.

Bradley stood up and carefully approached the paper. The moment he made contact, he was filled with an enlightened vision. In a flash of an incandescent burst of white light, he saw the faces of the selected three—a witch, an angel, and a queen.

The paper fell to the ground, and he thanked the heavens that he knew with certainty that he needed Chloe, Zaraquel, and

Amber to break the curse and to close the portal.

# Chapter 20

*Merlin, Underground Cellar, Present Day*

No longer tied to a chair, Merlin was hung by his wrists, chains holding him up to the ceiling. He tasted the salt and iron from his blood in his mouth. He spit it out and saw it as it spilled onto the floor. Merlin shook his head, trying to gain some sense of strength, but found that he couldn't.

*Crack!*

The sound of the whip broke the air.

He twisted his neck to look behind him and saw Nimue standing in the corner of the room, controlling the whip that continuously hurt him. *Crack!* One lash after the other, he winced in pain. He refused to give in and scream—he would not give her the satisfaction.

One more blow, and that's when he felt it. Not only was his body breaking, but he felt something else being affected. Like a part of him was being ripped open, Merlin felt a sharp pain in the middle of his chest. His heart raced as if it wanted to explode. He had never felt anything like that before. He turned to glance at Nimue, but it couldn't be her since the pain that she was inflicting was via the whip and nothing internal.

*It couldn't be her, could it?*

The pain deepened, more tragic and heart-wrenching than before. He caught a glimpse of shock on Nimue's face, but as quickly as it appeared, it disappeared. Something was not right; something was seriously wrong. He just had to figure out what.

He cleared his throat as he tried to gather up his strength. "So, he left you to do his dirty work, didn't he?" Merlin smirked.

The whip stopped, froze mid-air, and she walked up to face him. "What did you just say?" She was seething, he could see it.

He craned his neck to make a show of scanning the room. "You're alone, unaccompanied —"

"It is the 21st century, Merlin," she scoffed.

"Alas, you're here without him. What could he possibly be doing that's so important he would think to exclude you?"

She took a breath, and he noticed her hand was clenched into a fist at her side. He was getting to her — *perfect*. She looked down as if she were weighing her options, and her shoulders began to shake. *Is she crying?*

"You are not as important as you believe yourself to be, Nimue."

She looked up at him, not crying to his surprise, but with a smile on her face. "Oh, Merlin. You dense old man. You still don't get it, do you? I'm not the secret weapon, *you* are. I break you, I break the Order."

That was when the terrible feeling sank in: The Tall Dark Man was going to succeed in opening the portal.

She returned to her spot behind him and proceeded with her torture. And that was the last thing he heard before his world turned black.

~*~

*Bradley, The Order, Present Day*

He fell asleep on the couch in the library. Nothing could wake him, not even his loud snoring. With papers piled on top of him and beside him, it was safe to say that an adequate description of the state of the library was one word—messy.

Unbeknownst to him, the walls of the entire building were cracking, slowly but surely. The ground vibrated—not that McPherson noticed. He remained fast asleep, tired from last night's discovery. Books began to fall from their place on the shelves, and one heavy edition of the *Witch's Encyclopedia* hit the floor with a loud thump.

McPherson jumped up, discombobulated from the sudden and rude awakening. He rubbed his eyes, trying to wake himself. Another book fell—then another one, and another one.

The edifice was crumbling.

Because everything was falling, Bradley failed to notice that the front door was being pounded on loudly by what sounded like a mob of people. He looked out the window and noticed there was a puncture within the protective shield. "What the hell?"

He finally reacted and saw that the castle, and therefore the Order, was falling apart at the seams. *The perimeter has been breached, but how? That's impossible!*

"Rowe. Hey, Rowe!" Nothing. Not a peep.

Where could he have gone without telling him? Nothing made sense, and McPherson did not like having things out of his control. He had to gather the necessities to prove to Chloe, Amber, and Zaraquel that they were the chosen three to break the curse. But in doing so, he realized by the raucous noise of the mob that they may have entered the castle's premises.

"Oh, shit."

He attempted to gather as much as he could into his magical Mary Poppins-esque bag that never seemed to be filled—it was, in fact, endless. The thing was that he had to hurry before the intruders realized someone was in the castle.

~*~

*Krieg, The Order, Present Day*

He had no idea why Machiel had shipped him and his army of vampires to England with these exact coordinates to this ratty old castle. But he did as he was told. He got on the plane, along with the vampires, he arrived at the exact coordinates at midnight, and once inside, he was to raid the castle. Destroy everything and anyone who got in his way, and he was going to do just that. After all, he was a demon of his word.

He stood atop the large case of stairs and overlooked his army, who looked for instruction since they were programmed that way: to not act freely.

"Listen now and listen well, I will not repeat myself." He scanned the room, and each nodded, so he continued. "Everything in this castle is trash and must be treated as such. Tear books, break windows, knock down a few statues while you're at it. I don't give a fuck."

With that last statement, a hearty chuckle vibrated through the room.

"When we leave this place, it better look like a bomb went off. Nothing or no one is off-limits, understand?"

"Yes," they said collectively. And with that, they all got to it.

Krieg looked at the destruction below — the eager vamps were pillaging every inch. It seemed as if they ruined everything they touched. The books were ripped open, the pages flew through the air; precious statues and antique vases were crushed to bits; furniture upholstery was ripped apart. With Dimitri and Natalia leading the reckless group of misfits, they trashed each crevice like it was a 1980s rager.

Not only was the army causing damage to the interior, but the newly turned vampires desecrated the outside as well. The lawn was a mess—the grass that was once green was now uprooted in a muddy mess. They set fire to the trees that surrounded the building, and it truly looked like hell on earth.

While they laughed and continued to spread mayhem out on the grounds, inside, there was a crash upstairs, and Krieg knew for a fact that no one had made it that far yet. Despite his robust structure, he managed to walk up to the door from which the sound erupted with ninja-like stealth.

Slowly he opened the door and found someone ransacking the library. He was not ripping out the pages—rather, he was salvaging them. Krieg took another step, and to his misfortune, there was a loud creak. The man turned around, and before Krieg had a chance to attack, the man flew his hand over the bag and murmured a spell. "*Ut cum regina.*" Krieg's Latin was rusty, but he was sure he had said something along the terms of, "To the queen."

*Stupid witch.*

He was not going to let him ruin the plan. He lunged at him with considerable force, but in a blink of an eye, the man disappeared.

*Damn it.*

He stomped out and addressed the room with a loud whistle. They all froze at the sound of the command.

"Drop the shit and burn this place to the ground."

And that they did.

~*~

*Miriam, Seattle, Present Day*

During all the years spent away from her daughter and on the run, Miriam always sought reprieve within the confines of a church. Wherever she was, even if it were on the other side of the earth, she had faith that she could find a quiet place to gather her thoughts.

She walked down the aisle and knelt as she reached the cross in the middle of the church. It was grand and beautiful, the cross golden and encrusted with rubies, every ridge done so realistically that she couldn't help becoming entranced by it. And behind it was a majestic organ in all its glory. Miriam imagined all the choral harmonies that were sung in accompaniment, all the hymns during mass. She was simply amazed by the sheer tranquility she felt the moment she stepped into the holy building.

She stood and took her place in a pew. With her hands on her lap and her fingers laced together, she thought back to her childhood. She had been born a great witch with even greater power, but it had been taken by the Tall Dark Man.

No one should have suffered the fate she had — she wouldn't wish that on her worst enemy. Even so, her fate was sealed. Had she not been given up to the dark lord, she wouldn't have had that wonderful vision of hope for her future. No Nikoli. No Amber. And for them, she was forever grateful.

*My loves.*

She was who she was because of them.

Miriam caught sight of a glimmering light and prayed to the heavens that her Nikoli was resting peacefully. A sharp jolt hit her body so hard that she sat back in her seat. Her heart raced, her vision blurry. She knew this sensation — she knew it very well. Miriam closed her eyes and let her gift of sight take over.

*Nikoli stood before her, a dead look in his eyes. He didn't look the same — he didn't look like the man she loved. This version was like a shell of the man she once knew, with pale skin and a haggard appearance, his eyes slightly glazed over, his movements unnatural. His neck jerked, and his feet dragged against the hard concrete.*

*Shrill screams filled her ears as she accessed her vision and saw further into it. Behind him, she saw blood fill the streets from a trail of* bodies. *When his face came back into focus, his mouth was covered in blood, his lips salivating for more.*

Miriam lurched over to the side, now awake from her premonition, her body shaking in the pew. She became overwhelmed with emotion. She didn't know if it was grief or fear of what she saw, but she knew she had to do one thing; Miriam had to let her daughter know right away.

~*~

*Mozart, Seattle, Present Day*

With his hair blowing in the cold wind, Mozart got a hold of his lapel and stood atop the iconic Seattle Space Needle. He looked up at the starry night sky — inky with specks of white — closed his eyes and took a breath. Out of nowhere, his violin appeared in position on his shoulder, as if by command. With the bow in his other hand, he began to play a painfully soft melody.

It was so low only a dog could hear it, and on cue, the dead began to step out from every dark fissure in which they were hiding. The music from above mounted as Mozart let the notes take over his body, a man possessed by the music that haunted him.

Suddenly the music became faint background noise as screams filled his ears, as well as the streets of the city. He looked down and saw people running to and fro in every direction, some swerving, others hiding, and a few who actually had the guts to confront them. This was one thing Mozart had never understood. In all his years on earth, a human's behavior always seemed to boggle him. What caused them to act the way they did? Why did people, like him, cower and bend to the will of those superior? But alas, he didn't have time to doddle on the perplexities of life. He was bound to his word and had a job to complete.

He continued to play, and the undead's actions became more

violent as the music itself picked up speed. Mozart walked off the Space Needle and felt as if he were flying as he made his descent to the building below. *Whoosh!* Like a cat, he landed on his feet, the violin still nestled in the crook of his neck, like lovers not willing to part ways.

"Whoa."

He surveyed the destruction that had taken place before his eyes. He was feet away from all the action, and he saw it all up close and in high definition. The gore — the blood that covered the streets, all the horrified screaming that filled his ears, the sounds of bones crushing as the zombies cracked open the skulls of many innocents — it was all too much.

Mozart wanted to put an end to this — he couldn't stand to see the blood anymore. He played his violin and commanded the zombies to a halt. The Space Needle caught his eye, and he knew exactly what he had to do — destroy the sign of hope and wonder.

It was silent. The cries and whimpers got carried away with the wind, and the undead were frozen in place, waiting for their next instruction. He communicated with them via mindspeak. *Take down the Needle — do whatever you have to do.*

Like an army of robots, the zombies left the terrified people, or what was left of them, in their wake. They staggered with a lack of finesse that could only be attributed to those with limited brain function. They climbed up the tower and clamored with whatever they had in hand — crowbars, human remains, anything to bring it down.

Mozart saw this scene of lunacy and rolled his eyes at their antics. "Idiots."

Out of nowhere, a woman appeared before him. She was beautiful, with long dark hair, and her eyes glistened as she took in the chaos.

He gave her a lengthy perusal and smirked. "And you are…?"

She looked at him, annoyed by his meandering stare. "Here to finish what you started."

He scoffed, not impressed with her impertinence. No woman had ever spoken to him like that before. Mozart did not appreciate her attitude. "Who are *you*?"

"Nimue."

The name sounded familiar, but he didn't know where he had heard it.

"How d—?"

"*He* sent me."

Of course, his master had a contingency plan. Perhaps he had more than one in place—he certainly wouldn't put it past him. And that's when she saw her raise her hands in the air, chanting something. Latin?

"*Et iactata fatiscit,*" she spoke repeatedly. His Latin was rusty, but he knew it meant something along the lines of crumbling. He heard the rumble before he turned and saw the Space Needle tumble down.

The city was filled with screams, with corpses—dead and undead. It was as the Tall Dark Man wanted. It was the end and the beginning, and nothing was ever going to be the same. He looked over to Nimue to bask in the glory of the success of a job well done, but when he turned, she was already gone.

~*~

*Amber, Seattle, Present Day*

Amber's mind raced as she thought back to the moment where all this craziness—the prophecy, the magic, her past lives—began. It seemed so long ago when she was packing up her things and moving to a new place to start her job as a curator. Her worries then were along the lines of paying student loans and making a new archeological discovery. Now she was the queen, with the responsibility to save the world and unite the magical community.

*No biggie, right?*

It was through this journey that she'd made lifelong friendships, fallen in and out of love, met her mother, and welcomed her goddaughter. Had she not been thrust into this fate, she would not have gained a family. Amber may have been on her own—aside from her adoptive parents—for quite some time, but she was about to enter a room with all the people she cared about and who cared about her.

They were there waiting for her instruction. She was their leader, and she had to lead them—that was literally the definition. She knew what she was capable of, knew she had the power, the abilities—after all, she had been training for this since she'd discovered her heroic fate. Yet, there was this little nugget of doubt lodged in her stomach.

"You got this," she told herself as she began to pace the room, back and forth, one corner to the other. "This is ridiculous— you're just psyching yourself out, Amber. Ugh, listen to yourself. You sound like a crazy person."

She took a breath, removing her hair from the haphazard bun placed atop her head. She ran her hands through her hair and bit her lip nervously.

*Amber, relax.* Malakai's voice rang through her brain.

It couldn't be—she was merely imagining it. She wanted him there, so she'd manifested his disembodied voice. Yeah, that made sense.

She felt a warm hand on her shoulder, and she turned to face Malakai's shy smile as he looked down and then back up at her.

"You're here—like *here*, in person?"

He chuckled. "Yes."

"I, uh, tried looking for you, but…."

He scratched his neck and looked visibly uncomfortable. "I know, I had to figure some things out."

*Oh.*

As if sensing her train of thought, he interrupted her before she could say anything. "I was with Sabre and the dire wolves."

She looked behind him, looking for them. "Are they here?"

"They're just checking the perimeter."

Biting her nails, Amber didn't really know what to do with herself. She was nervous before, but now with Malakai standing in front of her with his ruggedly handsome looks and the stubble on his jaw and the tan that warmed his skin, she was even more nervous.

He took a few steps closer to her and grabbed her hand, removing it from her mouth and holding it firmly in his. She was so focused on their clasped hands that she gasped when he let go to tip her chin to look at him.

"You have no reason to be nervous. Not because you must face them, and especially not because of me." He took a breath as if he was searching for the perfect words. He cradled her face in his hands, his thumb gently caressing her cheeks. "I'm here. And I'm always going to be here, *always*, in whatever role you want me to be: friend, protector—"

"Something more?" She quietly asked.

A beautiful smile reached his lips. "Something more." His gaze turned serious, and just for a moment, her heart stopped. "But you don't need me. You can do this—you can do anything really, but this? You were quite literally born for this."

She let out the breath she didn't know she was holding and smiled. "Well, when you put it that way." Amber laced her hands around his neck, and he smirked. "But you're wrong about one thing."

He quirked a brow. "What's that?"

"I do need you. I may not need you to fight all my battles for me, but I need you in my life."

He was stunned to silence at her confession. She stood on the tips of her toes and placed the tiniest of kisses on the corner of his lips, teasing him of what was to come. Amber saw the lust in his eyes and knew she had to take a few steps back before his resolve slipped away.

She walked towards the door, feeling more empowered than ever. She was ready to save the world.

~*~

*Malakai, Seattle, Present Day*

He stood in the back of the room as Amber was front and center, demanding everyone's attention. Malakai watched as Chloe, Marcus, Zaraquel, and the rest of their close-knit circle of friends and family were enraptured by Amber's speech. He himself couldn't take his eyes off her. She stood her ground, majestic, as the queen that she was.

"The time has come." She scanned the room, and her eyes briefly met his, and she smiled but then continued. "We, uh, now know that Michael is no longer with us." She cleared her throat, as he knew her heart was still a bit bruised from the discovery that Machiel was who he was. But she soldiered on.

*She was made for this.* He beamed at her strength and her authority—he was so immensely proud of her. She knew who she was, and she embraced it.

"The prophecy states that those of differing magical lineage would come together because of the queen—well, me—but that's not the case. It's not because of me, it's because of all of you. Each one of you has a purpose. And now look at us. We are here, together—witches, werewolves, angels, vampires. We are here, united under one roof, under one common belief that we can change how the magical community treats us. And we c — "

Suddenly a hole swirled in the ceiling of the room. It was eerily quiet, like a vacuum sucking out all the air. Everyone was distracted, and then *plop!* A duffle bag fell to the floor.

*What the hell?*

The wolves approached the bag, sniffing it for questionable contents. Everyone circled the bag. When the hole in the ceiling grew bigger, the insides looked like a storm was brewing in all shades of grey and black.

Suddenly Bradley fell to the floor in a fetal position. Chloe crouched to the ground. "Oh, Bradley." He had a burn on the side of his cheek. Malakai and Marcus quickly helped him into a chair.

Zaraquel was quick to her feet, closing her eyes and performing a healing spell. The burn on his cheek disappeared, and his coloring returned to normal.

"The books. The books, did they get here?" Bradley coughed as he sat up.

He was bombarded with questions from the whole room, asking if he was okay, what had happened, where was Rowe, things of that nature. Malakai pinched the bridge of his nose, as he wasn't fond of dysfunction.

"Enough," he barked loudly so the room quieted instantly. He realized it was a little too harsh, so he apologized with a brief sorry and continued. "Bradley. What happened?" Malakai said in the calm tone that he was known for.

Amber looked at him appreciatively, and he nodded in response.

The doors pushed opened to reveal a frantic and scared Miriam. Amber and Malakai rushed up to her and saw the concern clouding her eyes.

"Mom, what's wrong? Are you okay?"

For some reason, Miriam avoided looking into Amber's eyes. She addressed the room instead. "It's the city. We're all in grave danger. The undead are roving the streets. Blood was everywhere. I...."

"M, why don't you take a seat?" Malakai guided her, and she sat down.

She continued, clearly shaken. "The city, it's in ruins. The Space Needle crashed down."

"The Space Needle crashed down?!" Zaraquel squealed.

Miriam clutched onto Amber's and Malakai's forearms and whispered so only they could hear her. "I...I saw Nikoli."

*What?*

# Chapter 21

*Krieg, The Order, Present Day*

He watched from the hills not too far away as the immense building caught fire. Dark smoke and soot filled the sky, which morphed into a filmy imitation of what was once a cerulean blue. With the rest of the vampires looting and hollering on the grounds, Krieg chuckled at their crazy antics.

Doing what Machiel had asked, Krieg was eager to see where his master needed him next. As if his thoughts summoned him, his cell phone rang. It was Machiel.

"What can I do for you, Master?"

~*~

*Tall Dark Man, Mona, and Rae, The Order, Present Day*

The Tall Dark Man as Briar ignored the smell of smoke, wafting down from the fires above. He knew very well what Machiel was up to, and he had to keep him busy, of course. He could sense Rae's hesitance and gestured for her to come and walk with him.

"Yes, Father?"

"Come here, child."

He placed his arm over her shoulders, and she snuggled up

beside him. This was easier than he'd thought it would be. He could wrap her up around his little finger in no time.

She looked up to him shyly. "Did I do something wrong?"

"Why do you think that, hmm?"

Startled, Rae jumped at the sound of the castle falling apart from the inside. "What's going on?"

Meanwhile, Elizabeth and Mona continued to soldier on through the labyrinth and into the Pit. They knew every turn as if they were looking at a map. The Tall Dark Man urged Rae on as he guided her to follow them. "That's nothing you need to concern yourself with."

As if seeing something in the distance, Mona ran along and knelt. "Go on," he said to Rae. She excitedly ran over to join her sister. She knelt beside her, and they peered down the manhole that led into an even darker tunnel.

The braver of the two, Mona braced herself and climbed down. However, in missing a step, she fell with a hard thump.

"Mona, be careful!" Rae chided.

"I'm fine, c'mon. Come down." Rae followed her sister. As the Tall Dark Man and Elizabeth shared a knowing look, they descended as well.

~*~

Down in the tunnel, a furious cold air blew against their skin, and the girls shivered as they clutched onto each other's hands. They looked around, and it seemed as if they had entered another world.

It was dark and damp. The roots that sprouted from the ceiling and the walls were like hands reaching out to touch them. If they were welcoming or warning them, they didn't know. But like magnets, they gravitated toward the end of the tunnel.

A low, crackly voice whispered, "Follow me." The girls didn't question it—they merely did as they were told.

Elizabeth and the Tall Dark Man followed closely behind, as they knew the young Tudor witches would lead them to the portal—much closer than their father had before them. They would accomplish what he never could.

Abruptly they stopped in their tracks—the girls had reached their destination. Once a reddish wine tint, the Pit now looked as if it was a living breathing thing, an entity with a life of its own. The Tall Dark Man approached the almost-open portal, a look of amazement in his eyes. Since he had been alive since the beginning of time, it was hard to impress him. But the portal before him? That was what he was waiting for.

It was time.

He turned with a gleam in his eyes and faced the Tudor girls. "Ladies, the time has come to make a brave new world. Are you ready?"

He held out his hands for the girls to take, and one by one, Elizabeth, Mona, and Rae each linked their hands together, a human chain standing in front of the immense gateway.

With their hands firmly pressed against one another's, the unification of their powers only amplified with the power of the spell they chanted in unison.

*"Open the new world, set us free. Set us free."*

Over and over, they repeated the enchantment until the foundation began to crack. As if it were taking its first breath, the orifice let out a breathy groan. It glowed a bright red, which only grew brighter and brighter until it was blinding.

One hand over her eyes and the other still in her father's, Rae couldn't help but look into the portal. "Whoa."

The Tall Dark Man grinned at the tiny witch, excited at the prospect of the wondrous things to come from the opening of the portal. A burst of fire unleashed as the gateway opened with a thunderous roar.

~*~

*Merlin, Underground Cellar, Present Day*

He could feel it. He could feel the fire burning inside him. Merlin's blood was boiling, his skin peeling off, revealing pink flesh. He knew the moment the Order was burning down. It was a part of him. He'd taken a piece of his soul, of his magic, and placed it in the heart of the castle. But with every artifact that withered away, the Order was dying.

Despite the lashings and his weakened state, he tried one more time to save the place he so cherished. He closed his eyes, and with every hope in his heart Merlin took the magic he had buried deep inside himself — but alas, it was to no avail. He was too feeble and powerless; he could barely move, let alone breathe.

It was useless.

~*~

*Amber, Seattle, Present Day*

Amber and her friends stood in the middle of the city during all the destruction. They were the first and only line of defense against all the horrid monsters attacking the city. She turned back to face all her friends and family, all in position: Chloe and Bradley, their hands swirling with magic; the dire wolves alongside Sabre in their wolf forms; Marcus with his fangs and talons in full display; Zaraquel with her wings spread high above them; and finally, Amber, floating inches above the ground, sandwiched in between her mother and Malakai. She had never felt stronger.

The undead came at full speed and hurled at them in reckless abandon, but they knew very well how to defend themselves.

Malakai morphed into a large majestic wolf and pummeled through them. Sabre and the dire wolves quickly followed suit. Their growls melded with the screams of the city goers. Amber was so entranced by the agility of the wolves that she didn't see the advance that was made towards her friends.

Thana jumped out and lunged at Chloe, but Marcus, all healed and stronger than ever, rebuffed her bombardment. Like a feral cat, Thana hissed, "You bastard!" and leapt to punch him, but she found herself floating in the air instead.

"Get away from my husband!"

Chloe, with a simple hand gesture, flung Thana across the shambles of bodies and discarded wood. Thana yelled as she was impaled in the heart with a stake. She sneered, and her body fell limp, as what was once flesh disappeared into a fine dust.

*Well, that was that.*

Amber looked across the plaza and saw that the zombies were rabid—they kept attacking anything and anyone that moved. Her mother gasped, and Amber turned to catch her line of sight to see a tall, strong, green eyed man who looked familiar. And then, in a flash, a memory invaded her mind from when she was an infant. She remembered seeing that same man that stood before her, alive and smiling down at her.

*Her father.*

Her father was there in the flesh. *Well, sort of.* He ran towards them with abnormal speed, lunging straight with one victim in mind, her mother. Amber stopped him, her hand raised in front of her, and he froze. Despite all the turmoil and fighting that surrounded them, Amber took the time to assess the situation. Carefully, Miriam and Amber approached the corpse that looked so much like the man of their memories.

Amber felt her mother clutch tightly onto her hand, and instantly they knew what to do with the shared gift of sight. With the tips of their index fingers, they touched his forehead in an attempt to access the memories that perhaps lie beneath. What they saw was more tragic than what they had hoped to see. They wished for some glimpse into the past—when he was a young wolf, when he met Miriam, when he held baby Amber for the first time.

Instead, there was nothing. Nothing was present. His mind was a void, a darkness that had no secrets. It was what it was, a cavity that held nothing. The man he once was, was no longer there.

They departed, her mother shaken by the disappointment of having no chance to see her husband again. Tears filled both of their eyes. "I'm so sorry, Mom."

Miriam brushed off the tears quickly and backed herself away from both Amber and Nikoli as she gathered her wits about her. Amber saw a sudden shift in her. No longer was she saddened by the loss—she was fueled by something different, something darker. Anger? That had to be it. She couldn't explain the fire in her eyes any other way.

Amber heard the end of the enchantment before she could stop her. Miriam spoke the words low and fast. "*Celeriter igne.*"

Her fists were balled at her sides, and heat emanated from her body.

"Mom?"

She knew her mother was powerful, but she did not expect what she was witnessing. She had witch fire, immense and powerful, but she could control it, despite its wild and unpredictable nature.

Miriam let out a loud battle cry—one of pain and anguish—just as she had years before. She screamed, and all the zombies and the zombie maker were set aflame, their screams heard from miles away. She targeted the enemies, and one by one, they blew up. Nikoli disintegrated before their eyes, and Miriam fell to her knees, Amber tried to reach to hold him, but ashes filled her hands, and he was gone.

All the undead were gone.

~*~

*Malakai, Seattle, Present Day*

The wolves and Malakai led the group into a safe place, a clearing, void of any remains of the undead. What they had witnessed and experienced was something out of this world. He could not imagine what Amber or Miriam must be feeling for the tragic loss of someone they desperately wanted to see again, only to have him taken away in an instant.

Still, in wolf form, he looked over to Amber to find that she was already looking at him. His heart broke at the sight of her teary eyes. He walked over, and she knelt to the ground and rested her head on him. She gripped his fur tight in her fingers, not wanting to let go. He didn't keep her from holding him.

He glanced over to Miriam, who was alone in the corner, standing by an old, worn tree. She seemed so focused on that tree — two trees that had become one — that the loss didn't seem to faze her. He knew she was resilient, but for her to completely disregard the events that had transpired? That was very unlike her. There had to be something significant about that specific spot, but what?

Bradley also walked over and approached the tree with the same keen interest.

What was so special about that tree?

~*~

*Chloe, The Clearing, Present Day*

Chloe had heard stories about the powerful witch imprisoned

by the Tall Dark Man, but she had no idea that woman was Amber's mother, Miriam. She was in awe of the incredibly powerful woman that stood only a couple of feet away. Chloe was cognizant of the loss that her best friend and her mother had suffered, yet she still couldn't wrap her head around what had happened.

The control. The control that Miriam possessed was transcendent.

"Chloe? Chloe, you okay, babe?" Marcus placed his arm around her waist.

"Just a lot on my mind."

"I know. I know that was intense back there."

They looked up to see their daughter flying in the air, keeping watch. She flew in a circle and then stopped. Chloe felt the hairs on her arms stand to attention—something was wrong.

"Mom?" Zaraquel flew down and landed on her feet.

"I know, sweetie, I feel it too."

Marcus's brows pinched in confusion. "What's going on?"

~*~

*Krieg, The Clearing, Present Day*

He didn't know why Machiel had sent him these exact coordinates, and he didn't bother asking why. Machiel did specify for him to come alone and to leave most of the "children" at home, save for Natalya, Dimitri, and a few others that had a special penchant for violence.

As always, Krieg did as he was told and made it the clearing. From a distance, he began to see why—they were there. They were all there.

*So, this was a trap? Perfect.*

He made his way to the clearing and approached one person in particular, Marcus. Since Valentine hadn't lived up to his word, Machiel put Krieg up to that task.

He commanded the vampires to charge in and attack with brute force. "Go!" The younglings leapt into action. Everyone was so caught up in fighting the vampires that it served as a perfect distraction to punch Marcus in the gut.

"Why can't you just die?!" Krieg gritted through his teeth.

Marcus jumped back and lifted Krieg by the throat with incredible strength, a strength that he didn't know he was capable of. He backed him up against a giant boulder and proceeded to crush him. Krieg felt his outer layer starting to crumble.

*What the fuck? Why can't I move?*

With his forearm, Marcus pushed him further into the hard rock. Krieg didn't like this sensation, rock against rock. It wasn't natural.

"Hold him still," he heard the wife say as she appeared beside them.

"That's what I'm doing, *honey*," Marcus said, his jaw clenched.

The wife made a gesture with her hand as if she were stretching something, and that's when he felt it. Krieg felt his atoms begin to separate — his bones, if he had any, were breaking. He yelled in pain. He had never felt such anguish in all the years he had walked on earth. It was unfathomable.

And then, just like that, he felt nothing.

~*~

*Zaraquel, The Clearing, Present Day*

She was just about to swoop in and save her father when she saw that he was up against the stone demon, but her mother stepped in just in time. Seeing them work together to destroy that monster made Zaraquel's heart swell with pride. Her parents were the definition of awesome!

Moments away from congratulating them, she felt a rush of

wind against the feathers of her wings. She didn't have to turn to see who it was. But she did anyway, knowing that simple act would break her heart all over again.

Loquiel.

Wanting to cry, she forced herself to buck up and get ahold of her emotions. The battle was not the appropriate place to talk about one's feelings, but what did she know? She was a teenager.

"What are you doing here?" She neared him, her arms crossed over her chest.

Loquiel tried to close the distance between them, but she flew a couple of feet back. "C'mon, dear Zaraquel, can we at least talk?"

"Isn't that what we're doing?" She stuck her chin out and turned away from him to sneak a peek at the battle below them. Her family was tearing the vampires apart, limb by limb. *Yes!* Grotesque? Also, yes. But hey, it was all in the name of good and for the prophecy.

Zaraquel was so distracted by the ruckus that she failed to see that Loquiel was inches away from her. He gripped her shoulder with his hand. "Zaraquel, *please.*"

She looked at his eyes, and they seemed earnest and full of love and sadness. But then she remembered that he had lied to her, and when she wanted to save her father, he didn't really support her. It was her father, for crying out loud!

"No!" She pushed him away with so much force he staggered. "No, you don't deserve a second of my time, do you hear me? You lied to me. You broke my heart, Loquiel."

As their argument escalated, she noticed that they got closer. It was a habit. She tried to pull away, but every time he got closer and closer.

"I didn't mean to, Zaraquel. I love you. I always have, and I just got tired of waiting for you to see it, to feel it too."

"That doesn't give you the right to toy with people's emotions, let alone control them. What the hell is wrong with you?"

He backed her into a tree. She could feel the tiny bristles and branches poking her wings, her back. She felt the splinters puncture her feathers, and she winced.

He grabbed her face in his hands, and she struggled to get away, but he held her in place. "I love you. Isn't that enough?"

She looked at him, with all the frustration and anger that she could muster. "Get. Off. Of. Me. *Now*."

Loquiel gave her some space, but not enough. She cleared her throat and looked him straight in the eyes. "I don't want to see you. Ever again. Please leave."

"But, Zara—"

She cut to the chase. "I don't love you."

He flew back as if he had been slapped. "What?" His voice broke. The air between them was thick.

She looked down, not wanting to see his somber expression. "*Please*, don't make me say it again."

*Whoosh!* A large gust of wind blew her hair into her face. Her hands were shaky as she wiped away the tears that threatened to fall. She looked up to see him flying away, and she knew in her gut that would be the last time she saw him.

Slowly she made her descent to the ground, where she was ready to fight alongside her parents. As she punched a vampire in the throat, her mom looked over at her, concerned. "Is everything okay, sweetie?"

Tired and exhausted and heartbroken, in a rapid movement, Zaraquel broke off a branch with her bare hands and plunged it into the chest of the vampire that her mother was in combat with. She dug the stake further in and twisted it.

"Just peachy."

~*~

*Bradley, The Clearing, Present Day*

Just as he believed they were finished with the current threat, another one would pop into place. The Order had burned down, and he didn't know where Rowe had disappeared to. Bradley felt like his mind was unraveling. First the zombies, then the vampires and the stone demon — what next? What could possibly be waiting for them now?

There was something about this place that seemed familiar to him. Since the moment he arrived, he was enthralled by a tree — well, two that converged into one. He remembered seeing trees like that during his time in the Circle. He stood beside Miriam, who was also analyzing the tree. This couldn't be the same, could it?

That would be impossible. The clearing and the tree were back in England. Had they transported somehow? He scratched his head in confusion. What was going on? Something was not right. Had something occurred with the portal?

He had been so distracted with all the commotion that he did not have a chance to tell the girls their roles in the Alchemy of Three. He needed to do it soon. He needed to warn them. Perhaps now was the ti—

Losing his train of thought, a haze of dark smoke rose to eye-level on the other side of the clearing. It smelled like sulfur and was opaque and dense.

*What the hell?*

Out of the smoke and onto the field walked Briar, Mona, Miss Arianna — who, as she stepped into the light transformed into a woman, he recognized from the history books as Elizabeth Hexham — and Rae. Little Rae had abandoned the Order to work alongside them?

He could not believe it. He scanned the clearing and found

that everyone else was as astounded as he was.

Mona was the first one to throw a stone, literally. With a tricky magical maneuver, she unearthed the stone from the ground and sent it flying towards them. She kept them coming as if they were grenades. Bradley managed to transfuse her attack. He transformed them into small pebbles, which he soon regretted, as they rained down on them.

~*~

*Machiel, The Clearing, Present Day*

Everyone was so caught up in the news that the little Tudor witch was working in his neck of the woods that no one saw him arrive. He had not been surprised, however. The moment they met, he'd seen the darkness within her. The acheri was too strong for her not to succumb to her advances.

Amber's red hair was braided and wrapped around her head like a crown. As much as he hated her and wanted to kill her, he couldn't help but admit that she was still nice to look at. She stood alone at the periphery, which was perfect for what he had in mind. The silver knife he held behind his back felt cool against his skin. He was careful not to touch the blade, however, since it was poisoned—a poison he so generously received from the Tall Dark Man himself, fashioned with the sole intention of killing the queen. That was exactly what he was going to do.

~*~

*Amber, The Clearing, Present Day*

Amber heard her mother take in her breath, her eyes trained on the man who stood beside a witch she didn't recognize and Mona and Rae. She was about to ask her why a stranger would elicit that sort of reaction. But she soon found that she couldn't.

Behind her, she felt his breath and the blade of his knife

piercing her skin before she could look up and face him.

*Machiel. Damn him.*

Right then, all she heard in her head were the words Zaraquel had spoken not too long ago. "*...Michael rips open your chest. He pulls out your heart. You die. Die. Die. Die.*"

Her vision blurred, but he was all she could see. She couldn't move — something cold in her veins prevented her from doing so. Poison? Nothing hurt, she didn't feel in her pain, but what she felt was her heart slowing down.

She started to lose consciousness when she felt herself being ripped open. The air was cold, but the blood that flowed out of her was warm. How odd. Wanting to move her hand to sense the severity of the wound, she found she couldn't.

Amber felt the world move beneath her feet and realized she was falling. Fast or slow? She couldn't tell. A scream filled her ears before she made her complete descent to the ground.

Feeling arms encircle her, she fought to open her eyes, her lids heavy. Breathing slowing, she could count her heart beats, as slow as they were.

*1....*

*2....*

*3....*

The last thing she saw was Malakai's face before everything went dark. She felt a smile beginning to form at the sight of him.

*What a way to go.*

Her eyes closed, and her heart stopped.

# Chapter 22

It was as if Chloe's world had stopped the instant she saw her best friend, her sister, fall into Malakai's arms, Miriam on her knees, clutching onto Amber's limp hand. She looked at Sabre, and with a nod, she knew that he knew what she wanted him to do. *Keep them busy,* she said via mindspeak.

From the corner of her eye, she saw Marcus pounce onto Machiel, his claws lodged into his former father's throat. Machiel was not moving. Zaraquel flew down seconds later, concern etched on her little face. But she looked at her daughter, and something shifted: she looked determined, confident.

"Zaraquel…." Her voice wavered.

Zaraquel met her eyes, and confidently said, "You need to freeze time, Mom."

"What?" she asked, flabbergasted by such a strange request. Chloe looked over to her lifeless friend and then to Malakai, who couldn't bear to let her go. She met his eyes, brimming with tears.

"Please. Save her, *please.*"

She knew exactly how he was feeling, and she wanted to put an end to it. She nodded and looked up to the heavens, her hands raised above her head.

"*Horae, minuto, secondo secundam. Frigidus in tempore iam.*" The sky cracked open, and a burst of blue light erupted, blinding everyone in the clearing. There was a loud ringing that caused everyone to cover their ears.

Time froze.

The boulders that threatened to sprout from the ground froze mid-air; everyone — save Chloe and Zaraquel — were in the midst of their actions stock-still: Bradley and the wolves battling Elizabeth and Mona; Marcus with his hand tight on Machiel's throat; and Amber surrounded by Malakai and Miriam.

She looked at her daughter and gave her the go ahead to save her aunt.

~*~

*Zaraquel, The Clearing, Present Day*

Zaraquel unfurled her wings and cracked her knuckles in preparation for the necromancy ritual. She could feel the sadness all over her body, and it finally made its way into the tips of her fingers. She absolutely hated seeing her auntie Amber in such a condition.

Nevertheless, she knew in her heart that this was the reason she was born, her role in the Blood Prophecy. She had to save her.

She slowed her racing heart — one breath and then another — until she was focused and centered. With her mind, she created circles on the ground that surrounded Amber's body. She knew very well that this was a dark magic ritual with a cost. But she didn't have any other choice. She would sacrifice herself if she had to. But just as a precaution, in each circle, she drew tiny crosses.

She closed her eyes and spoke the words Bradley had ingrained in her brain. "*Animatum, respirare, vita est vita. Vita est vita. Vita est vita.*"

She repeated the words until they sounded like a soft murmur, and gradually Amber began to rise from the ground as if she were light as a feather. Zaraquel fell to the ground beside her—that was how she knew the spell was working. She could feel her soul take flight, and when she opened her eyes, she was somewhere else.

~*~

*Alexander the Great, The Heavens, Present Day*

Alexander had this funny feeling in his stomach that told him today was the day Amun-Ra had prepared him for. Today he would meet the woman who was the key. He had been kept alive up in this special place for that sole reason, to assist when all was perceived to be lost.

The room was bright, all white, as it had been since his arrival. But on this day, the light flickered and continued to flicker wildly until the room was dark. He blinked his eyes a few times to adjust but found that when it returned to its normal state, there were also women a few feet away from him.

*Two? How could that be?* he thought.

He floated over to them and discovered that one was an angel, while the other.... He looked at her with keen interest and couldn't decide what was so special about her.

The angel stirred awake, and then in analyzing her surroundings, sat up. She looked at him, confused. "Where am I? Who are you?"

"Alexander. And who are you?"

"Zaraquel." As if remembering her purpose for being there, she was frantic, her wings shaking uncontrollably. "I...I have to save her! Therefore I exist! I...I said the spell exactly how I was taught. 'Animate, breathe, a life for a life. A life for a life. A life for a life.' I said it exactly like that."

That's when it clicked. He'd sacrificed so many birds; he was so obsessed with life that given the thousands of years he'd spent in this place, he realized why Amun-Ra had chosen him. He was there to save her.

A life for a life.

"All right, Zaraquel. I know exactly what to do."

She looked up with her doe eyes. "You do?"

He kneeled and leaned over to place his hand on the woman's wound. Her mouth was slightly open, so when his lips hovered above hers, he gave her the gift of life. His warm breath blew into her mouth as if he were literally resuscitating her. The more he breathed into her, the more his soul gave way.

His body, his essence, began to fade until he was no longer there.

~*~

*Zaraquel, The Clearing, Present Day*

She woke up, gasping for breath. She looked up and saw her mother helping her up.

"Are you okay? I saw you, and I didn't know what to think."

Zaraquel waved her hand, dismissing her mom's concern. "Mom, I'm fine. It was weird—I...I saw a man. He helped us, then he disappeared."

Chloe's brow crinkled in confusion. "A man? Who?"

"That's beside the point. Did the spell work? Is Auntie Amber okay?"

They looked over and saw that the open wound Machiel had inflicted was no longer there. Amber's eyes sprung open, and she was breathing.

~*~

*Amber, The Clearing, Present Day*

Licking her lips because her mouth was dry was the first thing she felt since she woke up. The second thing was the thumping in her chest — her heart. The third? Malakai's hands cradled around her, carrying her as if she was the most delicate thing in the world. She bit back her smile and slowly turned to see that everything and everyone was frozen, rendered immobile.

"Huh? What's going on?" she asked, puzzled.

She saw her mother, a sad statue, trying to keep it together, holding her hand.

Chloe and Zaraquel leapt to their feet and screamed with joy. "You're alive! It worked!" Her best friend snapped her fingers, and time returned to its usual pace. One by one, they unfroze, and everyone was moving and talking.

"Amber?" He said her name like it was a caress. *Malakai*. She warmed as she heard her name leave his lips. But the gravity of their current situation hit her hard and fast. She sat up as if nothing had happened in the first place. No knife in her chest, nothing. She was good as new.

She heard a hiss and whipped her head around to see Marcus on the ground holding Machiel down. Catching her gaze, Machiel's eyes widened in surprise, and for that, she was happy. That son of a bitch had tried to kill her!

The fighting continued, the wolves and the witches, along with Chloe and Miriam, fighting the good fight. It was loud, and it was messy.

She let Marcus get a few punches in, but then felt it was time to end the misery of their tragic love story once and for all. With great speed, she took Marcus's place and climbed on top. Placing all her weight on Machiel, she whispered an enchantment, making sure he couldn't move.

Taking pleasure in his fragile state, her eyes glittered with the anticipation of taking her revenge. She wanted to hurt him like he'd hurt her, if not worse. It was his turn to feel pain.

"You were supposed to die," he gritted through his sharp teeth. She took a moment to look into his eyes. They were pulsing with so much anger she could tell he was seething. He struggled to move but couldn't.

She chuckled at the thought of seeing him so powerless, bending to her will. Amber soaked this moment in for all it was worth and smirked as she bent down to whisper in his ear. "*I lived…so, you can die.*"

With one fell swoop of the poisonous blade that had threatened to take her life, she severed his head, blood spewing onto her face and clothing until his head rolled out into the middle of the clearing. His head was quickly squashed by one of the dire wolves in the midst of their battle with Rae, Mona, Briar, and Elizabeth.

She stood to attention when she saw a lithe brunette standing deep within the forest with what looked like an exact replica of the amulet Amber herself wore around her neck.

*Who is that?*

~*~

*Merlin, Underground Cellar, Present Day*

He didn't know where Nimue had gone off to, but he figured now was his chance to take what little strength he had and contact the one person he knew he could trust. Merlin closed his eyes and went into a deep meditative state as if he were floating between worlds. He had enough power to extract his soul from his body. His soul traveled and allowed him to project himself into the physical plane of existence. He was a voluntary spirit.

~*~

*Merlin, The Clearing, Present Day*

In this state, Merlin was able to see the battle that was being fought, the destruction that mounted because of the powerful forces of good and evil. He found Bradley defending himself against Rae with a barricade spell. *Smart.* He didn't want to hurt the child, but he didn't want to get hurt either. Merlin had taught him well.

Merlin approached him, and Bradley was alarmed, to say the least. "Rowe? Rowe, where have you been? Are you okay?"

The poor man was frazzled at seeing him in such a translucent state. "Bradley. Listen to me and listen to me well—this is important. There is a woman, Nimue, who was responsible for the fall of the Order."

"What? She helped set fire…. I don't understand. What's going on?"

"This is bigger than any of us could grasp, and there is no time to explain, but I need you to do something for me."

Bradley nodded as he listened intently to Merlin's instructions. He was to get the necklace no matter the obstacle, he emphasized. "You get that necklace; you save the Order. Understand?"

"Got it."

Merlin knew Bradley meant it when he said it. He floated off in the sky to see the remainder of the battle, wondering if he could be of some assistance.

~*~

*Bradley, The Clearing, Present Day*

Despite the heat of the battle, Bradley managed to reach into the minds of Chloe, Amber, and Zaraquel through a psychic link. Each were fighting the enemy, Chloe throwing punches through the air with tufts of wind, sending the opponents flying the opposite direction. Zaraquel took the vigilance route, trying to foresee any advancing attacks, and before they happened, she tried to swoop in and stop them — at times, she was successful, and sometimes not so much. But did she try? She did, and Bradley saw that. He smiled up at her, proud of everything she had accomplished so far, given her short time of life.

Now Amber, like her mother, was warding off Briar with her witchfire, Miriam, more so than Amber.

*Huh, I wonder why?* He scratched his head in contemplation.

They fought, shrouding Briar with a fiery wall of flame that felt like they were at the earth's center. However, he countered every assault with an even more powerful rebuttal — rain from the sky, transforming fire into ice, and so forth. Bradley didn't remember him being this powerful when they were younger. But then again, he remembered the darkness that had consumed Briar when he was in search of the tree of knowledge.

*Did he ever find it?* He thought to himself.

Distracted by his thoughts, Bradley soon felt the ground vibrating beneath his feet. He looked down and saw that although the ground was a rich brown with grass peeking through, there was a glow, a red glow emanating through.

*Oh, no. They opened it?!*

*Hey Uncle Mac, y'know we can hear you, right?* Zaraquel said through mindspeak.

*That's right, we're psychically connected.*

*Bradley, what is going on?* Amber said, frustrated and out of breath. He looked in her direction and saw that Briar was on top of her, his hands around her neck.

*Something's wrong, what is it?* Chloe chimed in not too long after.

He spotted Nimue. She caught him looking and ran deeper into the woods.

*Shit!* He ran after her, losing sight of the battle in the clearing.

A loud burst, like a volcano exploding, filled his ears. But he didn't let that deter him—he soldiered on and chased her. He dodged trees and hopped over roots that seemed like arms trying to reach out and grab him. Bradley ran out of breath, but he persisted.

*Bradley!* Chloe and Amber screamed after him. He winced at the loudness in his head but continued running after Nimue. He took a breath and gathered his thoughts, trying to make some sense of everything he had learned.

*All right, all right, listen. That glowing down there? I'm pretty certain the portal is open — the portal to the complete unknown. To darkness, evil? We don't know, but what we do know is that Rowe has kept it closed for over a decade, and with good reason. Now, you three are the chosen of the Alchemy of the Three. Yes, you are powerful on your own, but combined? You are unstoppable. By working together, you can destroy those responsible for opening the portal and save the Order. By saving the Order, you save magic. Your light will put an end to the darkness. Got it?*

*Got it,* they all repeated in understanding.

He stopped, no longer within seeing distance of the clearing. He was in too deep and had lost Nimue in the process. But he had to find her, there was no other option.

*Repeat after me,* he said, anxious to be finished with this whole ordeal.

~*~

*Amber, The Clearing, Present Day*

Amber struggled to breathe as the man she learned was Rae's father strangled her with his bare hands. She looked into his eyes and realized who she was looking at was filled with pure, undiluted evil. She wasn't scared easily, but something about the man had given her a sickly feeling in the pit of her stomach. Malakai growled, and she knew his intention of attacking, but she shook her head, motioning to him that she could do this on her own—she had to. He trusted her, so he backed away but stayed close in case anything went awry.

She said the words that Bradley had told her to repeat.

*"We are the three.*
*We are the light.*
*Vanquish the darkness,*
*Bring the light."*
~*~

*Chloe, The Clearing, Present Day*

She heard Amber as she tried to block the ambush from the ancient Hexham witch. Having heard stories about Elizabeth's relationship with the Tall Dark Man and the great power she possessed, she knew, based on what she was experiencing, that all the stories were true. That great witch had been practicing for millennia, but could her relationship with the Tall Dark Man be so significant to her that it blinded her to such depravity against her own kind? What hold did he have on her?

Instinctively she knew that now was the moment she had to say the words Bradley had spoken to her.

*"We are the three.*
*We are the light.*
*Vanquish the darkness,*
*Bring the light."*
~*~

*Zaraquel, The Clearing, Present Day*

Flying in to block an attack on her father, Zaraquel was finally face to face with Rae. Rae looked at her, a hardened stare.

No longer was she the little girl that laughed at everything and chased Zaraquel around the castle. The Rae that stood in front of her was someone completely different.

"Why are you doing this, Rae?" She gestured to all the fighting that surrounded them.

"This?" She arched her brow. "This is my destiny. You were born because of a prophecy, your fate sealed. But I am my father's daughter. I believe in free will."

Zaraquel sighed and shook her head. "This war is not the answer, Rae, and deep down, you know that. I know you do."

She grabbed onto Rae's shoulder and gave a reassuring squeeze, and saw uncertainty flash in Rae's eyes. She was getting through to her. *Finally!*

"You know what you have to do, Rae!" Her father barked an order, and she immediately shifted, darkness clouding her every move.

But before Rae could hit her with whatever attack she had planned, Zaraquel said the words she had heard moments before.

> *"We are the three.*
> *We are the light.*
> *Vanquish the darkness,*
> *Bring the light."*

~*~

*Amber, The Clearing, Present Day*

After Amber said the spell, Briar began to loosen his grip, and Amber overpowered him, flinging him up against a tree. He started to move, gritting, "You are not powerful enough, Queen!" Slowing, he began unsticking himself, but in a jolt, he was pushed back. Amber looked behind her and saw Zaraquel and Chloe raising their hands in the same stance. They were stronger together — Bradley was right.

In one fluid motion, Chloe and Zaraquel raised their other arms and threw both Mona and Elizabeth against the trees beside him. It was eerily still, for in containing the threat of those powerful witches, there was no reason for the chaos to continue. All slowly began to gravitate to where the prisoners were held against their will. They encircled them, not wanting to risk a possible escape.

Amber eyed Rae cautiously, wondering if she would also act, but she found that the little witch was entranced by something else entirely. Amber followed her line of sight and saw what Rae saw.

Briar's facade was cracking, quite literally. His skin was flaking off as if every blow of the wind did him more damage than good. Little by little, the disguise chipped off. His face was more angular than before; he looked younger, his skin supple; his hair longer, shinier. But it was his eyes that made them all jump in their skin. They were completely black, like newly mined obsidian.

That's when she saw her mother slowly approach this stranger. This sudden movement reminded her to look back at Rae. She was no longer there.

~*~

*Rae, The Woods, Present Day*

She couldn't breathe and felt a terrible lump in her throat. Her mind was racing, her body shaking. Rae didn't know where she was going, and frankly, she didn't even care. All she knew was that she had to get away from there, fast.

*Who was that? Does he even exist?* She asked herself. Who was the man that had disguised himself as her father? What the hell was she thinking?

Rae had so many thoughts she couldn't really make sense of that she had to stop. She stopped in her tracks, placed her head between her knees, and breathed. That was all she could do.

Just breathe.

But she couldn't. She was too enveloped in the shock, in the betrayal, so overwhelmed that she fell to her knees and sobbed. She sobbed until she felt her throat was raw, and her eyes wanted to fall out.

How could she be so stupid? She gave in to the darkness, the liberation that the acheri had offered. She gave in to her sister and the desire to have a living parent, especially one that was significantly absent. She was so incredibly blind that she didn't see what was right in front of her—she had a family in Chloe and Zaraquel, and at the drop of a hat, she'd given it all away.

If that man was not her father, who was he?

She heard a man clear his throat, and when she looked up before her was an ethereal version of Rowe floating above her. Rae stood up, shocked.

"Rowe? What are you doing here? Why do you look like that?" She asked as she quickly wiped the tears from her face.

He made his descent until his feet touched the ground a few feet away from her. "That man was not your father. It pains me to say that what I said before was true. I was the reason for your real father's demise."

She picked nervously at the sleeve of her sweater, but she nodded, signaling for him to continue.

"He was working for the Tall Dark Man, a source of great evil, to open the portal. The portal was and continues to be extremely dangerous. The man who pretended to be your father promised Briar great and unlimited power. But it came at a cost—it darkened his soul and his heart."

"So, he wasn't always evil?"

He shook his head at her innocent question. "Despite what you believe, one does have the power to choose their own fate and *not* the other way around."

Without a second thought, she said, "I want to close the portal."

"There is only one way to close it. Are you sure?"

"More than anything," she said confidently, hopeful she could redeem herself. Maybe they would forgive her?

"Very well then," he said with a tender smile. "Take my hand."

Despite his phantom-like appearance, she could feel his hand pressing against hers, and in the blink of an eye, she was transported elsewhere.

~*~

*Miriam, The Clearing, Present Day*

The instant she saw him across the clearing, she knew he was not who he was pretending to be. He was the Tall Dark Man, the man that had destroyed her life and haunted her dreams. She didn't know why her legs were moving in his direction, but when he spotted her, he smiled.

She spotted Elizabeth sneering in her direction, jealousy radiating off her body, whispering "Miriam," venomously.

The Tall Dark Man's gaze meandered over her body. "Time has treated you well, I see."

Walking up to him, she placed her hand on his face, just as he had done to her when she was in his clutches. She was merely returning the favor. She felt the fire racing through her veins until it reached her palm. He squirmed and screamed in pain as she held on tighter to his cheek, not minding that she had an audience. She wasn't going to let him get away unscathed. He didn't deserve anything less, and she was going to make sure of that.

~*~

*Merlin, The Pit, Present Day*

Although no longer inhabiting his body, Merlin still found the strength to transport himself and Rae to the portal. The light that illuminated the gateway was dimmer, but it was still open. He could feel it pulsing with life, yearning to break out.

He looked down at Rae, and she met his gaze with a determination he had never seen but had always known was in her. Placing his hand on her shoulder, he reminded her of the stakes. "Now, because your father opened the portal, only a Hexham can close it." Merlin took a breath, not necessarily fond of the next part, but she interrupted him before he could continue.

"It's okay, you can say it."

He studied her calm and poised manner. "Those that had *any* part in opening the portal are cursed with being sucked inside at the closing."

Looking at him with a sad smile stretched across her face, she reached out her hand and together, they approached the entrance. Closing their eyes, their intentions were strong enough that there was no need for an actual spell. Their hearts and thoughts were so pure the magic that electrified the air took control.

Hands clasped together, they rose until they were feet above the ground. Merlin felt something wash over him that in all his years of life, he had never felt. From the tips of his toes to the tip top of his head, he felt peace.

Rae and Merlin began to glow from the inside, slowly at first, but then as they rose higher, the light grew in intensity. They looked at each other, conscientious of their sacrifice, a small part in the greater scheme. They both knew what they were doing was right for the world, for magic, for the balance of good and evil.

With the blinding white light, Merlin heard a faint ringing and knew that Rae could hear it too as she clutched tighter onto his hand. The light that surrounded and eventually became one with them was warm, and they burst into a tiny million stars; only then did the Pit close once and for all.

~*~

*Nimue, The Woods, Present Day*

Tired of all the chasing and harassing from Merlin's little stooge, she finally stopped and took a stand. She faced him and found his look of academia quite charming. Nevertheless, she knew what he wanted, and she was never going to give it to him, not as long as she lived.

Nimue held to the necklace tighter as if her life depended on it, and it did. Merlin had caused enough pain and damage.

"You will nev —"

She never finished because she disappeared. Her entire essence, her body, was sucked into the gateway that was opened without her knowledge. She, like many others, was a pawn in his plan, an insignificant price to pay for accomplishing the impossible.

~*~

*Bradley, The Woods, Present Day*

*Whoa.*

He looked around to see if she had hidden away, but all he saw were trees on trees on trees — nothing but greenery. *What just happened?*

He waited a couple moments for her to return, but she didn't. Where had she gone?

The necklace was there for the taking. Could it have been that easy? He didn't care, he pocketed it just as he was asked to do. He left the woods with more questions than answers.

~*~

*Tall Dark Man, The Clearing, Present Day*

Aside from the burning sensation that sizzled his skin, he was quite surprised to see Miriam. She stood alongside her daughter, and he laughed at the sad scene that gathered around him. Did they really think they could defeat *him*?

He addressed his audience as if he were on a stage and not imprisoned to a tree. "You're only stalling the inevitable. This plan has been in motion since the conception of that little Blood Prophecy of yours."

He saw Amber flinch, which only made his smile more pronounced. He was really enjoying this, so why not have fun with it?

"Everything had been planned to the 'T' — nothing could happen that I don't have a contingency for. Say goodbye to the world as you know it. The power and infinite knowledge will be free, pure untapped magic; creatures beyond your wildest imagination will roam the earth."

He looked at everyone's faces, accounting for their presence at his time of glory. Wait. She wasn't there. Where the hell was that little witch? His smile faltered.

"Something wrong?" Miriam pressed.

And then, as if reading his mind, Mona caught on, her voice small. "Where's Rae?"

*Shit.*

Could Merlin have escaped and convinced Rae? He didn't have to wait long for his answer. The Tall Dark Man felt it in his bones, his skin snapping to attention. He looked at his hands and saw the particulars pulling apart.

Whispers traveled, and he didn't have to listen to know what it was they were talking about, what was happening.

Mona, Elizabeth, and the Tall Dark Man screamed in agony as they unstuck from the trees. The other two didn't know what fate waited for them, but he did. He felt the pull of the darkness so unlike his own.

~*~

*Tall Dark Man, The Pit, Present Day*

He saw it there waiting for him, taunting him.

With a rush of wind, it pulled in Elizabeth and Mona, the white light amplifying with each new victim. The gateway was only waiting for him. The Tall Dark Man did everything he could think of — magic spells, enchantments — but none of his tricks kept him from being sucked inside.

He refused to resign, but the pull was far too strong for him to continue fighting. His resistance was futile, and despite the countless charms and vulgarities that he screamed out into the void, the Tall Dark Man himself was a victim of the Pit.

Gone, as if he were never there, to begin with.

# Epilogue

*Three Years Later....*

After the destruction the Tall Dark Man, along with Machiel, had caused, it was up to Amber and all the witches—including Bradley, Chloe, Zaraquel, as well as the Tudor Coven—to clean up the city of Seattle. With their combined abilities, they were able to return the city to its original, pristine condition. The Space Needle was intact, and those innocent bystanders that had witnessed the magical undoing had their memories of the incidents wiped. However, they were unable to save the lives that had been lost during the battle.

Because Bradley had managed to save the amulet, he, in turn, resurrected the Order in all its former glory, as Rowe had neglected to mention that all his artifacts were under a protection spell tied to the necklace. It turned out that the tree in the clearing her mother was so intrigued by was one of the original entrances of the Order. Those trees represented the tree of knowledge, and one was found anywhere there were any magical creatures present. It was a safe haven for those in the magical community, as Rowe had originally intended.

It was funny, but sometimes when Amber walked the grounds of the Order, she swore she could see Rowe's spirit mulling about, never too far from Bradley himself. She chuckled at the thought of Rowe, guiding him even then as a spirit.

Her mother finally found peace. Having suffered the loss of her father once more and facing her attacker was a tough break for anyone, but particularly her mother. But Amber was there for her and helped her heal, to find new meaning in her life. Miriam became a counselor at the Order, helping other wayward families find their paths and assimilate into their new lives.

Chloe and Marcus, on the other hand, lived not too far away from the Order, owning a cabin in the middle of the woods. She and Marcus split their time between the order and Yakima, with the Tudor coven. Meanwhile, Zaraquel wanted to live a semi-normal life as a teenage girl, with her weeks spent in a human high school and her weekends at the Order. Amber, nevertheless, found her niece sitting in front of the monument made in the honor of Rae's sacrifice. She knew in her heart that Zaraquel missed Rae, but Amber also knew that loss was what motivated Zaraquel to live her life to the fullest. If Rae couldn't experience a first date or the tedious difficulties of high school finals, the least Zaraquel could do was try her best to live the life Rae would have if she'd lived.

Amber sat there now, in front of the life size statue of Rae Tudor. It was carved in white marble exactly to her liking, a certain kindness in her eyes. Oftentimes she found herself collecting her thoughts, centering herself. The memories of the past, although painful, grounded her and made her extremely thankful for the life and family she had.

"I thought I might find you here," Malakai said as he brushed her long silky tresses aside and nuzzled her neck with little kisses.

She sank into the feeling of having him there, wrapped in his arms. She loved it…it felt like home. He walked around and sat beside her. She was his, and he was hers.

"Hi," she whispered softly as she reached up and placed a tender peck on his cheek. She could see his eyes crinkling at the sides through his lashes — he was smiling. And every time he did, she felt an unmistakable flutter in her heart, one that told her she'd finally found her home.

# About the Author

Having been born and raised in Hawaii, I loved telling stories ever since I was a child about vampires, werewolves, angels, demons, and witches. I was a little girl who loved scary stories, much to my mother's dismay. The scarier—the better. Hawaii was a perfect place for stories until I moved to Seattle. I decided to turn a love for the supernatural into writing stories to see if others would love them as much as I do. Currently, I live in Florida, but since I'm a Seattle girl at heart, my stories take place in the Northwest. I continue to write supernatural stories of vampires, werewolves, witches, and more while enjoying the beaches and sunshine.

www.ingramcontent.com/pod-product-compliance
Lightning Source LLC
Chambersburg PA
CBHW031132210626
46816CB00014B/234